Advance praise for *Perfect Little Angels*

"*Perfect Little Angels* is a brilliant debut bookended by blood; Vincent Anioke's prose slices with the heft and certainty of a meat cleaver. Readers will hang on the fates of goats and the voices of lost family, while betrayal, shame, and circumstance enlace and entangle as characters' desires meet dogma. A vivid reminder of the danger, joy, and depth of love."

—DEREK MASCARENHAS, author of *Coconut Dreams* and *100 Chapatis*

"Vincent Anioke's brilliant, harrowing short story collection *Perfect Little Angels* is populated by characters who are struggling, for the sake of those who in equal measure love them and judge them, to become someone else: someone with sanctioned desires. In these brutal, sad, funny stories, Anioke considers what culture demands from men and women and how to survive these demands intact."

—KIM MAGOWAN, author of *How Far I've Come*

"Steeped in violence, family turmoil, and broken dreams, *Perfect Little Angels* captures the rawest of emotions in the finest of prose. This debut collection marks the arrival of a phenomenal talent. Vincent Anioke writes with an honesty rivalled only by his compassion, and I'm first in line for whatever he does next."

—JENNIFER WORTMAN, author of *This. This. This. Is. Love. Love. Love.*

"Vincent Anioke has created such a compelling, memorable cast of characters in *Perfect Little Angels*, where the lines between victim and perpetrator are blurred and where surviving the stranglehold of a pietistic society is not always a given. Anioke is a masterful storyteller."

—CHRISTOPHER ALLEN, publisher of *SmokeLong Quarterly*

stories

Vincent Anioke

PERFECT LITTLE ANGELS

ARSENAL PULP PRESS
VANCOUVER

PERFECT LITTLE ANGELS

ARSENAL PULP PRESS
Suite 202 – 211 East Georgia St.
Vancouver, BC V6A 1Z6
Canada
arsenalpulp.com

The publisher gratefully acknowledges the support of the Canada Council for the Arts and the British Columbia Arts Council for its publishing program and the Government of Canada and the Government of British Columbia (through the Book Publishing Tax Credit Program) for its publishing activities.

BRITISH COLUMBIA | BRITISH COLUMBIA ARTS COUNCIL An agency of the Province of British Columbia | Canada Council for the Arts Conseil des arts du Canada | Canada

Arsenal Pulp Press acknowledges the xʷməθkʷəy̓əm (Musqueam), Sḵwx̱wú7mesh (Squamish), and səlilwətaɬ (Tsleil-Waututh) Nations, custodians of the traditional, ancestral, and unceded territories where our office is located. We pay respect to their histories, traditions, and continuous living cultures and commit to accountability, respectful relations, and friendship.

The following stories were previously published in different form: “Ogbuefi” in *adda*, September 14, 2021; “The Stars Yet Undiscovered” in *Peatsmoke Journal*, Spring 2022; “Nwanne Mu” under the title “The Smallness of Asking” in *Split Lip Magazine*, September 14, 2021; “My Americanah” in *SmokeLong Quarterly* 76; “Hey, Stop Blaming Your Dead Mother’s Fists” under the title “Hey, Stop Blaming Your Dead Father’s Fists” in *The Masters Review*, June 27, 2022; “All the Failures of Her Being” in *Passages North* 44; “Mama’s Lullabies” in Writers’ Trust of Canada RBC Bronwen Wallace Award for Emerging Writers 2023 Finalists; “The Alchemy of His Mirror” under the title “The Alchemy of His Own Mirror” in *Carve Magazine,* Winter 2021; “Perfect Little Angels” in *The Ex-Puritan* 55.

Cover and text design by Jazmin Welch
Cover art by Julian Adon Alexander, *“Was Anything I Did Worth It?”*, 2023, 8.5″ × 11″, graphite on toned paper
Edited by Catharine Chen
Proofread by Alison Strobel

Printed and bound in Canada

Library and Archives Canada Cataloguing in Publication:
Title: Perfect little angels / Vincent Anioke.
Names: Anioke, Vincent, 1996– author.
Description: Short stories.
Identifiers: Canadiana (print) 20230549721 | Canadiana (ebook) 2023054973X |
ISBN 9781551529431 (softcover) | ISBN 9781551529448 (EPUB)
Subjects: LCGFT: Short stories.
Classification: LCC PR9387.9.A55 P47 2024 | DDC 823/.92—dc23

For Dad, Mom, Chimdi, Ozo, Chioma, Johnpaul, and Chidera.
Long live our Polo Park days.

CONTENTS

OGBUEFI

When Papa returns home in the evening, I am curled up on the lemon grass carpet by the TV, watching cartoons. On the screen, red-tailed mice shuffle in widening circles, their arms interlocked, and Papa says, over their lilting chorus, "Chibuike, it is time. This weekend you will become an Ogbuefi."

That night, I barely sleep. Through the large windows of my darkened room, I watch the wind rattle the frangipani tree in our backyard, its long and skinny limbs peeking beneath clusters of white and green leaves. Two weeks ago, lightning flashed and thunder growled, as if the skies were prying loose a great beast. I scurried into Mama and Papa's room. Between their bodies was a span of space warmed by deep breathing. Mama snored like an airplane passing overhead, and I fell asleep to the sound in my ears. Before dawn, Papa shook me awake and pulled me aside. He said seven was too old to be scared of the mind. A boy became a man by trying.

Friday mornings are bright and quiet. The sun wakes me up to the smell of toasted bread and honeyed tea. I like two cubes of sugar in mine and a spoonful of powdered milk; the heat amplifies the sweetness, and I savour each sip carefully, the way Papa does on long evenings when he gets home and fills his glass halfway. He does not drink tea, he never has, but I see the way he samples his cup of dark-brown whiskey. Slow and measured, the long-blink pauses taking him somewhere far away—somewhere beautiful.

But I do not drink my tea now, not even at Mama's prodding. She sighs and flips my cup upside down in the sink. With her back turned, I step outside into a hot and windless day. Sweat sticks to my skin, tapering down the length of my face.

A large tar-coloured goat is tied to the frangipani tree. In past weeks, I have been content to spy on it from the safety of my window, this lazy thing that scratches its pointy ears with its hind legs and naps in the shade. Now we stand so close that its stench steals the air. It sits on a bed of wilted petals shaken loose by winds and passing birds. Branches sag low enough that the goat can eat with hardly any motion. There is no joy in its face when it chews, nothing like my bliss when Mama buys suya meat from the mallam two streets away—red, juicy meat flavoured with a pepper that stings my tongue twice over and brings tears to my eyes.

The goat munches slowly until it is full. Then it turns toward me, its eyes pale yellow, its ridged, scaly horns curled in two twists. I want to graze its head with my fingertips, but I fear that the movement would provoke anger. Instead I pick up a small twig and twirl it in the air so that the goat's eyes follow the arc of my hand. The animal soon tires of my charade and turns to survey a portion of bark where red ants cluster. If I were to burst into song and dance like the mice on TV, perhaps it would watch me again.

The thought makes me flinch. I will *not* dance for a goat.

Today is Friday. Tomorrow I become an Ogbuefi, like my older brothers, Toby and Nonso. They are in boarding school, where life somehow moves on without Mama or Papa. I wonder what they smell on mornings when the sun wakes them up, if it ever even does. I wonder if, on the day before they became Ogbuefis, their hearts pulsed in their throats.

Mama yells my name, but I do not move. She finds me outside, watching the goat look at nothing, our united silence a sort of covenant.

"Come inside," she says. "Get ready for school."

Before the bus arrives, she calls me to her room, a nail clipper in one hand, and I place my feet on her lap. She says my toes look like the claws of a hawk—they need to be short and smooth for Saturday. It has been months since she cut my nails, crescent clippings gathering around her feet like baby moons. She once belonged to me, her tender hands soaping and brushing my dandruffed hair, her stories about Amadioha and the river goddess guiding me to sleep, but now she mostly belongs to the house. Every afternoon, the windows and countertops gleam, and the smoke-wreathed stockpots are filled with diced vegetables and achicha.

When the last claw is conquered, she glances at her watch.

"The bus is almost here," she says. "Put on your socks and go."

My legs are back on the ground, my bag is on my back. I am ready, but I do not move.

"Mama," I say, "I'm afraid."

She takes my hands in hers. I wonder whether she would do so if Papa were here.

"Ten seconds, nwa mu," she says. "No. Five seconds. You hold on for five seconds, and it is over. You can do it."

"What if I can't?"

Her eyes scan mine, and it feels as though she is peeking past the layers of my skin. Finally she says, "You will."

After school, I come home to find Toby and Nonso in the living room. Mama is napping upstairs, and they are watching a movie. A man is clutching at his cut-open throat, blood seeping between his fingers. Before I can turn away, Toby grabs me, his fingers on my sides, and lifts me into the air. He twirls me until I think I might vomit.

"Ogbuefi!" Toby sings, while Nonso cackles.

Over dinner, as we dig into jollof rice and stewed beef, Nonso tells us about boarding school. An older student, Victor, tried to make Nonso wash his clothes. Now, Victor has a black eye. Papa laughs—the deep belly kind. He has not laughed in weeks. His thumps on the table rattle my almost-full bowl. Mama is silent.

I stay awake through the night again, thinking of the warm space between Mama and Papa. I wish I could crawl into their bed and freeze time. Rain pellets would hang halfway between treetops and ground. A streak of lightning would burn the sky forever white. My eyes scan for shooting stars darting beyond the velvet atmosphere. None streak past.

In the morning I walk up to my window. Through the wet glass, I see the frayed brown rope, one end of it looped around the tree but the noose empty, as if nighttime ghosts quietly whisked the goat away. Staring at the space it once inhabited, I decide on a name.

"Solomon," I whisper. It seems fitting for a creature with a king's size and silent, palpable authority.

The name takes on a cadence in my head and loops and loops and loops, like a song on the staticky radio that accompanies us on our drive to the village.

The road shimmers, its smooth grey surface broken up by pools of water. Toby and Nonso flank me. They argue over which anime character is strongest. Papa whistles along with the radio's ode to African queens and eternal love. His body bounces. His fingers tap on the steering wheel. It matters little that he is out of sync; an inner music hums within him. Mama's fingers are pinched on the shifting beads of a rosary.

I know we are getting close when the car starts to rock and crest, as though bobbing on ocean waves. The road is now a brown snake. When we arrive, a scorching heat beats down on us. Distant music is playing. Papa parks under the shadowy frame of a giant iroko tree.

We approach the swelling sounds in the village square. Beneath the rainbow sprawl of tall canopies, plastic chairs are populated by men in lion-patterned shirts and women in periwinkle wrappers. Their faces are only vaguely familiar, if at all, flickers of memory from past visits during Christmas. The air buzzes with their conversation, and around them, children clap and sing and play all manner of instruments: tambourines, beaded ichakas, and drums.

It takes a moment for Papa's presence to be noticed. Silence descends. Papa leads me to the centre of the square, where twenty-one men—seven sons, seven fathers, seven grandfathers—stand shirtless in a loose triangle. Their backs are straight, their faces painted a stark chalky white. They part to let us in and then, just as smoothly, they close the gap.

Papa crouches before me. Whenever he smiles, his eyes are often on some other thing: scantily clad wrestlers tussling on the TV, an approaching plate of Mama's eba and leafy ogbono soup, Toby and Nonso. But now his eyes hold mine, his hands grip my shoulders, and he beams. Like magic, my legs grow solid beneath me.

"Chibuike Anyanwu," Papa says gently. "My dear son. A village raises a child so that a child can raise a village. Today, you show our people that you can provide for them. Today, you become a man. Do you understand?"

I nod.

He walks away and joins Mama, Toby, and Nonso in the front-row seats reserved for us. Ululating voices and strummed ubos compel the men around me to dance, their steps sharp and precise. They preserve the triangle even while in motion.

The village chief, Ichie Okolie, approaches the edge of their dance. He is a wiry man with milky eyes, his face like the shapeless dough that Mama kneads into sweet chin chin. He sports a gold-threaded isiagu shirt that swallows him whole and lifts his walking staff to the cawing birds above. I face him, because I know that I must. My eyes are steel, my teeth are clenched, my fingers are curled into tight fists.

Ichie Okolie calls on the wide-eyed spirits of our ancestors, who commune in the unseeable heavens. Each year they bless the chosen Ogbuefi and, through him, our verdant lands, our fertile soil, the undulating hills that encircle us, cross-stitched atop our holy grounds. We are *one*: heaven and earth, here and now, elevated afterlife, afternoon sun, the glistening fireflies of night.

When Ichie Okolie finishes, I hold my breath. Footsteps approach from behind me. I turn around. The triangle has parted once more to let in two men. They resemble Nonso, although their chests are bigger and their stomachs are lined with muscle. The man in the front holds a blue bucket in one hand and, in the other, the end of a long, waxy rope tied around a goat's neck. The man in the back holds a machete. It scrapes along the ground as he moves.

It takes me a moment to realize the goat standing between them is Solomon. He has always moved so little unless he was eating, but now, his mammoth black head swings left and right, his eyes darting between the men, the sky, and the silent, watchful crowd. Upon seeing me, he lurches forward but is pulled back sharply by the man in front.

All my trapped air escapes in one breath. The man lets go of the rope. He sets the bucket beneath Solomon's twisting form. He accepts the machete from the man behind him, and my knees quiver. In my mind, I seek strength in Papa's face, his lessons, his smile. But every image of him blends into static.

An oja flute warbles, its sorrowful notes pricking my skin. I am focused on Solomon. His gaze finds mine a final time, yellowish eyes dilating.

The man in the back lifts Solomon by his hind legs, turning him upside down. The man in front takes my right hand, curls my fingers around the machete's handle. Our hands are fused.

He nods at me. "Together," he says.

We move slowly at first, then I am taken by surprise when he dives forward, my grip with his, and drives the blade deep into Solomon's neck. I feel the slight resistance of muscle, sinew, and tissue. Solomon's throat opens. The rain is red and warm, the air reeks of silver coins, and my stomach is unrolling. The man is still moving, but I don't want to anymore; I want Mama, I want Mama, her face and her arms and her hug and her smell—nutmeg, Maggi cubes, and freshly laundered pillowcases. I want snug bedsheets warmed by her breathing, I want home, I want the long night's thunder, I want anywhere but here.

I seek Mama. I hear gasps and feverish mutterings. I hear the flute die out. I hear a man yell for me to come back. I hear Solomon's final whimpering grunts. But I don't see, because my feet thud fast, faster than they ever have, and my head roars, and my hands swing so that blood sprays the air. I see Mama still perched on her chair and Papa next to her. He is rising, but I only want Mama.

She is close enough now, and I wrap my body around hers, my tears breaking free. She does not touch me. When I look up at her, she looks away, as if I am a lost wanderer from the dirty streets. Papa yanks me by the shoulder and forces me into an empty chair beside him, his face blank. I think he's broken one of my bones, because pain splits my body, and the tears spill harder.

"Shut up," Papa whispers, leaning close to my ear. "Shut up now, you stupid boy, or I will give you something to cry about."

My stomach heaves, but the storm does not end. I pinch my lips, Solomon's bitter blood catching on my tongue, and my voice falters. Even then, I can't stop shaking.

I focus on a spot of dirt before my feet. An indented circle hollows the ground there, perhaps from an idle finger or a shifted chair leg. I focus on this and imagine a family of serpentine worms twisting beneath the surface, their tiny tongues lapping up the rich, damp earth. Around me, whispers rise, words churn, and Ichie Okolie urges the people to relax. He says that the goat's body will be cast into Nshe

Forest at midnight, and skinned and smoked cows await our hungry bellies. He calls out to unseen men with a clap. Music resumes.

Calabash bowls stuffed with fresh meat are passed around like handshakes, their flecks of pepper tingling my downturned nose. The stench is overpowering. Papa is offered a plate but declines; he says his family cannot eat today. I push myself deeper into the chair. I do not look up, not until the oja's last note trails off and the afternoon light washes away.

"Get up," says Papa.

All five of us march wordlessly to the car, and it is a silent ride home too. Toby and Nonso grant me my favourite spot in the back seat, the left-side window, where I like to press my forehead against the cool glass and watch the trees race past. I close my eyes. In the dark, I see Solomon's thrashing body, his hind legs caught in two grips, his front legs slashing the air.

At home, we are barely through the front door before Papa explodes. His words are garbled, and although I keep my eyes on the marble tiles, I know that his are red and wet, that a Y-shaped vein bulges on the side of his neck, that his mouth sprays spittle between the refrain of *shame* and the ceiling-scratching high of *coward*.

At the very end he tells Mama, "You wanted three kids. Talk to your son."

He storms up the stairs and slams a door shut.

Toby rubs his fingers through my dry hair. Nonso punches my shoulder lightly. They disappear to their beds. Mama watches, standing by the front door with her arms crossed, and when she starts to move, I bound up the stairs and into my room.

The walls are baked by a blue-dark heat. I scuttle under my blanket, a room within a room, and I crave yet another opening, another hole to crawl into, until I am small and compact, folded like a beetle.

The door opens. The smell of honeyed tea trails the sound.

"My son," Mama says. "Come out. Talk to me."

When I do not, she kisses the fabric above my head. She whispers that everything will be okay. The door groans a second time, a dying echo.

Everything will be okay.

Mama has always moved as if that is true. Like the skies never scream, and the storm is only a graze, a mother's graze, offered like a sin. My tears are a tight ball in my chest, on the thinnest edge of release. I refuse to let them out.

I shake off the blanket and spot a green mug on my desk. Freshly made tea cools beneath a plume of steam. I lift the cup with both hands and raise it above my head. With a shuddering grunt, I let loose. The window shatters, jagged pieces of glass sparkling. A hot trail of liquid stretches from the floor to the ledge, past which I see ceramic shards gathered around the frangipani tree.

In the next room, Papa curses. His footsteps pound the hallway. I look around, my fingers digging underneath my bed, rummaging through neatly arranged drawers, shaking loose the innards of nearby boxes. I search for another cup, a glass bottle, anything that can shatter. My body trembles. A fire grows inside me. I want it to swell until its heat melts my skin. I want it to swallow this house, to devour Mama and Papa and Toby and Nonso and me.

I want it to burn with all the power of an Ogbuefi.

THE STARS YET UNDISCOVERED

On the evening of their three-month anniversary, Chibuike Anyanwu took his girlfriend, Ginika, to a restaurant on the city's outskirts. It was a roadside shack of stylistic contradictions: low wooden stools beneath slick mahogany tables, insect-covered bulbs above glimmering menu screens. A curtain partition separated the dining area from the kitchen, thin smoke oozing through the fabric's gaps. Chibuike found the resulting whole distracting until the first bite of their shared appetizer—isi ewu pepper soup—redirected his focus. He followed it with a sweet-sour sip of chilled palm wine.

"Oh my," he said.

"Exquisite, right?" Ginika replied. She swirled her glass and looked around slowly as though memorizing the mangroves and distant lakes. Chibuike was used to this habit, her attempt to familiarize the unknown. She was roughly as new to Port Harcourt as the length of their relationship. On her twenty-fifth birthday, she'd fled an overbearing father eager to marry her off to a "carefully selected" suitor. Her first stop in the city had been the nightclub where Chibuike spotted her nervously tracing a circle on the rim of a shot glass. He'd sidled across the dim, sticky-floored room to say hello. To his surprise, she'd responded with an outstretched hand and a full smile.

"I could drink this forever," she said now, waving away a small tornado of gnats. "Too bad tomorrow's a workday."

He groaned. "Don't remind me."

"I thought you loved the company of your students."

"Well, this morning, one of them clogged the senior bathroom. It was out of toilet paper, so they used a T-shirt. Graduation's only a few weeks away, you know? They do well on my calculus mid-terms and make me think they're ready for university, then this."

Ginika reminded him that he wouldn't have to deal with such infantile nonsense at Wazobia, the school he planned to build, a school where quantum physicists doubled as poets.

"Madam Angelina keeps saying that she can't run Rivers Transit without me though," he said. Behind Ginika, the waitress drew close with their mains.

Ginika scoffed. "Madam Angelina will manage."

Chibuike's dish was a spicy yam porridge with chunks of fried fish. Ginika leaned into the restaurant's foreign sensibilities with a double cheeseburger.

"Your ancestors would be disappointed," Chibuike said, sticking his tongue out.

"My ancestors thought birthing twins was a sign of satanic witchcraft. I'm happy to disappoint them."

Chibuike thought, *Here it comes.* A moment later, right on cue, Ginika laughed. They'd spent enough time together that he now possessed an internal blueprint of her many characteristics. She made fun of her ancestors. She liked her fiction full of robot-paved boulevards and Igbo slang and floating skyscrapers, so he bought her West African sci-fi novels when he was book hunting. She often spoke with her jaw angled high, but she glanced downward whenever thanking him for a new necklace or a Silverbird Cinema ticket, as if she found an unnamed shame in his provisions.

Still, there was a different kind of knowing, wasn't there? Not of wants and tics, but of pain, memory. Ginika scarcely existed before Port Harcourt. She only mentioned her father on the rare nights she allowed herself a few strong drinks, and often, it was the same reminiscing loops. His proclivity for Russian cigars. The handcrafted dresses he'd contracted a village tailor to make her each month, most of them abandoned in her escape. His claim that he could see her even if they were rivers apart, his loving eyes watching from every cloud she glimpsed.

If ever Chibuike probed further into Ginika's past, she insisted they remain in the present. She had other strange insistences, like saying they could only meet in public spaces: cafés and museums and parks, but never his penthouse in Pitawka Estates or her dingy apartment across from the bakery where she worked. Despite Chibuike's easy acceptance of this arrangement, Ginika often apologized for it. She said their restraint would give meaning to their first time alone together, but he sensed her father's background presence in her words.

The weight of the past mattered little tonight though. As they ate, Ginika stole forkfuls of Chibuike's porridge or leaned across the table to kiss him or laughingly wiped a smudge of beef from the side of her mouth. Each time, a warm wave surged in Chibuike's chest. He recalled the small hill he'd glimpsed on the taxi ride over, surely no farther than a twenty-minute walk. An intoxicating image came to mind: them standing on its summit, awash in starlight, *I love you* professed for the first time.

After dinner, when he suggested the walk, Ginika rubbed her stomach.

"Yes, please."

The darkened sky was dotted with gold. A warm breeze rustled the leaves of the trees flanking the road. This time of day possessed a gentle solitude: the occasional passing car, the harmony of unseen crickets, him and her, their hands interlocked. She talked about all the items on the restaurant's menu she'd considered getting, and his mind slipped elsewhere, played with variations: *All my worries—they seem so small in your presence. We are two heartbeats, one soul.*

Ginika stopped abruptly. It took Chibuike a second to notice that someone had just jumped out of a bushy dirt path snaking off the main road: a scrawny boy of twelve or thirteen, a backpack clinging to his shoulders. The flesh over his cheekbones was taut, his eyes were red, and in his hand he held a meat cleaver, moonlight glinting off the steel blade.

Chibuike's legs shivered. Their chill spread to the rest of his body, and when he opened his mouth to speak, no sound emerged. Ginika's grip on his hand tightened so much it hurt.

The boy scanned them from head to foot. He pointed his weapon at Chibuike and barked, "Oga, remove your watch. Put it on the ground. Your phone. Wallet too." Then at Ginika: "Your purse, madam. Phone. And that necklace."

Chibuike unstrapped his watch unsteadily, lowered it next to his phone and wallet. Ginika did not move.

The boy's voice rose, his blade slashing air. "*Madam, you too.*"

Ginika finally complied, slowly setting down her belongings next to Chibuike's. A car roared past, and Chibuike thought of calling out, but the thought didn't morph into motion. The orange trail of the Volvo's tail lights lingered mockingly and then disappeared. The boy ordered them a few steps back. He scooped their things into his bag and retreated backward into the path from which he'd emerged. He was soon out of sight.

Chibuike inhaled deeply, each lungful of air vibrating in his throat. Ginika fell to her knees. When he reached for her, she shrank back.

"Don't touch me!" she said, tears running down her face. "Don't touch me, you *coward*."

Chibuike felt it then, the disintegration of a thousand tiny daydreams.

✦

They backtracked to the restaurant in silence. Ginika shakily relayed to their waitress what had just happened, giving no indication of the thief's age. The waitress disappeared behind the curtain and returned minutes later with a middle-aged man who had tribal marks sunken in his cheeks. He shook his head apologetically and stepped outside to flag a taxi on their behalf.

He was gone for almost ten minutes. Chibuike stared at Ginika, searching for the smallest word of consolation to offer. On finding none, he stared at the customers around them, tucked into the safety of their bubbles. A man sat by himself, dunking balls of fufu in peanut soup. Two women shared a large foil of kilishi, one of them uproariously thumping the other's shoulder. To think laughter had come easily mere minutes ago.

The taxi driver made three stops. The first was at a nearby police station. An officer grudgingly took their statements. He handed them supplementary forms to fill out and return at their earliest convenience. Chibuike knew not to bother. Next, the taxi driver dropped Chibuike off at Pitawka Estates, a set of enormous apartment buildings surrounded by bougainvillea, neatly trimmed hedges, and water fountains. Before Chibuike stepped out, he leaned toward Ginika—she pushed herself back against the side of her door.

"I just need time," she said. "Maybe we can meet tomorrow evening at seven. Our usual spot. Is that okay?"

Chibuike managed a nod. He waited until the taxi rounded a corner before he started off in the opposite direction. He pushed away from the sharp cones of towering street lights, the gentle drone of gas-powered generators. A half-hour later, he was in a smaller, darker neighbourhood. His apartment building loomed ahead, candlelight stirring from behind shuttered windows. The five flights of stairs up to his flat had never felt so endless, as his misshapen shadow twisted along the walls. His roommate, Fikayo, responded to his knocking almost immediately. Behind Fikayo, a table lantern threw shadows around the kitchen. A charred pot of fried rice steamed on the stove. Afrobeats blared from Fikayo's speaker.

"What happened to your key?" Fikayo asked.

Chibuike shouldered past him and into his windowless shoebox of a room. Fikayo followed, lingered by the door.

"Bro," he said, "what happened?"

Chibuike settled into bed and said nothing until Fikayo scoffed and walked away. Then Chibuike rolled to face the wall and closed his eyes tight against the rush of inner voices. In a former time, he would have told Fikayo everything. They had been close friends at the University of Benin, where Chibuike had studied economics and Fikayo international relations. After both graduated with first-class honours, they had moved to Port Harcourt together, reiterating their biggest dreams on the bus ride over. Five years had passed since then. Fikayo never got past the doors of the city's United Nations office, instead settling temporarily and then permanently into cashiering at a supermarket. Chibuike's seed loan applications for starting a selective private school gathered cobwebs in the cabinets of various banks. Their three-months-at-the-max apartment, with its cigarette-smoke corridors and sparse electricity, was never upgraded for a penthouse atop Pitawka Estates. Fikayo no longer cared to indulge Chibuike's lofty plans. Chibuike would start, "A new bank opened on Dhamijah. I want to make a revised pitch to their investment analyst," and Fikayo would smile, look elsewhere, ask how work at school had gone, as if the present was all that would ever exist.

Their conversations withered into minutiae: the day's rain, the month's rent. Chibuike stuffed his stapled, handwritten sheets of pitches into the suitcase beneath his bed. He passed endless nights in Bonny Club, losing track of the naira spent from long-held savings—the "quantum physicists' account," as he'd once thought of it—on beer cans and bourbon, on making passes at random women in solitary corners. Invariably, they turned away. Until Ginika. That first night, they drank till closing, then walked to Boro Park, where the night wind and his grand stories sobered her up. Convinced that she would vanish come sunrise, Chibuike spun tales from the life he'd never lived. He taught math at a prestigious secondary school and was on the verge of running his own. He overlooked the city's river ports from a penthouse balcony. Every December, he travelled to a new distant country. Enthralled, Ginika asked if they could meet again the next day, perhaps right there at the park.

They met many times at the park, at restaurants with crystal chandeliers, in the VIP sections of neon-lit cinemas featuring Nollywood's latest blockbusters. He funded their outings via the quantum physicists' account. In her presence, he rediscovered his capacity for soul-stirring conversation, and even when he returned home alone, that gulf between present self and future possibility felt minuscule. Late at night, by candlelight, he fell into old habits. He reworked Wazobia's payment models and advanced curricula, introducing derivative equations one class earlier and adding a section for European languages (surely, someone in Nigeria spoke fluent German). He looked up various funding contests with grants up to ten million naira and printed the applications in Madam Angelina's office when she was away. After work, he walked to the post office whistling P-Square jams, his shoulders squared high.

At night, in the rare moments that electricity flooded his room, he could suddenly see things for what they would be, the ordinary portending the extraordinary. The bedside fan that hardly ever spun was really an air conditioner set into painted walls. He lived in a mansion with parapets and long driveways, its marble staircases shaped like spirals. His lamp's glow was sunlight streaming through floor-to-ceiling windows, tugging him awake. On his ocean of a mattress, Ginika lay pressed beside him, tucked safely in his arms. She smiled in her sleep, her face free of lines. She baked his skin with her love and therefore made him worth loving.

Even now, as he listened to the shuffle of Fikayo's footsteps, he held on to that smile, how it softened her eyes. Outside, the uneven crooning of lovers on Fikayo's speaker stuttered into silence from a dead battery. A plate clattered into the sink, where it would sit atop a stack of other crust-covered plates for days. A door slammed. Then there was silence, and against it, the gathering of thoughts Chibuike had been straining to keep at bay. The look on Ginika's face earlier tonight, as if she'd glimpsed a diseased thing. *Coward* shrieking through the void. The boy with the cleaver. A fluttering terror gripped Chibuike. He was back on that road, frozen in hellish time, wondering if this was it. If all his daydreams and longings, all the stars yet undiscovered, could be undone at the whim of a child.

For hours, sleep evaded him.

✦

He dreamed briefly of lightning, a night sky with fevered white cracks, and awoke in a puddle of sweat. It was nearly seven a.m., which gave him just over an hour to prepare for work. He showered quickly with icy water and shovelled two hardened slices of bread in his mouth. Next, he foraged beneath his mattress and within his drawers for all the cash he could find. The notes totalled nearly seven thousand naira, enough for a cheap new phone and a few bus fares. He took the first bus to Fidelity Bank. There was only one other customer around, a short man with patches of grey hair.

A bespectacled teller shook her head as Chibuike recounted last night's robbery.

"Port Harcourt," she said. "My sad and sickened Port Harcourt. We are losing our state to common hoodlums, you know? God will punish our useless governor. Six months in office with nothing to show for it. I'm so sorry, my dear. Did you cancel your debit card?"

"That's what I'm here to do. And get a new one too. Jesus, I have so much shit to replace."

"Language, young man." She typed, the edges of her daffodil-painted nails clacking on her keyboard. "Last name, first name, date of birth, please. Digits of your debit card if you recall them." She typed some more as he replied. She frowned.

"What's wrong?" he asked.

"Why didn't you cancel this card last night? We offer online—"

"My phone was stolen!"

"What was your last transaction?"

"Dinner with my girlfriend yesterday. About fifteen thousand naira."

"Sir, I'm sorry, but there's nothing in your account. There are two ATM transactions here following this dinner, one last night for 180,000 naira, which is the daily withdrawal limit at all our machines. Another from this morning for the rest of it ... 22,000 naira and change."

Chibuike blinked. "You're joking."

"Sir—"

"How is that possible? I didn't give him my PIN."

"Did you write it down, maybe on a piece of paper tucked in your wallet?"

"*No!*"

"Sir, calm down, please. I am here to help. He took your ID, yes? So, he knew your birthday. Was your PIN created from those digits?"

To admit this seemed like defeat, a cruel loophole the bank could turn on him.

"I don't see how that matters," he said. "I did not make those transactions. I did *not*. Cancel them and give me my money."

"The money has been withdrawn, sir. There is nothing to give right now."

"What the fuck?" Chibuike said. The grey-haired man turned in their direction.

"*Language.*"

"Just cancel my account," Chibuike said. "Now, please."

"Sir?"

"If you can't offer basic protection to your customers, I'll find another bank to work with. So, I would like to close my account. Thank you very much."

Before she returned focus to her screen, the teller gave him a final look over the thick squares of her lenses, and he hated the expression they held, a pitying softness far worse than anger or contempt.

✦

Outside the bank, sunlight scorched his neck. Too much life thrummed around him. Motorcyclists twisted their handles and weaved through the maze of growing traffic. Schoolchildren in blue uniforms and long socks ran along the sidewalk, their bags skipping on their backs.

Nearby, a line of yellow buses waited. Chibuike stepped onto one bus, paused, and stepped back down.

The walk to Rivers Transit Secondary School was thirty minutes. He'd be slightly late, but his chaotic thoughts needed more space than the confines of an overcrowded bus. Yet, when he arrived and greeted Madam Angelina and took his position behind the monitor in the corner of her office, a strange calm engulfed him.

He sent out the usual weekly reminders to the parents' mailing list. Mid-terms were fast approaching, and students who performed badly risked spending the midyear break taking remedial classes. Sign-ups for the inter-class sports tournament were still ongoing. The school was accepting donations for its new state-of-the-art library.

Ordinarily, the monotony of his secretarial duties wore him down, with the days painfully measured in milliseconds. But here, now, was a world with definition, with event flyers to design, meetings to accept and decline, emails to categorize and reply to and forward. Here was a semblance of routine, and it gave shape to the remaining hours. He'd have too-salty lunch at the school cafeteria and make small talk with the handful of teachers who cared to indulge him. The school bell would ring a final time, and then a hundred feet would march outside. Afterward, he'd walk to Boro Park and wrap his tired arms around Ginika on a patch of grass flanked by sky-scraping trees.

He whistled as he worked, buoyed by a sudden cheery energy. At ten a.m., Madam Angelina stepped out for her usual round of class inspections, and fifteen minutes later, Mrs. Esther Ukwu walked in. She'd co-led a few PTA meetings in the past, and her daughter, Anita, was one of the school's star pupils.

Mrs. Ukwu glanced at Madam Angelina's empty chair. "Where is she?"

"She will be back soon, ma. Should I leave her a message?"

Mrs. Ukwu sat down on one of the plush stools lining a wall. "No, I can wait." From her purse, she withdrew a novel, *The Requiem of Amadioha*, and flipped toward the end. Chibuike pretended to work but looked up at her occasionally. Her presence always seemed to clog the air until he was conscious of every breath he took. He didn't know if it was the rarity of her appearance, marked by her giant loops of starry scarves and her sleek patterned dresses, or the sophisticated way she carried herself—the soft tapping of her heels on linoleum, her beautiful head held high. But she was the kind of woman who could overlook Pitawka Estates from the height of her own balcony, who could take vacations on white-sand beaches a thousand miles away. And she reminded Chibuike that power wasn't merely a state of having but a way of *being*, its ripples palpable in every room you entered.

He imagined himself, Ginika, Mrs. Ukwu, and a dozen other men and women like her in a soft-lit room, gathered around a long table covered in white linen and hourglass-shaped wine cups. They were laughing at something funny Ginika had said.

Chibuike cleared his throat and said, "That book—I read it a few years ago. It is amazing."

Mrs. Ukwu looked up at him, said nothing, looked back down.

"Did you read the last book he wrote?" Chibuike started again. "*Willows of the Old Ikeja*. It trapped a special kind of sad in me. Unforgettable."

Mrs. Ukwu sighed, reached into her glittering purse. She took out a pair of earphones and stuck them in—left, then right—and returned to her book, flipped a page. Chibuike stared at her. Watched her scan one line and then another until she was flipping a page again. And he remembered.

That he'd always hated Mrs. Ukwu, how her sickly sweet, overwrought perfume stained the air, how she moved so slowly, as if the bones in her legs were congealed mud, how she spoke to him without ever meeting his eyes, and how her voice sometimes resembled a dog barking. He remembered that he'd always hated this job. In his nighttime dreams, there was no corner desk in another's office, no small intonations of *sir* and *ma*. He remembered that on some days, like today, the millions of seconds spent in this room seemed to coalesce into a single wave that descended on him suddenly, bringing forth the urge to pull air into his chest, fill his lungs, and scream until every student and teacher was crowded outside the door, wanting to see what the fuss was all about. He remembered that someday, with all those eyes on him, he'd pack his bag and push back his chair and rise, step out into the sunlight, walk beyond the soccer fields and cracked driveways, beyond the confines of this damned school.

But there was no screaming to be had. Not today.

He stared at his screen, the words like a new language. Ten minutes later, Madam Angelina returned. She hugged Mrs. Ukwu, and they laughed over a joke Chibuike didn't hear, and Madam Angelina asked how Mrs. Ukwu's husband was doing, and Mrs. Ukwu laughed again.

"He's fine," she said, her gold hoop earrings dangling. "So very fine."

✦

Chibuike's mind was a litany of pending tasks. The phone to replace. IDs too, including his driver's licence for a car that did not yet exist.

His next monthly paycheque was three weeks away, so he'd need a new account in a new bank. But when the day's last bell clanged and the corridor outside filled with youthful chatter and pattering feet, he felt no desire to do any of those things.

He barely registered Madam Angelina wishing him a happy weekend, her eyes on her phone. Outside, he stood for a moment, watching fathers and mothers compress their children in hugs, lead them into Hondas and Toyotas idling in the school parking lot. Although it was too early to meet Ginika, Chibuike headed for Boro Park.

Its steep and rolling lawns were filled with the proceedings of family picnics: knives spreading butter on soft white bread, juice boxes punctured by straws, the windswept scent of sticky mangoes. Couples flocked to a nearby bridge. A heartbroken woman had flung herself off it years ago, sparking a still-growing mysticism. Love from her shattered heart, the legend went, still clung to the railings.

"That is preposterous," Ginika had said on their fourth date here, pressing her palm to her mouth to suppress her giggles.

"Or maybe there are things in the air our eyes cannot see," Chibuike had replied, picking up a stone. On the railing, he carved their initials with crooked lines: CA + GS. He found the marks now, unblemished by time, and traced the curves of the G and S.

It was just past seven when Ginika appeared. The sun was sinking, the outlines of slow-moving clouds tinged a fiery pink. With most of the kids gone, the remaining adults—mostly students from a nearby university—had started cracking open beer cans and lighting cigarettes. Ginika walked around the maze of bodies, moving slowly, and Chibuike hurried toward her. The hug she pulled him into had never felt so frail. They sat down on the grass, and he realized her right hand was bunched into a fist.

"Good to see you," she said, unsmiling. "Did you go to work today?"

Chibuike kept his voice steady.

"I did! Went to the bank first, though, cancelled my cards, made sure my money's all there. Poets and physicists don't grow on trees, you know?" He chuckled. "But yeah, it's all good. I told my students what happened. They laughed, little rascals, promised to help me find the crook. But that's life, right? Shit happens. We move on. How are you?"

"I'm ... not good. My money is there, thankfully, and I replaced my phone with some ancient Nokia from GSM Village this afternoon. But my heart hasn't stopped pounding. I see that boy's face everywhere. And I keep hearing myself, the cruel things I said to you."

"Babe, you were shaken." Chibuike reached for her cheek, brushed it with a thumb. "So was I. It's okay."

"I want to get this right, so please listen. Just listen. This crazy fear I'm feeling now, it's familiar. Felt it the day I left Pa, a man who loved me more than life itself, in his own crazy way. That morning, I couldn't get myself to move until I made a list. A reminder of what I was running *to*." Ginika relaxed her fist, revealing a piece of crumpled brown paper on her open palm. Chibuike took it, smoothed it out. By the day's waning light, he deciphered the untidy loops of Ginika's handwriting:

> Get a temp job. Cashier. Janitor. Anything. Just a week or two while you get settled.
>
> Apply to accounting firms in the city.

Get your own apartment. Bisi seems nice, and her place doesn't look like a dumpster, but she's still a stranger from the internet.

Save 3,000 naira a month. 1,500 if it's too tight.

Learn to drive. Ideally, manual.

Treat yourself to a trip to Ghana with your new savings account.

Day trip to Ma's grave at Aboki—remind yourself she's more than a cross in the dirt.

Solo road trip across the country, from Sokoto to Akwa Ibom. A week. A month?

Taste a few lips.

Get yourself a present for leaving home. And then another each time you do something on this list. Could be a pack of gum. Or a massage. From you to you.

Make another list when this one is done.

Never let fear paralyze you again.

Forgive Pa.

Chibuike read and reread the list, searching for where he fit in. Ginika continued speaking slowly, her eyes on the grass.

"Writing my hopes down helped a bit, got me moving. But then I got here, this city full of strangers, and all that fear rushed back in."

"But you're still here. You're still here."

"That first night at the club, I was getting ready to leave. Figured after a drink or two, I could face calling Pa. I could apologize. Tell him I would see him soon. But you showed up, like something out of a fairy tale. And that instinct Pa put inside me all my life—to feel safe and protected, to be another's—came back so quickly. In a different way, but there all the same. Within a week, I didn't need the scary list, didn't need to quit my job at Agege Café, didn't need anything but you. And last night, terrified as I was, I wanted to fight. Or run. Anything but freeze again. I didn't move, because I had you."

"I should have tried harder, I know—"

"*Listen.* These last few months, I've been in awe of you. Your accomplishments, your ambitions, and the incredible kindness you've always shown me. It's far more than I deserve, but it's also made me forget. I close my eyes at night, and I dream of shiny white walls around some of the smartest kids in the country. Your kids. But I still don't know what my dreams are, my limits—just mine—the shape of me. It's why I left Pa. And it's why I have to leave you."

Cold tinged the tips of Chibuike's fingers, and it scared him, how he could burn and freeze all at once.

"*Babe—*"

Ginika started to rise, and Chibuike saw in her motion the last seed of his possibilities. He lay flat on his stomach, the ground's bladed tufts prickly on his neck. His arms wrapped around her ankles, and he opened his mouth to say that he was lost too, afraid too, all the time. He was nothing and no one.

Instead, he whispered, "You're all I have. Only you. Please. Babe. Please. Please."

Ginika's eyes widened. She wriggled her legs, bent low to pry his grip loose. Once free, she half jogged out of the park, never stopping to look back.

✦

For hours afterward, Chibuike sat cross-legged on the ground. He rubbed his palms in small circles over his lap. The distant bobbing lights of cellphones and cameras soon vanished. It was dark when he rose, darker still when he finally started moving. He walked out of Boro Park as he had a dozen times before, but always with Ginika in lockstep, Ginika standing so close that strands of her hair tickled his nose when she looked up to marvel at the sky. At how gold seemed to drip from it over all else—the stars winking at every intersection, the fireflies with vivid, swollen tails, the haloed street lights.

Chibuike didn't realize where he was headed until he came across a familiar billboard: a PDP presidential candidate pointing out of his rectangular confines as if to say, *I'm here for you.* Not long after that, Chibuike walked onto a snaking paved boulevard. An hour ago, it would have been crawling with buses ferrying home fishermen and weary market women. Now, it belonged to the pedestrians. A handful of them ventured into lantern-lit superstores or patioed bars. Most, however, made their way to the road's end, where Bonny Club stood.

The usual bouncer nodded at Chibuike, not bothering to ask for an ID, and the usual albino bartender took his first order, a glass of tequila on the rocks, and the same strobe lights pulsed to the blare of Tiwa Savage's vocals. The same acrid, face-screwing taste on the swallow. The same heat as the liquor travelled down his throat. Even the same legs twisting on the raised platform in the middle of the dance floor.

He downed a second glass of tequila. Then a third. He counted the money remaining in his pockets, all the money he owned now. He watched the club slowly fill until it stank of sweat. The room spun in circles, and yet every woman's face seemed crystalline, the tiniest mole magnified beneath disco lighting. There were women grinding on men, women twerking against women, women squatting low in backless blouses, women laughing and singing along and chewing gum, women swiping on their phones in the corners, where the light barely reached.

Chibuike had a feeling that witnessing this communion of heat and bodies and thumping vibrations would offer relief from the gnawing in his chest, the gnawing that couldn't exist if he paid no attention to it. He added a thousand-naira tip to his fifth order, and the uncertainty on the bartender's face vanished after that. But it wasn't until the seventh glass that he spotted her.

It was just past midnight, and his remaining cash was down to three digits. Across the bar counter, a thin, mousy woman—likely in her early twenties—leaned against a pillar. She was overdressed, sweating beneath a jacket, idly watching the room's frenetic motions as if uncertain of her place here. Her left foot started to tap to the beat. Then it stopped. Started again. Occasionally, she raised an orange juice cocktail to her mouth, sipped, grimaced slightly.

Chibuike watched how she held the glass against her stomach, with a tenderness that seemed like instinct. As he lumbered unsteadily toward her to say hello, at one point grasping the back of a barstool for support, he noticed the tiny curl of her lips. Half a smile. He knew it reached her eyes. Knew that in a few years, they would sit side by side on the summit of that hill by the restaurant. There would be no chase, no school, no money, no penthouse apartments. No little boys with giant cleavers. There would only be him and her and the sleepy little town sloping below them—rooftops with satellite dishes, truck smoke, a shadowy church. And when the vast, unvarnished sky opened into a storm, she would take his hand tenderly and follow him home. Up the darkened stairs, into his small, windowless bedroom. The mattress would creak beneath their tangled bodies, his head weightless on her chest. In the blissful dark, every sound would assert itself. The loop of her breathing. Fikayo's snores drifting from the other room, dispossessed of urgency. The rain pattering outside, nothing more than rain.

MR. YEMI'S REVENGE

It was that halfway point in the school trimester when mid-term tests provoked frantic nights full of rote memorization, and the two-week Christmas break seemed centuries away. Mr. Yemi, our hostel master, banged his walking stick against the metal sides of our bunk beds. We shuffled sleepily to our feet. A glance out the window told us this was not the usual shower-time awakening. Dawn still resembled dusk, the sky not yet tinged with blots of pink.

"Go to the common room *now*," Mr. Yemi spat, an *or else* in his voice. Then he continued to the next room. We heard the repeated clank of his stick, reverberating like a discordant wave down our floor.

The common room slowly filled with all sixty of us. We took to rows of wobbly chairs or leaned against curtained panes. Yawning, stretching, squatting low, we wondered why we had been summoned. One of us noted that Mr. Yemi seemed to have gathered only our set, the SSS3 students. Perhaps it was related to our upcoming graduation ceremony, another suggested, to skeptical looks.

The last of us trailed in, shortly followed by Mr. Yemi. Our voices retreated into our throats as they often did near him, even though he was petite in stature. His white razor-creased dress shirts were perpetually tucked into dark khaki pants, their cuffs ending above his ankles. He silently hobbled on his blackwood walking stick, his bald head sparkling with moisture of unknown origin. (This mystery was number three on our list of seven unsolved mysteries. Sweat seemed unlikely, because even on windy Harmattan mornings his slick head shone, the rest of him dry.)

Mr. Yemi scanned our faces. We were used to his slow-turning examination, but it seemed mixed with an unusual hardness in his eyes.

"Over the past several weeks," he began, enunciating each word, "I have confiscated at least twenty contraband devices from all of you. Your cellphones and tablets and filth-music MP3 players. That this is all I have done, seize your items until the term ends, is mercy. I know how you students in this ajebutter school get when graduation approaches. You become unruly. Rebellious. I was one of you once. In a school not averse to canes, yes, and in a town where electricity was for the imagination, but one of you regardless. Boys will be boys, so I let you be boys. Yet, just a few hours ago, while I slept, at least one of you broke into my office. Damaged my door in the process. Busted my locked drawer and stole the devices. I already have every hostel supervisor going through your lockers and beds and bags as we speak, but in the interest of time, I want whoever did this to confess.

Now. I cannot promise that things will be good for the thief. Only that things will be bad for all of you if no one comes forward."

We exchanged glances, scratched the sides of our cheeks.

"Your office is on the JSS1 floor," Hassan volunteered. "Maybe it was a junior student."

"Don't even bother with that line. We have eyewitnesses. They heard the commotion and saw someone in *green* hostel wear running up the stairs. If you know who did it, you will save yourself trouble by confessing."

"But snitches get stitches," Babani said in a singsong tone. We called him Captain Clown because he hyena-laughed at small nothings and forced his jokes onto inappropriate moments. Even now, he followed up with a hoarse chuckle. It faltered as Mr. Yemi's calm finally disappeared. It was ten steps from where Mr. Yemi stood to the front of the room where Babani sat, ten steps during which Babani rose and tried to back away and mumbled that he was just joking, just joking sir, please sir. Our stomachs dropped in anticipation of a slap, but Mr. Yemi grabbed Babani by the shirt and, for the first time ever, screamed in his face. "Do I look like I'm joking, you stupid waste of oxygen?" He released Babani and turned toward us. "You all have until Saturday to produce the culprit and return everything that was stolen. And I mean *everything*. Or I will show you that I'm not your classmate."

He walked out, his stick and curly-toed boots impossibly silent on the hardwood. Babani stood stunned. When one of us, Yusuf, reached out to him, Babani flinched and cursed Yusuf in Hausa. We followed Babani's retreat and returned to our rooms in time to catch the supervisors departing. Our mattresses leaned lopsided against their frames, and white sheets and blankets lay coiled on the floor. The padlocks to our lockers had been forced open, our clothes and books flung into corners. Yusuf found his wristwatch by his bed, cracked and no longer ticking. Ibrahim scooped up our head prefect Nathaniel's journal from beneath his own pile of smelly socks and flipped through its pages. We quickly learned, before Nathaniel snatched the journal back, that he wrote bad poetry mostly concerned with the same character, an "Ijebu Sugar Mummy." In their world, she bought him gold-panelled cars, flew him to Morocco, and even let him suck the milk from her "obstinately untamed" breasts. Chikemka's photo of his ex-girlfriend was passed from floor to hand to hand before he finally recovered it two days later. His nickname morphed from Father Christmas Thighs to either Lover Boy or Werey for Babe, depending on who you asked. We wondered why he still held on to her picture when she had broken up with him so shamefully at a packed museum—an angry dressing-down about suspicious texts from night-owl skanks. We also wondered which of us had provoked this new-found layer to Mr. Yemi's ire.

✦

In the following weeks, we would see growing deviations in Mr. Yemi's behaviour. Normalcy had been our curse, after all, every routine mapped out to the millisecond. Every day at five a.m., a hazy hint of morning light rolled down the six floors of our hostel building, from the top floor, where we lived, to the orange ledges of the ground level, inhabited by JSS1 students, most of them a year away from puberty. We were stirred out of dreams by the whistling and clapping of Mallam Ahmed, our floor supervisor. We dashed toward the five-stall bathroom at the end of our corridor. Two of them were often initially occupied by Nathaniel, who awoke even before the supervisors, and Suleiman, the biggest of us and the oldest at nineteen. We formed queues and mostly avoided talking (a combination of residual lethargy and rank morning breath) unless someone took longer than five minutes to shower. In that case, we banged on the stall door and asked if they were in there fucking their mother.

The bravest of us slipped back into bed after Mallam Ahmed vanished to his room. It was a calculated gamble—an extra hour of sleep versus the 30 percent chance that Mr. Yemi decided to patrol our floor with his jug of stinging-cold water. He'd cup the water in one palm and fling it at the snoring daredevils. Then he'd march them, held by one ear, toward whatever remained of the queues.

"Back in my boarding school days," he often said, "all the boys fetched their water in buckets from a tank one kilometre away. We showered outside too, in the middle of a big, open field. Whether you were in JSS3 or SSS2, your penis and buttocks were on full display. And if you dared go back to sleep, if you had that kind of death wish, our hostel master found you with his whip. Yes, he had a whip. He beat us till our skins cracked."

At seven, we ironed our uniforms, stretched our long socks over our ankles, and marched toward breakfast in the café atop the class building. Eggs drowned in grease. Crisp orange juice diluted with gallons of water until it held only a sliver of its original flavour. Assembly followed at eight on the cobbled grounds flanked by the hostel and the class buildings. The sun scorched our skins through our navy-blue uniforms. We lined up in columns, prying slack the noose-like knots of our ties, but never too loose. We did not want to risk Mr. Yemi double-tapping our shoulders, a signal to fall out of line. Out-of-liners also included those with unironed uniforms, unpolished black shoes, noisy demeanours, or overgrown hair. (A barber visited us on Saturdays; his price was no issue at two hundred naira, but he was ill-versed in the aesthetics of tapered hairlines and low fades.)

Assembly was the day's first hint of a larger world beyond our school's confines. The day-shift security guards unlocked the barbed wire gates for the arrival of non-hostel staff. First was Principal Akande, who lived a street over. He was mild in his manner, gargantuan in his cowardice, and ran the school only on paper. In truth, these grounds were Mr. Yemi's kingdom. Vice-Principal Obiora was similarly ineffectual, but we liked his dry humour and kind face. At forty, he was childless and unmarried. (This was number two on our list of unsolved mysteries, suspicions ranging from homosexuality to erectile dysfunction to the existence of a secret family somewhere in the rural north.)

We especially cherished the arrival of Miss Jimoke, the senior mathematics teacher. Of our three female teachers, she was the youngest at twenty-four. We secretly called her Auntie Nyash in appreciation of her heaving backside. We also appreciated her jewel-free fingers and her laughter at all our jokes, even Babani's.

For us, assembly was a bifurcation: one half of us here, the other half astral-projecting onto the partly obscured rooftops of surrounding hotels, banks, and multi-purpose plazas, buildings we only ever saw in full during the brief holidays demarcating each trimester. As VP Obiora read the morning's announcements and we chorused off-key through our national and school anthems, "*Thanking thee, evermore, for the bounty of knowledge*"—*thee* sometimes substituted with *pee*—we imagined ourselves perched like kites on those roofs, the edges of our backs glinting yellow, our legs readying for flight. We soared into a universe not constrained by two school buildings.

After assembly, we marched up the stairs into our classrooms, watching from the windows as Mr. Yemi punished the out-of-liners. He made them squat low and hold their fingers to their ears. At his command, they frog-jumped across the assembly grounds, usually for under ten minutes, occasionally for twenty. The determining algorithm seemed to be a mix of their crimes and his mood.

"Pay attention," our teachers invariably shouted, clapping their hands to recapture our focus. "Or else I'll make you join them."

Classes ran till two, followed by lunch in the café. The teachers had their own table at one end. The most discerning of us listened to their chatter for stray gossip, which was supplied mainly by Mr. Yemi, who positioned himself at the table's head. Afterward, there was a migration: the teachers to their cars, Mr. Yemi to his office in the hostel, and us to our rooms. We changed out of our school uniforms into colour-coded hostel wear. For us, it was a green T-shirt with the school logo emblazoned over the breast pocket and pleated white shorts. We prepared for nap time, although we hardly slept, choosing instead to watch the departing cars from the window or to lie on the floor to play the handful of board games we were permitted. Around this time, Mallam Ahmed mostly kept to his room. This allowed Suleiman, our early-bird giant, to conduct his business.

While most of our parents could afford the school's seven-figure tuition, students like Suleiman and Nathaniel were only here thanks to generous scholarship awards granted after entrance exams to the highest-scoring students. Suleiman kept the logistical details of his side hustle to himself, but we understood its basic shape. He somehow snuck in cartons of Indomie noodles, which he then sold to us, each ramen packet inflated by 500 percent. We knew to mourn this injustice privately. For one, an uppercut from Suleiman would surely land us in the sick bay, which always reeked of insecticide and had no female staff. For another, Indomie tasted better than anything the café ever whipped up.

Cooking the noodles was a masterclass in stealth. We made our purchases in bathroom stalls or behind the wild shrubs encroaching on our hostel backyard. Then, just as covertly, we moved to the toilet and filled our bathing bowls with boiling hot water. This served as a makeshift pot for the ramen block and its spices. Once the water turned milky and every strand soft to the touch, we used our curved palms to scoop noodles from bowl to mouth. Attracting the attention of hostel staff signified trouble, but we were far more fearful of running into each other. Whenever we spotted one of us going about his Indo-business, we followed him; we even helped him. We kept a lookout. If the water on our floor ran too cold, we fetched some from the lower ones. We offered our own bowls so much that "cleaner than your father's anus" became a catchphrase we dearly hoped was true. In exchange for these services, our caught mate would grant us one palmful of his Indomie. Knowing that we could later regain that palmful from a begrudging other allowed us to grudgingly give.

We never forgot the afternoon that three of us spotted Hassan with *four* noodle blocks.

"I'm hungry, wallahi," he told us. "I don't want to share."

Still, we offered him a bowl, fetched the water, and looked out for trouble while he turned the mix by the toilet, leaning against a toothpaste-speckled sink. Suddenly, we were jolted by a retching sound. Hassan horked a ball of spit into his bowl of noodles and swirled it with his fingers.

"Still want it?" he asked, smirking.

Without hesitation, three curved palms extended toward him.

✦

Nap time was sometimes followed by sports at five. We had a single football field, its photogenically green grass in our school brochures dulled to bristly yellow by reality. Mr. Yemi tacked the week's evolving soccer schedule to our notice boards, but we often commandeered field control from the junior sets. Our social hierarchy permitted us this power. In the absence of nearby hostel staff, we could also make the SSS2 students handwash our clothes, and they could demand a piece of chicken from a ravenous JSS3 student, who could slap a JSS1 student for looking at him funny. The JSS1 would bear the slap, knowing his power would come with time, would grow year after year.

From six to eight and from nine to ten, we returned to our classrooms for study time, with dinner in between. We copied homework answers off the most diligent of us, knowing when and where to alter our sentences to erase hints of plagiarism. Mallam Ahmed and Mr. Yemi patrolled each class, seeking loudmouths and head-on-desk nappers. Around this time, Mr. Yemi would be sipping from a beer can, which softened his mood. His nighttime admonishments were softer, the words coloured a vaguely parental hue. He was a moulder of clay, a master of destinies.

"I know you are all ready for bed," he would say, swirling his can, "but the work you are doing here is crucial. Work that will determine the rest of your lives. Every subject you study and every assignment you diligently complete brings you one step closer to becoming a functional member of society. Did you know that, in my day, we studied with candles and not light bulbs? My classmates dispatched early, but me? No." He raised a thumb above his head. "I never returned to my room until the burning candle was smaller than this finger. Father, dear Father, was a fisherman, and Mother mended sandals in our kitchen. See, she had to work from home to properly care for my siblings. I was the only one they could afford to send away, the *only one* with this gift of education. I knew that it could not go to waste. Would it have been fair to them?"

"No," we chorused. He smiled as though delighted by our capacity for tiny wisdoms, then cocked his head toward the ceiling for a final can-draining gulp.

"No," he continued. "It would not have been fair to Mother or Father, to my dear brother Ope or my sweet sister Moromoke, all of them stuck within the mud walls of our village hut. So I studied until unimaginable headaches pounded me, and I studied some more. I passed every class with nothing less than an A. I graduated at the very top. Now, here I stand in one of this country's most accomplished secondary schools." We thought this characterization a stretch; we were no Loyola Jesuit, no American Academy. We were prestige by virtue of cost rather than intellect. Still, we never corrected him, not even among ourselves.

"I am here," Mr. Yemi repeated, "begging you: Save your little naps. Save the hot gist you want to tell your friends. Save all that for later. Seize your future now. In ten years, you will thank me."

His eyes were always gentle at the end, almost liquid. It was as if he were not looking at us but backward in time, lost in a drafty, ceilingless room with low desks. He'd told us these words enough times that we knew them by heart. Yet, his gravitas rendered each proclamation fresh.

After study time, we returned to the hostel building. Room lights went out at ten-thirty sharp. An hour later, Mallam Ahmed and Mr. Yemi ceased their mischief-seeking patrols. Most of us fell into snores. The dark of the night thickened. Those still awake tiptoed against its shroud. We pulled our smuggled cellphones and iPods from various hiding spots: inside secret backpack compartments and soapboxes sitting innocently in lockers, beneath mattresses. We watched porn on mute. Texted girls we claimed were ours, hoping for a response in the heartbeat-heavy dark. Plugged in our earphones and listened to all the songs that reminded us we had once been babies and would someday grow old, our current reality no greater than a speck on nostalgia's windscreen.

In truth, only a handful of us could outline the coming years. Suleiman and Nathaniel had mailed out early admission applications to Stanford, their acceptance letters an enviable no-brainer. Hassan's father had all but guaranteed him a spot at Abu Dhabi University, freeing him from the final-trimester hassle of WAEC, NECO, and JAMB exams. Okonkwo, our bulky sports prefect, had already secured an athletic scholarship. For the rest of us, uncertainty seeped in. The slow march to graduation. SAT and TOEFL textbooks. Universities in unknown cities. Our future was a swirling black portal. Enticing because it meant getting "out of here." Terrifying because it asked, "To where?" The quiet, moonlit hours offered us a temporary reprieve from the day's numbing monotony and the night's fearful wondering. Yes, there remained a non-zero probability of looking up from our screens only to find Mr. Yemi suddenly beside us, his hand outstretched as if for a palmful of Indomie, which surely meant that we would be frog-jumping beneath the next day's sun, double-burned by its heat and by the gaze of our watchful peers. But routine made such risks calculable. Acceptable.

At least until the phones went missing from Mr. Yemi's office.

✦

During assembly, Principal Akande spoke about the incident in his usual unconvincing manner. We could practically see Mr. Yemi's ventriloquist hands jammed up his buttocks, forming the words: "One or more SSS3 students are suspected of breaking into Mr. Yemi's office. These ruffians stole a box containing confiscated devices and some of his personal items. Please, please, please, if you know anything about this, come forward to him or me. We will not tolerate theft or disorder under any circumstances."

His statement was so passionless that we assumed the incident would vanish to the realm of the occasionally referenced, normalcy reigning supreme. If only. The days afterward were a collage of accumulating deviations. For starters, neither Mr. Yemi nor Mallam Ahmed returned to his room after shaking us up for shower time. They patrolled so unceasingly that it would have taken a Herculean effort to sneak in that extra hour of sleep. Not that it stopped Lover Boy Chikemka from trying. One second, he was lying against the wall edge of his bed beneath his caramel blanket, the next, Mr. Yemi was emptying a bucket of freezing cold water onto him.

Soon, the out-of-liners group was mostly populated by students from our set, and twenty-minute frog-jumps became the rule rather than the exception. Classmates returned to us stinky from sweat. Nathaniel, prone to approaching his head prefectship with overzealous communality, started checking our hair, nails, ties, and shoes as we readied for the day, a clipper or comb in his hand. "Something has entered Mr. Yemi," he whispered beneath the frenzied din of breakfast and lunch. "We have to be perfect."

Some of us prized our stubbornness. Okonkwo, for instance. Given his six-pack and the *V* shape of his torso, frog-jumps had never fazed him. On Friday, only days after Mr. Yemi's outburst in the common room, Okonkwo was pulled out of line for rocking bushy, uncombed hair. This time, though, he was sent to Mr. Yemi's office. He resurfaced during second-period Christian Knowledge, the collar of his shirt raised over the top of his head. Mrs. Ugwu asked him to take it down, but he only complied when she threatened to find Mr. Yemi. Gasps and laughter followed—Okonkwo's hair was now a messy patchwork of thick hair and random bald spots. He skipped lunch that day, too keenly aware he would be subject to a litany of new nicknames.

That same evening, when the setting sun released us to dinner, we found Mr. Yemi standing next to the serving chefs rather than already seated at the staff table. Several JSS1 students were queuing up and grabbing steel plates. The first of us to arrive cut in front of them as usual, and they stepped back in hasty deference as usual.

"*Hey*," Mr. Yemi snarled. "What do you people think you are doing?"

We gaped at him. It was like asking why we breathed.

"I know you people are dense, but do you really not understand the concept of first-come, first-served? Before I count to three, you will return yourselves to the back of the line."

"Sir," one of us started.

"*One—*"

We moved.

✦

We experienced a collective feeling of surreality.

Routine, it turned out, had held a certain comfort. Not in its macro structures, which were still largely unaltered, but in its foundational microcosms. The tiny traditions now intercut by venomous *heys* and wordless glares. Hassan, formerly one to pretend our bland morning tea was actually cream liqueur, stopped lumbering drunkenly toward assembly, a chorus of our laughter in his wake. The diffusion rate of homework solutions from the brainiacs to the brain-dead during study time dwindled. As did our accompanying low-volume chatter that, in some small way, had given our days together a sense of finality. Gone were the mathematical analyses of Premier League predictions, of which SSS2 students were mutually jerking off in secret, of which of us—based on the latest English mid-term scores—would bloom into rap aficionados, pot-bellied politicians, hooker connoisseurs. Even the rate of finding new unsolved mysteries was impacted. In the last five years together, we had accrued seven mysteries. This trimester alone, we accrued three more.

Number eight, of course, was the identity of the phone thieves. Theories abounded in whispers. The least popular: Mr. Yemi was wrong. He'd invented his eyewitnesses, or they'd mistaken the colour of hostel wear, or they were in fact the guilty ones. We weren't quite convinced. The act did speak to a courage only those almost out the gates could possess. Therefore, we considered the most reckless of us. People like Hassan, who openly flirted with Auntie Nyash in the staff room until Mr. Ezeudenna, our geography teacher, chased him out. We considered the poorest of us. Who better than Suleiman, versed in the ins and outs of smuggling Indomie? Or Nathaniel, whose father worked as a trader in GSM Village and therefore had the means to quickly unload a dozen high-end smartphones come Christmas. We considered hatred. Had Lamawal really forgiven Mr. Yemi's comment from six months ago that his dead mother would be disappointed with his unacademic ways? We considered personal stakes. Hadn't Yusuf's laptop been confiscated as well? A latest-brand model stocked with five hundred movies, each one painstakingly downloaded from sketchy websites.

We also considered that Mr. Yemi's actions possibly stemmed from a deeper wound. What were the "personal items" Principal Akande had said were also missing? Like Chikemka, had Mr. Yemi held on to a picture of an expired love? A beautiful woman? Or a handsome man? Or perhaps he'd possessed a secondary school transcript riddled with Cs and Ds and Fs, proving the exaggerated fluff of his intellect. Perhaps the shame of his lies, exposed to at least one of us, had metastasized into rage. Or perhaps the simplest answer was the truest: his ego had been damaged simply because some of us refused to fear it. Regardless of what had or had not been taken, some of us had dared to break into his office.

Mystery number nine arrived on a Thursday evening two weeks after Okonkwo's monkey-with-a-clipper haircut. We returned to our floor after study time and pooled into shocked clusters at the top of the staircase. A near-spherical blob of feces was attached to a corner of the ceiling. There were no smears on the wall or around the sphere, as one might expect, had it been flung upward. No, we imagined the culprit Spider-Manning up the wall and letting loose at a perfect gravity-resistant angle. Upon sighting the atrocity, Mr. Yemi cursed us in Yoruba. He ordered head prefect Nathaniel to fetch a sponge, a ladder from our supply closet, and a bucket of Dettol-infused soapy water. "Lead by example." In the days after the forced cleaning, Nathaniel said little, a shadow of anger locking his jaw in place. For us, a connection existed between the Spider-Man poop and the missing phones, a link at once inevitable and yet deeply inscrutable.

Mystery number ten was, therefore, necessary, a constructed myth whose answer we could never voice because it only mattered that we wordlessly understood, and in our understanding, there was control.

Mystery number ten: what happened to Adamu Babangida, son of *the* Mr. Babangida?

✦

The sky was a perfect blue parchment, ripe for our joy. Rainy, grey afternoons had plagued the last few days, dampening our most recent football game. By Mr. Yemi's schedule, the field belonged to the JSS3 students; indeed, they were kicking, laughing, and spectating when a number of us descended upon the grass, led by a clean-shaven Okonkwo.

He caught the soaring ball with both hands.

"Una don try," he said, grinning. "But na time to bounce. Or if una like, you sabi watch." In the old world, they would have grumbled and sighed and stalked off. This time, Adamu Babangida, tall as a tree and just as thick, stepped forward, moving so close to Okonkwo that they could have kissed.

"It's our turn today," he said. His voice wavered, betraying his bravado. "Check the notice boards."

A few awkward laughs petered out of the other JSS3 students.

Okonkwo cupped a hand to his ear. "Sorry, e be like say I no hear you well. Talk am again."

"I said it's our—"

Four of us gathered around Okonkwo, with Babangida standing alone, diminished. When he turned to his classmates for support, they backed away, some even departing the field. Babangida had enough sense to fall back and follow them. About five minutes later, though, just as we were starting to sweat, Mr. Yemi entered the field, snapping his fingers until our game stopped.

"Are you all blind?" he said, gesturing wildly. "Or is it that you lack the ability to read ordinary English?" His voice was raised high enough that we instinctively avoided direct eye contact. We regarded the clouds, our dusty shoes, the field's entrance ... where a smiling Babangida stood, arms crossed and head high. We dispersed, glowering, and the JSS3 students resumed their game.

At dawn, the freshly awoken JSS3 students hurried into their floor's bathroom to shower. They were stopped in their tracks by the sight of Babangida's naked body propped against a stall door. His face was a swollen pulp, red tears leaking from a puffy left eye. Mr. Yemi drove Babangida to the hospital. An hour later, he summoned us to the common room. He pointed at Okonkwo, who cried panicked tears and swore on the heads of his ancestors that he knew nothing about it. Mr. Yemi pointed at Nathaniel—"What kind of a useless head prefect are you?"—and then at all of us, promising fire and brimstone, promising the end of days: "Just you wait. Once Babangida wakes up and lets me know which of you evil thugs attacked him, just you wait. You will see."

But Babangida had no names for Mr. Yemi upon hospital discharge. He returned with one eye bandaged, his bruised lips quieter, his shoulders hunched downward. Senator Abdullahi Babangida screamed down Principal Akande's office door, pledging a media firestorm. Flustered, Principal Akande threatened expulsions. But with no evidence and no confession, the best he could manage was to strip Okonkwo of his prefectship and suspend him for two weeks under the charge of inciting violence. Not that it stopped the senator from pulling Babangida out of school shortly afterward. From our floor, we watched the boy wheel his suitcase past the gates and into a sleek black Mercedes. Some of us even laughed at his limping leg. Yes, we could appreciate the violence of his fate, but violence had always been the contract of our existence. The metamorphosis from suffering to birthright: first, we gave and gave; then, we took. Mess with that balance, as Mr. Yemi had, and something else would give. Every drop of Babangida's blood that had stained the JSS3 bathroom was on Mr. Yemi's shiny head.

✦

We also lost Suleiman's tasty, overpriced packets of Indomie. Mr. Yemi's patrol was now too active for us to buy and cook them, however discreetly. The bastard also ripped our notebook pages out if he even suspected we had so much as glanced at our desk neighbour's assignment answers, demanding we start afresh. When he did this to Babani, he followed it up with a smug question: "If you ever become a surgeon—just allow me this fantasy—will you call Suleiman here to operate on *your* patient?"

Unfazed, Babani laughed and said in his sincerest tone, "No sir, sorry sir, I'll start again, sir, this time on my own." We saw how his easy acquiescence deepened the lines on Mr. Yemi's forehead, how Mr. Yemi stared and stared at Babani as if searching for an opening to pounce through before shaking his head, muttering, and stalking off. From that interaction, we finally understood that our despair fuelled him. The perfect antidote existed in the stability of our demeanour.

We became perfect.

Without Nathaniel's interference, our shoes shone, glossy enough to reflect our faces. The creases on our ironed shirts were sharp enough to pierce skin. We watched Mr. Yemi circle our queues over and over, unable to pull anyone out for infractions. Watched him march down corridors, in and out of classrooms, staring.

One night, barely a minute after lights out, Mr. Yemi crashed into our room, uncharacteristically explosive, as if surprise were the missing piece to his unsuccessful investigative efforts. As if we hadn't stopped taking even the smallest late-night risk. He shone his torchlight across our various beds, then walked off, his stick thwacking as he departed. Babani laughed that hyena guffaw of his. Its melody followed us into sleep.

✦

Before we understood the need for perfection, a few of us had pestered Suleiman about resuming his sale of Indomie noodles. Our promises were plentiful: we would counter Mr. Yemi's increased vigilance with renewed stealth; we'd pay more money; shit, we'd drop his pants and drain the semen from his penis until his toes fluttered. The last one made him stroke his beard as if in deep ponderance before responding with a flat, stoic no. Our only source of "nutrients" became the tragic café.

There, the chefs were stingy with the chicken but generous with the oversalted rice. When they served us beans, the oil overflowed from our bowls. We could probably find stones in the hostel backyard with softer textures than their garri, and their ogbono was even more watered down than the breakfast orange juice. Worst of all, they served the same handful of meals every week; we tasted the greyscale palette of our lives in every bite. By contrast, Suleiman's noodles had been spicy, flavourful, and steeped in the quiet thrill of a stealthy cook gone undiscovered. In their sudden absence, we had only one culinary saving grace: Visiting Day.

One Saturday per trimester, right at noon, the school gates opened to our families. Mothers showed up with reluctant fathers, eager sisters, mathematical sets featuring new protractors, bags, books, and best of all, food. Burgers and shawarmas from Drumstix, the reddest assorted meats from Yahuza, home-cooked jollof rice, achicha and amala, zobo juice, ice cream, strawberry yogurt, pepperoni pizza, and leafy okpa, in plump nylon bags. We dined together in the café and classrooms until our bellies swelled, traded stories and assurances—*It's all good, doing great, studying hard, miss you every day*—and held back tears when the sunset announced their departure.

But on that breezy November Saturday, as we headed into the class building to ready our desks and chairs for the feast ahead, the joy of anticipation morphed into a disbelieving confusion. There were new additions to the notice boards that dominated every corridor. Each of these identical sheets of paper, embossed top and bottom with our school's logo, bore a list of ten names: the worst ten SSS3 students in the entire school, ranked by mid-term average across all subjects. An introductory paragraph framed this list as a new technique to motivate and inspire the younger students.

All day, the notice boards functioned as a magnet, drawing students, supervisors, and hordes of parents. Hassan—number five on the list—avoided any suspense by marching his father directly to it. His father stared for a long time and sighed. He led Hassan away. They ate cross-legged beneath the canopy of trees clustered near the gates. At first, they were all serious faces and vigorous nods. Then laughter followed, the kind we added to our envy box because we knew it came from an airy and unburdened place, a place alien to us, even outside those gates. Hassan's father was a conundrum, proud in attire and demeanour, a local government chairman by profession, and somehow still unembarrassable. Before he left, he kissed Hassan on the forehead.

Leading the blacklist's charge of dunces was Babani at 38 percent. To no avail, he begged Mallam Ahmed for a call to his parents—"I'm feeling sick." His mother, Mrs. Hauwa, arrived in a bejewelled ankara, his two younger brothers marching behind her, all of them holding transparent boxes of skewered beef. We watched them depart the school fifty seconds later. Babani, the ever-laughing Captain Clown, chased after them. He dropped to his knees when his mother reached the gates, yelled her name when she walked past it—"Mama, please!"—his words frightening in their intensity. Pieces of beef from the discarded boxes littered the cobbled grounds around Babani, who refused to rise even after his mother drove off, not even when we hurried toward him, tried to pull him up—*get up, dust yourself off, don't beg*. Not in front of the juniors, not in front of these strangers, not in front of a watchful Mr. Yemi.

✦

We were not surprised when the blacklists disappeared on Sunday, their purpose served. No, our shock came when Mr. Yemi apologized during Monday morning's assembly, even though there was a lilt to his voice.

"Over the Visiting Day weekend," he said, "I made an attempt to inspire all of us toward more ambitious standards of performance. This involved highlighting the members of our senior class whose graduation chances seemed uncertain. I admit now that it might have been overzealous on my part. I know we all strive for excellence, so in the future, I will aim for more encouraging avenues." Principal Akande clapped afterward, leading to a smattering of applause from the teachers behind him. None of us were out-of-liners that morning; this had been the case for a few days, but it was also clear Mr. Yemi had hardly tried to find offenders today.

Whatever demon had overcome him recently seemed fully exorcised. He no longer paraded around our floor at nap time. He did not perch by the field at soccer time. During study time, he even exchanged his eagle-eyed vigilance for a relaxed and grinning personality, regaling us again with familiar stories about his secondary school days and how its many fires had forged his inner strength. His eyes flitted toward Babani's at every weak joke's punchline, as if hoping for the compromise of a smile. But Babani remained as he had ever since dusting himself off the ground and walking into the hostel two days ago: cold and rigid.

The next morning, as we starched our uniforms, we saw Babani crumple his own uniform to make wrinkles. We laughed, then we frowned, then we pleaded. Okonkwo, back the previous evening from his suspension, pulled Babani aside in the bathroom for a heart-to-heart discussion. Still, come assembly time, there Babani stood, already one step out of line, his collar popped high, his tie wrapped around his fist like a glove, and the zipper of his unironed pants pulled low enough that his maroon underwear showed.

Mr. Yemi spotted him just before we started our off-key anthems. His shock quickly gave way to amusement, a brand of it at once cold and familiar. War was back on the menu. He tapped Babani's shoulder twice. We held our breath, waiting for Babani's resistance. To our relief, he fell out of line. Minutes later, during first-period geography, Mr. Ezeudenna readied his notes. We ignored him, our focus past the windows, on Babani and Mr. Yemi.

The day felt like it should be shadowed by imminent rain, sunlight dimmed by a congress of clouds. Instead, there was scorching heat, the worst temperature possible for an undoubtedly prolonged frog-jump. But Mr. Yemi had something decidedly more creative in mind.

"Focus on the board," Mr. Ezeudenna cautioned us, between drawls about regolith formation. Our eyes remained glued to the glass. Mr. Yemi disappeared into the hostel building while Babani waited, bouncing restlessly on his toes. When Mr. Yemi re-emerged, his pace was slowed by the weight of two metal buckets, one filled with water, the other empty. He placed them about twenty steps apart and directed a compliant Babani behind the full bucket. Mr. Yemi took a fork out of his pocket and handed it to Babani. He pointed at the full bucket, then the empty one, making a scooping-and-transferring gesture.

Babani stared unblinking at Mr. Yemi.

Mr. Yemi pointed again. Fork. Full bucket. Empty bucket.

Babani laughed. He dropped the fork and started toward the hostel building. Mr. Yemi called after him, his small frame vibrating, and when Babani did not turn back, Mr. Yemi dashed forward. We were muttering now. Those of us farthest from the windows rose to draw nearer. Even Mr. Ezeudenna gave up on any sense of decorum, his eyes affixed to the unfolding scene, a piece of chalk dangling from two pinched fingers. We felt our lungs become pits, air finding its way inward and then falling ceaselessly. Felt it even before Mr. Yemi grabbed Babani's shoulder, and Babani turned around, and Babani swung, his fist catching Mr. Yemi's throat, bowling him backward.

Our held silence exploded. Gasps, laughter, scattered applause. *What the fucks* and *shits*. Babani turned his back on Mr. Yemi, who scrambled to his feet in a way that should have been comical but for our ice-cold skins. Mr. Yemi pulled his belt loose in a fluid motion, raised it high, and struck, the buckled end catching Babani's neck. He struck and struck. When Babani dropped to the ground, attempting to protect his face with his raised elbows, Mr. Yemi kicked too. We saw the arc of his spit, his crunching boots. We saw it from the window and from the cobbled grounds we suddenly found ourselves running across. We saw it as we drew closer. Nathaniel was there in a flash. He caught Mr. Yemi's belt just as it rose again, tore it from his grip, and flung it aside. He stood between a quivering Babani, his lacerated elbows still raised, and Mr. Yemi, his eyes red as Harmattan dust, his chest rising and falling, spit tinging the corners of his mouth. Then Mr. Yemi noticed the audience he'd drawn, all the students from various classes, VP Obiora, Auntie Nyash. Mr. Yemi uncurled his fists and marched silently into the hostel building. Nathaniel pulled Babani up and held him against his shoulder. Held him for a long time.

✦

We waited.

VP Obiora, Auntie Nyash, and two hostel supervisors shepherded us back to our classes. As we scribbled words from board to book, we waited. Those of us sitting closest to Babani stole glances at the parts of him we could see: jaw half-clenched, spots of reddened skin, dust smears lining one side of his shirt. Through the sleepless hours of nap time, we waited. Routine had already reasserted itself, but we felt the falseness of it in Mr. Yemi's absent footsteps. When dinnertime rolled along without fanfare, though, we started to breathe a little. Hassan stabbed the last cut of his chicken with a fork. He said he'd half expected Nathaniel to carry Mr. Yemi like *this*—he raised the fork—and bounce him off the ground. Or for Nathaniel to whip Mr. Yemi with his own belt, Suleiman added, drawing smiles from even Babani, who had licked his plate clean. When Babani reached over and grabbed Hassan's meat-topped fork, Hassan granted him that final bite.

Mr. Yemi didn't show up during either round of study time, leaving only Mallam Ahmed wandering from class to class. Okonkwo utilized Mallam Ahmed's periodic lapses to pass around a page-long note torn from one of his exercise books. He'd overheard two teachers saying that Mr. Yemi's actions might cost him his job. To Okonkwo, perhaps we finally had a chance to capitalize on Mr. Yemi's overreach. Until Mr. Yemi agreed that he would apologize at assembly to Babani, in front of everyone, we would not leave this classroom, not even for food or sleep. If we needed to use the bathroom, we could simply shit our pants. It was just like Okonkwo to deem himself an activist after two weeks of playing FIFA and guzzling Fanta at home. In fact, most of our comments as we read his note concerned his chickenshit cursive. Still, we felt an immovable thing lodge itself within us, birthed by his words.

When Mallam Ahmed tried to shepherd us back to our rooms in preparation for lights out, Okonkwo said, "With all due respect, sir, we won't leave here until we've spoken to Mr. Yemi." Never one to tolerate our shifting moods, Mallam Ahmed sighed and walked away. We crowded into a singular classroom, five dozen bodies warming it so fast our foreheads turned slick. The lights in the adjacent hostel building winked out synchronously from first floor to fifth. Square windows still glowed on the sixth floor, and we quite liked the image of it, how we shone in the dark.

By midnight, we had remixed rock, paper, scissors into rock, paper, scissors, Ijebu Garri, Auntie Nyash's nyash. The final round was ongoing—Lamawal vs. Suleiman—when Mr. Yemi finally walked in, a notepad tucked under his armpit. A new weariness coloured his expression. Some of us focused on it. The rest of us continued cheering as Lamawal's double-fisted Ijebu Garri finally vanquished Suleiman's scissors. Only when Mr. Yemi cleared his throat a third time did he have our complete attention.

Casually, he asked, "Why are you all not in bed? It is past lights out."

Nathaniel raised his hand but spoke before Mr. Yemi could call on him. "Sir, we have things to ask of you before we leave this classroom."

"Oh. Is that so?"

"First of all, we want you to apologize to Babani—"

"Head boy, I'll stop you right there before you embarrass yourself any further. I know that for too long you've all lived in this wonderful reality where you're kings of the jungle. If my Ope and my dear old Moromoke had had a fraction—a mere fraction—of what you're so willing to disrespect ..." A cloud took hold of Mr. Yemi's face, and just as quickly, he shook it away. "Head boy, do you know what is happening in the junior rooms right now?"

Nathaniel stared at him. "Sir?"

"They're awake, every soul. Even the JSS1 students. All of them gibbering like baboons instead of falling asleep. They see you boys masquerading as men, and it's stirring all kinds of devious thoughts in their heads. Do you think Mr. Akande likes that? No matter. At least you can bear witness to their voices. But do you know what is happening outside these gates? Because remember, there *is* a world outside these gates. One that is less keen to shield you from genuine consequences. This little act where you all band together like the disciples of Christ and make demands, it might have worked if you hadn't laid a hand on Babangida. But you did. And his father still wants blood. He's been rallying other parents to pull their kids out, calling this school a den of lawlessness. A few parents have even started to pay attention, which means that you are in no position to make demands. You are in a position to reap all the seeds of discord you've sown. This is the end."

The surety of Mr. Yemi's words increasingly numbed our stomachs. It buzzed against our ears until they rang with tinnitus.

"So," he continued. "I had a long talk with Mr. Akande and the senator. A very long one. I'm done with wasting my time, and you're done with wasting yours. We are ready to expel anyone who continues to cause havoc. The last six years—poof, just gone. Starting university next year? You can forget about it. Unless we end this here and now."

Okonkwo stepped forward, unrelenting. "You heard Nathaniel, sir. Full apology at assembly, and there will be no more havoc. I promise. But I also promise that if you expel one of us, you will have to expel all of us."

"That is not true."

"It really is, sir."

Mr. Yemi slanted a pen against his notebook. "Okonkwo Onwuchekwa, will you return to your room right now?"

"No, sir. I'm okay right here."

"Okay." Mr. Yemi scribbled. "Nathaniel? How about you?"

Nathaniel shook his head. "No, sir. I'm with Okonkwo."

"Stanford will be disappointed to hear that, head boy. I don't think they would want to welcome insurrection into their campus. I hope it's okay with you if I tell them tomorrow that your letters of recommendation no longer apply." Nathaniel started to say something, his face knitted with concern, but Mr. Yemi quickly moved on. "Now, let's see. Hassan Aliyu. Your room?"

Hassan rubbed his hands and licked his lips. "Ahn ahn, sir, you get hot babe for me in my room abi wetin?"

Mr. Yemi laughed and continued to scribble. "We can only hope your mother has a hot babe waiting for you at home." He turned his head in a direction that quickened the pulse of our bodies. "Babani. I'm going to ask you to listen carefully. What happened this morning was unfortunate. I won't apologize for not tolerating your disrespect, but I admit some regret here. I do not want to see you suffer anymore. I even called your home and explained as much. Everything that happened and why it will never happen again. It was not an easy conversation, but they listened with both ears and full hearts. In fact, they want to speak with you." Mr. Yemi took out his flip phone and pressed some buttons. He listened for a sound before extending the device to Babani. "Take it."

"I'm good, sir," Babani said, his words cracking.

Mr. Yemi continued to stretch the phone Babani's way until a woman's voice sputtered out of it: "Yaro na?" Babani trudged forward slowly and pressed the phone against his ear. For too long, it felt like we were watching the genesis of a signature Captain Clown moment. An overseriousness that would soon defuse into comicality. We held on to that belief even when he started fidgeting, his shoulders sagging from the weight of words we couldn't hear, his gaze lowered to the floor. Only one soul had the power to extinguish his will. We knew exactly who, and still, we waited for the gotcha moment. Instead, Babani handed the phone back to Mr. Yemi. With hardly a glance in our direction, he walked out the door.

Mr. Yemi let us simmer in our silence before resuming his operation. "Looks like one of you has sense. Suleiman. Mr. Brain Box. How about you? Will you return to your room? Keep Babani company?

Or will you join Nathaniel on Stanford's blacklist? Is that the reward your father reaps for breaking his back on your behalf all your life?"

Suleiman shook his head. "Fuck this. I'm out."

Okonkwo spun toward him. "What?"

"Babani just left, and you want me to still stand here like a mumu. What kind of joke is that?"

As Suleiman started toward the door, Nathaniel jerked forward and yanked his elbow. Suleiman pulled away and departed, his retreating steps dropping like anvils down the hallway.

Mr. Yemi did not miss a beat. "Lamawal, would you like to return to your room? Or would you like to be on the—"

Lamawal was already leaving, with Yusuf not far behind. A chain reaction commenced, dozens of footsteps following suit. In the aftermath of sudden exodus, about twenty of us remained. Mr. Yemi regarded our diminished numbers with a surprising absence of pride. He almost seemed sad. "I will return in one hour. Those of you whose names I've written down, you can expect immediate repercussions. Anyone else who is still here remains at his own peril. Think of your future. Return to your rooms."

He left.

The minutes until his resurgence were interminable. Mere steps away, the ajar classroom door possessed a gravitational pull, beckoning our heads toward the promise of peace beyond its hinges. But we remained. Hassan swore and cursed. Ibrahim reiterated our pact of unity. Lover Boy Chikemka attempted to divine the murky hours ahead. Okonkwo paced about in a heaving, stomping manner, promising to slit Babani's throat the moment he laid hands on him. At some point, Nathaniel zoned out of our hypotheticals and took to the back of the classroom, silently mulling over thoughts we could only guess at, never mind the clarity of his wrinkled forehead. *We*, after six whole years together, now a tense collection of *I*'s.

Cleaved though we were, we waited for Mr. Yemi's return, determined to catch dawn's light from within these walls, even if it blinded us. Next door, on the sixth floor, a row of square lights flickered out.

NWANNE MU

The craving was instant. We had just gotten home from school, my sister Nneka and I. As I changed out of my uniform in our shared bedroom, I looked out the netted window—crusty home to a dozen dead bugs—and saw two boys across the street. They stood under the shade of an umbrella tree sucking tangerines, the best thing God ever made (after small dogs), and licking bits of fruit off their fingers. Nneka would soon be going to Ogbete Market, a place she deemed "not for little boys." She was fifteen, and I was eight, and she treated our age gap like an ocean, as if she were older than Mama. Usually I tried my best to avoid her until nighttime, when Mama and Papa returned home from their bookstore in the city. But this Thursday afternoon, I was willing to bear the penance of Nneka's company, saliva already frothing on my tongue at the imagined taste of cold, delicious tangerine slices.

I found her in the kitchen frying plantains. Oil hissed in the pan.

"I'm coming with you to Ogbete," I said.

She didn't look at me. "Why?"

"It's none of your business why."

"Then no."

"I want to help you. Keep you company."

She turned around, smirking. "*You* want to help me?"

"Yes."

She examined my face, her brows raised. Then she shrugged. "Okay. Why not? After lunch."

We left the apartment at four p.m., walking down our twisting street of tenements and hair salons. The sun licked my skin, and sweat bathed my forehead. Already, part of me longed to be back home, curled up on my bed, but I pushed my thoughts to the tangerines, their sticky-sweet pulp, the juice in every bite.

Every seat on the bus was occupied, so Nneka and I stood swaying in the back, squeezed between limbs and rancid armpits. She refused to let go of my hand, glaring at me each time I pulled away. She didn't let go at the market entrance either, bending low so that our heads were level to whisper, "Hold on at all times. *At all times*, Chijioke."

But I was looking over her plaited scalp, my eyes wide. In either direction, the road crawled with taxis, three-wheeled keke napeps, motorcycles, and feet—the most feet I'd ever seen at once. Stalls lined the sidewalks, marked by wide umbrellas looming over carts of wrappers and blankets. Nneka led us inside Ogbete, into an overwhelming rush of sound. Music blared from thumping speakers—gospel songs and Afrobeats and American pop. Trilingual chatter rose over the tunes: "How much for that one?" "Tufiakwa! Chineke ga-ata gi ahuhu." "Fine madam, wetin you want, we get am for here." The stony lane flanked by shops was crowded, as were all the roads it forked into, replete with men pushing wheelbarrows loaded with cement bags and noodle cartons, children lugging baskets of bananas on their heads, women handing out pamphlets about the town's newest church. The air changed with every step, wafting scents from fried fish to acerbic paint to the rusty tang of coiled wires.

My heart thumped, and I clutched Nneka's hand ever more tightly. I marvelled at how effortlessly she moved, her lightning pace pushing us past tight gaps and brimming corners. A plump woman grabbed her wrist and smiled through brown teeth—"I can do your hair!" Nneka shook her off without missing a beat. We took a few more turns until finally she stopped at a shop stocked with rice pouches and spices. The owner, a big man swallowed by an even bigger sports jersey, smiled in recognition. Without Nneka saying any more than a greeting, the man stuffed a nylon bag with cans of Peak milk powder, sugar cubes, spaghetti, and garden eggs. Nneka handed him several crumpled nairas. Then we were off again.

My initial terror soon settled into weary distrust; we had seen other stalls selling milk and sugar minutes ago, but she'd whizzed past them. My feet ached. Was she trying to tire me? To punish me for tagging along? A fruit stall appeared on the right, its wooden table topped by pyramids of gooseberries, pockmarked jackfruits, and tangerines. I'd barely pointed before we turned left, the juicy goods vanishing from my view.

At one stall, Nneka asked a man for a hundred-cube pack of beef-flavored Royco. He pulled it from a rickety shelf, said, "Five hundred naira." Nneka laughed, that half-scornful sound she sometimes made with me.

"Do I look like Yemi Alade?" she asked. "Other stalls are selling this same pack for 250 naira."

The man glared at her, his face steeped in wrinkles. "Then go to the other stalls. I will not go lower than four hundred naira."

They came to a mutually reluctant agreement at 350 naira. As we left, Nneka mumbled "thief" under her breath. At our next stop, she laughed at the initial price and walked away, only to be called back. At another, she pointed out wear and tear on a flour bag's packaging, shaving off sixty naira. She was transformed, animated, and I sensed her joy in the tango of back and forth, her swell of inner pride. It was like discovering a new sibling.

After Nneka had purchased some new lace wigs for Mama, she could no longer hold all the bags in one grip, so she released me to free her other hand, screaming, "Stay close!" over the commotion. We were separated and reunited by the motion of things and people—a man on a bicycle, a stray toddler, two women interested in a nearby stall filled with DVDs. As Nneka rounded a corner, the distance between us widening, I quickened my trot to a run. I missed one step and fell sideways into a gutter overflowing with mango pits.

Sickening pain bloomed on the left side of my head. I wailed, the sound intensifying when I rubbed my hand against my temple and saw blood. Something tugged at my shirt, lifting me up. It was Nneka, nylon bags discarded at her feet.

She wiped smudges of dirt off my clothes, cupped my face in her hands. "Are you okay? What happened?"

Behind her, a bare-chested boy and his mother watched from their stall. They were smiling.

I shoved Nneka's hands away. "Can we go home now?"

"You're bleeding, Chijioke."

"I'm fine."

"We need to get you some bandages. Jesus, Mama is going to kill me."

She balanced the handles of her six bags over the palm of one hand so she could again hold me with the other. I glared down at my stained cleats as we walked to a medical stall. There, a white-skinned man dipped balls of cotton in methylated spirit and rubbed them on my wound. I resisted the urge to scream at the fiery sensation.

"No wahala; the cut no dey deep," he told Nneka as he applied a bandage to my head. "E go better on its own. Oya, my guy, high-five." He raised his hand, but I did not reciprocate.

"Don't mind him," Nneka told the man, handing him two hundred naira.

We moved toward a section of the market marked by an archway where the words *OK Line* had been crudely painted.

"This area is called okrika," she said. "Most things here are second-hand, but they come from abroad. I'll buy Mama and Papa some Kenyan jewellery so they don't disown me when they see your head. Then we can go, okay?"

I shrugged.

She sighed, lightly squeezed my thumb with two fingers. "You still haven't told me the real reason you came, Chijioke."

I kicked a stone, watched it soar.

Unlike the rest of the market, the OK Line stalls were less exposed, connected overhead by sheets of protective zinc. Loose sunlight spilled through the gaps. The day seemed impossibly hot; my damp shirt was matted to my skin. We passed rows of clothes hanging from nails in walls, colourful bedsheets, oversized purses. Toward the end of the path, a teenage boy of seventeen or eighteen stood over a glass table beset with all manner of ugly bracelets and necklaces. Nneka dropped her bags on the edge of his table, and he pulled her into a brief sideways hug. They beamed at each other like old friends, like something more than old friends, and I suddenly understood that we were not here on Mama and Papa's behalf. Not entirely.

"Long time, long time," the boy said, exuberantly rolling his *l*'s. "I thought you had forgotten me."

"I have o," Nneka replied with a grin, pinching at the skin of her elbow. I had never seen her do that before. "I am getting married next week."

"Oh, yeah? Who's the lucky man?"

"A sixty-year-old grandpa with big thighs and an even bigger bank account."

The boy laughed, and Nneka laughed, and I hated it, the tangle of their voices, the way he crooned when she tried on a gold-coloured rosary, the way I stood at the edges, invisible. Across from me was a shop stacked with irons, hair dryers, and extension cords. Near the entrance, two bowls of fruits were set atop a small shelf, one full of green apples, the other tangerines. The shop's owner was a portly bald man. A generator buzzed next to him, powering the television angled high into the wall. He was distracted by a movie.

I glanced at Nneka, who was now rotating the beads of a band around her wrist. Nneka, who seemed to have aged ten years in Ogbete, who blended seamlessly with its chaos. Here, legs still marched in droves. A dozen conversations mixed with the shriek of songs. I could disappear into the storm. It would only take five seconds.

I moved to the other side of the teeming market road. The bald man remained distracted, enraptured by the tiny lives on his television screen. I stood on my tiptoes and reached for a single tangerine. It was soft in my grip. I spun around, shoved it into my pocket.

"Hey!"

A furious, high-pitched shout from behind me.

I pushed my legs faster, toward Nneka. She was staring my way now, frowning. A hand twisted my shoulder, fingers dug into my flesh like claws. The bald man dragged me back toward his shop. He reached into my pocket and pushed the tangerine against my nose. "Is this yours?"

Nneka seemed to teleport right beside me. "Don't touch my brother!"

"Your brother is a thief," the man said, waving the tangerine like a weapon. "A thief in Ogbete, of all places! With just one word, I can have all the agbero boys in this market flogging the devil out of him. I will teach him a lesson."

Nneka looked back at her more-than-a-friend, her lower lip sweat-slick and trembling, but he remained at his stall, his gaze fixed on his own little trinkets. Nneka turned back to the man and dropped to her knees, her palms pressed together in prayer.

"Please," she whispered. "I will pay."

"You think I want a thief's payment?" His voice was rising. "He deserves a bloody beating!" People were stopping in their tracks to stare. A man holding a thick bamboo stick over his right shoulder started to approach us. An uncontrollable shiver took over my body. Urine filled my underwear, forming a dark oval on my shorts.

Nneka reached into her purse for all her remaining naira. She extended them to the bald man. "Please, biko, o nwanne mu—he's an idiot, but he's my brother. My only brother."

The man considered the money dangling in her hand. His face relaxed and his mouth curled into a smile. He bunched the cash in one fist and nodded at me. "Get this criminal out of my sight."

Nneka yanked my hand and dragged me forward with a force that made my neck creak. She picked up the nylon bags at her more-than-a-friend's stall, rebalancing them in one hand so the other was free to keep dragging me. The boy started to say something, but the look Nneka gave immediately silenced him.

The path out of Ogbete seemed endless. Gravel crunched beneath my feet, and my head was throbbing anew. It felt as though the eyes of every man, child, and wandering hen were on us, unseen pinpricks poking at my sides as lines of urine dried on my calves. Once, I dared to look up at Nneka. I wanted to break the silence, to explain what I had done.

I knew you wouldn't have bought the tangerine if I asked seemed insufficient. No, it had been something about the smallness of even asking. Here, she loomed larger than life, the things she wanted hers for the taking. I opened my mouth, unsure of what would come out, but when I saw the droop of her shoulders, the sadness pulling down her eyelids, I said nothing.

Outside Ogbete, a gloom had settled over the sky. The sun was a receding half sphere. Taxis honked. Conductors clung to the roofs of buses, screaming their destinations. We moved away from the vehicles and started down a sidewalk. We would have to walk all the way home.

I tried again.

I'm sorry. I didn't mean to.

The first was true, the second not so much. In any case, the words still wouldn't form. What came out instead was a hacking sound, a rasp caught in my throat. Nneka looked at me, and I came undone at her gaze, my reflection in her pink eyes. I was a boy, a tiny, foolish boy, and I cried my little boy tears. Snot bubbled, popped, and clumped around my nostrils.

Nneka released my arm.

We were still within the commercial stretch outside of Ogbete. A woman carrying a box of used bibles approached from one end; children selling frozen yogurt approached from the other. Nneka made no attempt to move out of their way. She pulled me into her body. My face pressed against the plantain-scented warmth of her stomach. I hugged her back, harder than I ever had, and refused to let go.

MY AMERICANAH

My firepit glows in the darkening backyard, corn cobs—Kayode's favourite—roasting atop the coals. Fresh off the airport taxi, he slides past the rear gates. I help him prop his luggage against a wall and throw myself into his arms to remember his scent. The pinewood on his corduroy evokes no memory. His hug fails to bruise my spine. And when he says, "I missed you, Mom," it sounds rehearsed, his accent diluted.

We sit on white plastic chairs flanking the flames, and I feel the distance of the last three years more thoroughly now—our perfunctory Sunday afternoon calls, his one-word replies to my paragraphs of texts. I worry that this two-week summer visit will not fix us. But when I mention that the neighbour's wife finally snapped and broke a bottle on her husband's head, when Kayode gasps and then laughs and says it's about time, when he unwraps a cob and bites into it and licks the butter off his lips, when he tells me about the Fulani businessman who caused a scene on his flight just before takeoff, I become younger, time's separating ocean almost a droplet. Almost.

"What changed?" I ask. "Why did we grow apart? Why did you stop trying?"

Our first cobs are naked rinds at our feet. Kayode fidgets and looks away. I place my hand on his shoulder, which makes him turn, makes him speak, even though he cannot meet my eyes.

"I like men," he says.

My palm retreats to my lap.

"Even before leaving," he says, "I always had this feeling deep inside."

I start on the next cob, eating just to keep busy, to drown the falling in my stomach. He could never say it to me, he says, because he knew I loathe his kind—just like his friends do, our priests, the government, every force in his life. He says it took him all these years at Columbia to finally accept himself.

"I'm only telling you because I miss you," he says. "We used to be friends."

I've heard the stories. The neighbours' tongues still carry the name of Madam Ozioma's son, even though he died twenty years ago. How his vomit-soaked body had been discovered in Maryland on graduation's eve, a bloody needle in his arm. Then there was the hairdresser's teenage daughter, turned pregnant by some white Canadian old enough to be her grandfather. The night before Kayode left Nigeria, I tossed in bed, reminding myself that he'd be fine. I'd taught him, in gentle bedside lullabies, "Your body is the Holy Spirit's temple." I'd filled his spiritual diet with twice-daily prayers, Gwagwalada bible camps, choir practice at St. Mary's. I'd done everything to ensure his soul would make it to heaven, even if mine didn't.

"I tried to be with women"—he's still talking—"my freshman year at Columbia. But they felt all wrong. Their lips, their breasts, their night breath on my neck. It was so different my first time with a man."

A man. He says it so casually. I rise, my chair scraping against gravel, and look up at the crescent moon. Except I don't see the moon, don't see the stars. I see a grey-haired white man—maybe Kayode's bio professor, who teaches a new and westernized bio—saying that it is okay, it is how bodies move in these lands. I see the white man's mouth sucking Kayode's tongue, the white man's trousers falling, the white man's penis hairy and red with bumps, that penis entering Kayode's anus. I squeeze my hand into a fist, put the fist to my mouth. I bite hard but cannot draw blood.

"I'm still your son," Kayode says in that hybridized accent, *your* into *ya*. He closes the gap between us, takes my hand with his greasy, quivering palm. The next house over, a gate creaks, and I know the bottle-wounded husband has returned from his barbershop; he always returns. I imagine low whispers over supper—in these lands, a mother's deepest failures never stay buried—*her son is back, yes, the New Yorker doctor wannabe, about to graduate, him, guess what he's become*. A tale for the ages. I listen to what he's saying now, my Americanah son: "I hadda tell ya before I went back, back to Columbia. I hadda, I just hadda, because I'm still ya son." There, within his twisted syllables, I see the answer.

"Can you get me a paper towel?" I ask, my fingers dabbing at my eyes. He nods eagerly, ready to grant me the universe. He disappears inside the house. His home. First time in three years. I steady myself and square my shoulders to resist the heavy weight of the months ahead. I am capable. I always have been.

There is a lack of rhythm to his pattering feet; I know that he is reorienting himself to the locations of things—the cupboards, the pots, the windows. A spark from the pit catches my shadow as I turn toward the rear gates. Beyond this life, a congregation of sparks will consume the sinner forever. But here, now, the heat is salvation. I reach atop Kayode's wall-propped luggage for the folder from which his return flight ticket peeks out. And his Nigerian passport with the US visa too. I say a silent prayer and toss the folder into the bright-burning flames. As the pages shrivel and blacken, I learn to breathe again.

FAKE HYDRANGEA

Aunt Nkiru says, "My home is your home," but my focus is on the fake hydrangea in a vase centred atop the living room table. We sit in a parlour of plastic-looking things: shiny white walls, sunsets trapped in portraits, couches shaped like vowels, strained smiles. The old maid, Ukamaka, wears time on her face in a way that Aunt Nkiru does not. She stands in the corner in a black uniform, arms crossed, silent. I will see her on some mornings dusting the fake hydrangea, brushing its eternally green petals.

"Your room is to the left," Aunt Nkiru continues, motioning at my sixteen-year-old sister, Helen. "And yours to the right." She gestures at me, her glassy pendant necklace making tricks of refracted light. "Remember, you start your new school on Monday. I will drive you there at seven a.m. and pick you up at three p.m."

Helen launches into a speech, her gratitude theatrically heightened. "We already feel so welcome here," she says at the end of it.

"Thank you, Auntie. You will not regret this." The same Helen whose attitude provoked Mama to such anger that Mama's voice ran hoarse and her shoes arced across the room. Who habitually fled from home while Mama sat weeping by the door. Who vanished midway through her classes to smoke cigarettes in abandoned fields with her dropout friends.

Aunt Nkiru nods fervently.

She believes the lies.

✦

The last time Helen ran away was the night of Mama's birthday. We ate sponge cake with too much icing for dinner and drank tall cartons of Lucozade Boost. My post-meal stomach ache forced me onto Mama's lap. I awoke on the floor to their usual sparring, scrubbed my eyes to the tempo of Helen's "wish you were dead" scream and rose just in time to watch a cartwheeling vase shatter against a swinging door.

"She thinks I'm her agemate," said Mama, breathing heavily, eyes aflame, fingers raking patches out of her greying bun. "Me, her mother, her own mother! I'll cut her dirty tongue when she comes back." She staggered to a corner of the room, rattled her pill bottles in a fist, swallowed a handful. She turned to me. Crooned. "Sweet angel. My baby. Come here." We cuddled through the night. Her stomach pushed and pulled against my back, the movement slowing down as her sobbing turned to snoring. There was the briefest sleep, then another awakening. Our windowless room hid dawn's arrival, but the sun must have been rising. And even though Mama's arms were still tangled around my stomach, something had changed. There was no rhythm of sound, no warm nostril air on the nape of my neck. I closed my eyes again, refused to turn, refused to move, to see, not even when Helen came back in the evening, reeking of beer, when she screamed at the sight of us motionless, when she pulled and pulled at me.

✦

While Ukamaka takes our duffle bags to our rooms, Aunt Nkiru empties a kettle of boiling water into three mugs.

"Adanma," she says, dunking a bag of Lipton into one cup, her eyes on me, "you have not said much today. Do you have any concerns?"

"When can we visit Mama?" I ask. Mama is Ezeagu soil under a mango tree, but still, Mama is Mama.

Aunt Nkiru sighs. She adds spoonfuls of powdered milk and spins the mix slowly. "Don't worry about that for now. It will happen." When she turns her back to hunt for sugar cubes, Helen prods my knee with hers in a way that says, *Shut up, stupid girl.*

Aunt Nkiru's television is a long black window. We gather around it with our steaming cups and watch the local nine o'clock news. Two trucks collided on Maitama Highway. There were no survivors. Helen downs her drink in three gulps. Says the tea is wonderful. My first sip scalds, and I decide it will be my last. On Sunday mornings after Mass, Mama used to buy two cans of condensed milk from a nearby store—old newspapers lined its walls, and airplane-shaped balloons dangled from its ceiling. We'd sit on the floor mattress in our bedroom, and she'd puncture both cans with a knife. We drank slowly. She swirled her can between sips to create a stronger flavour, called it "queen's tea." I don't know what Aunt Nkiru has made, but it is too hot, not sweet enough. It is not tea.

When the news ends, Ukamaka emerges from her room. She rounds up the cups—mine is still full and mostly cool—and washes them in the sink.

"I am tired," I mumble, rising. "Good night, Auntie."

I pretend not to notice Aunt Nkiru's arms open wide for a hug.

✦

There is a fake hydrangea in a vase on the nightstand next to my bed. I will find several of them all over the house, like hidden toys—beneath standing lamps, on bathroom countertops, around the perimeter of the green backyard.

I graze its petals, sniff its nothing-smelling base, and think of how Mama grew her collection of potted anthuriums in our basement apartment. The room I shared with her, small as it was, overflowed with treasures she'd gathered over the years. Beaded bracelets, moth-eaten paperbacks, and bleached dresses filled several checkered bags. Beer bottles lined one wall in widening rows. The anthuriums stood next to our bed, each identical but for the newest, which showed its youth in the burning red of its leaves. Mama would water its coarse potting mix for weeks and shine a lamp on its bending fronds in lieu of sunlight. Eventually, though, the anthurium would sag until it was brown and decaying, but it never met the trash. Mama said that there was life even in crumbling death.

"Can't you smell it in the air?"

A rich, earthy musk that drowned out all else. The many nights I couldn't sleep, I closed my eyes and listened to the discordant ticks of four wall clocks, imagining that the smell came from Mama's skin, overpowering, the way comfort is.

✦

My eyes refuse to close.

My tongue feels like sandpaper, my body full of turns. I wander into the kitchen, where silhouetted machines hum, and I drink from the tap until my belly is swollen. The dryness in my throat does not go away. It will linger through the coming months until I hardly notice it anymore.

Near the sink, a sliding glass door leads to the backyard. An ocean of grass stretches out onto a small enclosure where two shadows stand hunched together, their backs to me. For some reason, Helen and Aunt Nkiru are scanning the sky. There are hardly any stars in this city.

Helen points at lumpy clouds. Aunt Nkiru looms on her tiptoes. I watch them, longing for thunderstorms to force them inside. When they are done moon-gazing, Helen walks past me as if I am not there. She pulls open a cabinet, rummages within. Aunt Nkiru blinks at me in surprise.

"Adanma," she says. "I thought you were already asleep."

Helen scoffs. She fills a glass cup with rattling ice cubes from a hole in the fridge. "Without Mama to hold her, that one does not sleep anymore."

"And that is normal," Aunt Nkiru says, crouching so our eyes align. I look over her shoulder, studying the veins along Helen's thin neck. "Just know that if sleep proves elusive, you can always wake me up. We will talk, watch a movie, whatever you want."

"She doesn't talk anymore either," Helen says. At first, her face is twisted in amusement, but something she sees in mine strips it away. She places the cup on the sink's edge without looking.

It is like the dropping of a bomb. Helen quivers behind the shards, her sudden jitters reaching her fingertips. She unleashes a frenzied torrent of *I'm sorrys*. Aunt Nkiru quickly sidesteps the jagged fragments to pull her close.

"It's okay," says Aunt Nkiru. "You're okay."

I wear a smile until I return to the room. It disappears when the bed sags beneath me and my body tangles beneath the cold sheets. For hours, I pinch along the fabric, searching for stray threads.

✦

The new secondary school is called American Academy, even though the only American there is the red-faced principal with fingers like sausages. Classrooms have colour schemes with matching walls. I am in JSS2 Blue, and Helen is in SSS3 Purple. The paint looks fresh, but the plaster is dry, and there is no paint smell in the air. There is a cafeteria with free lunches: burgers and salad and vanilla ice cream. The sun does not bake our skins through cracks in the concrete here, but the chill of the buzzing air conditioners cuts through bone.

"Only ingrates complain," Mama used to say, so I keep my thoughts to myself, shivering in the back row, taking notes from the tidy loops of writing on the blackboard. At the end of each week, Mrs. Kingsley, the school secretary, hands us "summary reports." On Friday afternoon, after Aunt Nkiru drives us back to her house, she goes through the papers while Helen and I watch.

"Adanma, this is wonderful!" she says of my first report, waving it in the air. "Excellent penmanship. Focused listener." The third line says, "Could speak up more," but Aunt Nkiru ignores it, moving on to

Helen's report. "Let's see here. Highly engaged. Funny but respectful. A model introduction. Girls, these reports are *amazing*."

Somewhere out there, a former home economics teacher sports a purple bruise on his forehead from Helen's stone-flinging aim. A landfill bears the ashes of the exorcised child that another put inside her. That year, they called Mama nnukwu ọdịda, a great failure. Yet, this same Helen grins sheepishly before Aunt Nkiru now, a model introduction. I am eaten up by the ground beneath my feet, and for weeks, I am falling, falling, falling.

Breakfast, lunch, and dinner have new names: bacon, waffles, s'mores, lasagna. The kind of food Mama and I saw in movies on the hair-salon screens slanted above our craning necks while Miss Ujunwa pinched our hair into cornrows. Food eaten by white families living in giant dollhouses, with peeks of square hedges and water sprinklers beyond the curtains. Strangest of all: although Helen and I still barely exchange words, she is *here*. Present. Location consistently known. She curls up on the couch next to Aunt Nkiru, and from my room I hear them laughing, losing their voices to unfunny things. Sometimes, the door creaks slightly, and Aunt Nkiru sits down on the edge of my bed, poking and prodding my feet.

"Come join us," she says. Pats my hair before giving up.

On some weekend afternoons, she leaves novels by my door. One of them has her name on it. *A Father's Wounds*, by Nkiru Okpara. Her face is an expressionless square on the back cover. I flip through it without taking in the words until I am consumed by a desire to rip page after page from the spine.

"It was inspired by our lives in Ezeagu before I moved to Trans-Ekulu in the city," Aunt Nkiru says one Sunday evening. "Your mother stayed behind to look after Grandpa. I watered my words and became a writer." We are eating jollof rice, dry and overcooked, all of us except Ukamaka, who appears only when there is cleaning to be done.

"It is the best book I've ever read," Helen replies, twisting her fork into her rice like she's looping noodles. In this house, utensils clink against ceramic. Bowls have curvatures and floral patterns. I want Aunt Nkiru to follow up on Helen's claim. *Go on. Explain. Tell me why.*

Instead, she says, "I am glad to hear that."

Helen continues. "I'd love my friend Ogemdi to read your book. He's never been patient enough to sit through anything so long before, but this one might get him there."

Aunt Nkiru beams. "Such a thoughtful suggestion. I'm glad to hear you're already making friends. I moved around a lot myself, so I understand how scary new faces in new spaces can be, but—"

"Oh no," Helen replies, her eyes on her plate in a way that makes me sit up. "He doesn't go to the Academy. We were friends back in Nasarawa, but he's thinking of visiting me here. I really miss him, Auntie. He helped me a lot, especially in my last few weeks there."

A moment of silence passes.

"But he's in Nasarawa?" Aunt Nkiru asks.

"Yes. If he takes a bus, it's only a two-hour trip."

Aunt Nkiru dabs the corners of her lips with a napkin. "Perhaps another time. For now, I want you girls focused on proper integration here. Acing your schoolwork, making new friends, all of that. Goes just as well for you, Adanma. Your teachers say you're still too quiet."

I nod, but my eyes are on Helen. She is talking now about the jollof rice's exquisite peppers. I don't know who Ogemdi is, and Mama never knew who Helen's friends were, but I remember the screaming about wayward fools with evil intentions, the violent slamming of doors. I remember this Helen, sly and mysterious, her lips full of unfamiliar names.

✦

One Friday morning, Mr. Salau walks into class with his box of coloured chalk. His bald head is shaped like an egg, shiny from the morning's light, and I picture it cracking open, a great vulture unfurling from his bloody scalp. On the blackboard, he writes in green letters, "The Formation of Gametes."

"Every one of you," he says dryly, as though we are putting him to sleep, "is the union of two haploid cells—a father's sperm and a mother's ovum."

I doodle shapes on the back of my biology textbook. Stick-figure classmates with tiny eyes and sewn lips. A coffin with dangling crosses. Mama. Papa. He is absent from memory, from photographs, from every word Mama ever uttered. He is fuzzy and wrinkled on the page. I look like Mama and Helen does not; I wonder if Helen wears his face, if she carries a shadow of his soul.

At three p.m., Aunt Nkiru picks us up. She pulls out of the school's driveway and onto the adjacent street, where beggars gather on the sidewalks to catch the post-school crowd. She inquires about our day.

"Did you know our papa, Auntie?" I ask.

Aunt Nkiru glances at me in the rear-view mirror. "Why do you ask?"

I shrug. "Just wondering."

"I didn't know him well, no. After your mother married, she kept her life as private as possible, even from me. But he looked very much in love with her at the wedding. His eyes never left her face, and he smiled so wide I feared the moths would find his tongue."

Helen interjects. "In love, keh? Mama turned old like a turtle, and Papa ran for the mountains. It is what men do." She smirks. "I'm sure that is why you never married, Auntie."

Aunt Nkiru chuckles. "There are many shapes the heart can take. Marriage love was never for me, but take the kind I've found with you girls, for example. Nothing can ever change that. I hope you both know this. Nothing at all."

Afterward, the ride is silent. Helen turns to the window. She watches the cluster of people blend into whirling trees and skyscrapers, a vaguely familiar smile on her face.

Spiders, invisible, dance on my neck.

✦

That night, I dream of Gungere, the thatched-roof bar where I had palm wine for the first time. I'd grimaced at the sour taste. Mama laughed. She was eleven when she had her first sip too. She said the drink had taken root in her inner pores and started her march toward womanhood.

As usual, sleep is a brief flash. I wake to dawn's bronze hue and a deep thirst. Low voices drift in from what sounds like Aunt Nkiru's television. I shuffle into the living room. The table catches my eyes first, freezing me in place. The fake hydrangea has been replaced by a potted anthurium, its spindly stems rising out of dark-brown mulch. On the TV screen, a man dangles from a rope attached to a burning helicopter, screaming at the wind. Helen is lying on the sofa, her head on a strange man's lap. Her fingers stretch upward, ruffling the sides of his scant beard. When they see me, Helen says, smiling, "Ogemdi, this is my sister, Adanma. Adanma, my friend Ogemdi. See what he got us?" She motions at the anthurium. "Be nice!"

Ogemdi waves.

I simply stare.

Helen's tone is casual, as if all past Saturday mornings have begun with a stranger in our midst. Without a word, I turn back. Helen whispers, "Some days, I think she is deaf." Ogemdi laughs.

I plop into my pillows, hovering so close to the bed's edge that the slightest motion would send me tumbling. With my eyes closed, I think of Helen, her friend, the anthurium. I am hammered by déjà vu. My stomach contracts. The day has barely started, but I know I have lived it a hundred times before. Waiting in the dark, counting the seconds until—

Ukamaka's voice comes first, a high-pitched "*Madam!*" followed by running feet and Aunt Nkiru's gasp. I remain on the bed's cliffside, war drums pounding in my chest.

"Helen, who is this?"

"Good morning, ma, I am—"

"*Helen*, I'm talking to you."

"Auntie, you told me I could invite him."

"I said no such thing. He needs to leave immediately."

"You did, Adanma was there." Helen's voice swells. "He took two buses to get here. Woke up at four a.m. just to catch the first one. He's my best friend. Auntie, please!"

"Young man, I will call the police if you do not get out of my sight in the next thirty seconds. Helen, to your room now. *Now*. Helen! Come back here. Where are you ..."

There are rapid footsteps. A thump on the ground. A door slams shut.

✦

Minutes later, Aunt Nkiru knocks and prods my shoulder. I pretend to awaken.

"Adanma," she says. "Helen left the house with someone I don't know. Her friend Ogemdi. Did she tell you anything about him? Or where they might be going?"

I shake my head.

During lunch, I dunk spheres of garri in egusi, tearing white fish from bone, licking my thumbs between bites. Aunt Nkiru gazes at the table, one finger twirling her soup.

The sun is disappearing into reddening clouds when Aunt Nkiru emerges from Helen's room with a brown file folder. On the dining table, she spreads out Helen's summary reports in a half circle, searching for clues in the pool of words. But there is no line to draw between *model introduction* and Ogemdi.

At night, she approaches my bed again, lips chafed.

"When Helen would leave home," she says, sitting next to me, "for how long would she disappear?"

I am surprised that she knows even this much.

"Sometimes two hours. Sometimes six weeks."

Aunt Nkiru nods, and she keeps nodding until I worry that her neck is broken. This I can handle, the physical after-effects of Helen's indifference. I sidle closer to Aunt Nkiru.

"This house used to be such a lonely place, Adanma," she says. "The sound of my own footsteps just echoing against nothing. It started to drive me crazy. I was grateful when Ukamaka moved in. I still am, of course, but she's only around because I pay her well enough to support her family back in Onitsha. She avoids anything that starts to look like a friendship. I appreciate her stance, but ... I guess my point is that you girls, your presence—I've needed it, and I regret that it took your mother's passing to get it. I wouldn't be where I am today without her efforts, and I've been trying so hard to do right by her. But I don't know. Tell me, Adanma, do you feel at home here?"

I give her what she needs. "Yes, Auntie."

"I thought Helen did too. I thought she was slowly stepping away from her pain."

"Helen feels no pain."

"She does."

"She creates pain." The words tumble. "She killed Mama."

A misty cloud settles over my vision and turns the floor to shifting rubber. With two gentle fingers, Aunt Nkiru tilts my head toward hers.

"Adanma, Helen is hurting. In God's name, I know that your mother loved you girls with all her soul, but she was very much your grandfather's daughter. Papa used to say, 'The oldest cub guards the den.' He raised your mother like a wolf, with harsh words and a farmer's hands. She did the same with Helen, for your sake. Do you remember, Adanma? You must. How sometimes she would beat your sister."

"Helen was always breaking Mama's heart. Always running off to do bad things."

"Maybe. But why was she running, Adanma?" When I turn away from Aunt Nkiru, forcing myself to rise, she adds, "Helen has opened up to me these last few weeks in a way that I hope you can too. Someday. At your own time. Do you know that she wishes you two were closer?"

Her words are starting to buzz. I think of Mama swatting at droning mosquitoes on prickly walls, the web-like spread of their blood, sharp smelling in the sticky humidity. I refuse to look back even when she stops talking. Before she leaves, she kisses the side of my cheek.

✦

Street lights lance through Helen's bedroom windows, forming gold petals on her rumpled sheets. I sniff the air for hints of her, searching for signs Aunt Nkiru missed, the shivery tang of days-old alcohol, the scratch of unvanquished smoke, secrets tucked beneath pillowcases. Ironed clothes hang in her closet above an empty duffle bag. A copy of Aunt Nkiru's book sits on the nightstand, its pages annotated, phrases underlined. On the last page is a sketch of an anthurium, neither red nor brown, trapped in stasis between life and death. I stare at it for minutes. It is strange to picture Helen curled over her blanket, her feet kicking the air, her fingers flipping through these pages with a pen. It is strange to think of her placing Ogemdi's anthurium on the living room table one floor below, brushing its red petals the way Mama did.

I lie down, push my legs against my chest. Shadow and light turn this posture into a funny-shaped mouth on the wall. Large. Hungry. I close my eyes and wonder again if this is all Mama sees now, this black nothing, forever. Or if a part of her remains, privy to the destination of Helen's legs. Helen, always running, out of morning classes, down a flight of stairs—

Into the next room, the one that is Helen's alone, just beyond a door that swings closed too late—Mama pulls through, something raised in one hand. A fist or a belt buckle or a thorny stick. This time, there is no blink between Mama's vanishing into Helen's room and her resurging. Helen's pleading ("Biko, Mama, biko, I'm—") is cut off by a thud. Her pleas morph into a rising pitch of sound that doesn't quite drown out Mama's sharp, continuous thwacking. I screw my eyes even tighter, as if I possess the power to see through walls. I shrivel into my own body to suppress the noise, but my mind leaps above me, out of me. It makes a video of its perceptions. This film has no people, only a gust of wind that cracks bottles against tiles, upends shelves to empty them of books, pulls curtains by the hem, and the rods that hold the curtains in place too. A clanking, clattering, furious wind, a wind that—if I rush into the bedroom—might stop the noise, unmoor us from gravity, up, up, and away, couldn't we fly, all three of us, wouldn't it be fun?

No.

I don't move.

Not until the end.

My nostrils flare and I mark time in rapid flurries of breath. Then a door squeaks—the genesis of relief—and Mama's slippers thud on the stained wood floor. She wipes her palm on her wrapper and reaches for the tin can of biscuits next to our pillows. Often, they sit crumbling in the container for weeks, their salt fading. Still, I favour their softness, how they dissolve in my mouth after she feeds them to me. Then she wipes the crumbs off my face, and she takes me in her arms long enough for sleep to find me.

Now and then, I wake in the middle of the night, stirred by some unsettled sound in the distance, something without form. Something like the remnant of a bad dream.

✦

I rise, my arms numb from pins and needles.

Helen's bed does not smell like Helen.

I do not want to be alone in her room any longer, so I guide myself down to the darkened parlour by feeling along the smooth walls. The front door is wide open, and Aunt Nkiru is perched on the porch steps. She turns at the sound of my approach.

"Adanma," she says, glancing at the clock. It's 1:32 a.m. "Do you need anything?"

"No."

"Water? Tea?"

"I am okay."

She shifts to make space for me. We sit side by side, close enough that our knees touch. From this angle, her features are sharper in the moonlight: the calluses on her palms, the strands of whitening hair bunched behind her left ear. From this angle, she looks like Mama's sister.

"I sent Ukamaka to drive around," she says. "The city bars are still open. Maybe Helen and the boy are at one of them. Maybe she'll even come stumbling right through those gates."

"Maybe we'll never see her again."

Aunt Nkiru sighs. "Is that what you want?"

I open my mouth to reply, but no word emerges. I remember this too, the seeming permanence of Helen's absence. The sliver of unease that came with the thought of Mama and me by ourselves forever, as if our stability somehow depended on Helen's existence, her endless capacity to reflect and absorb chaos.

I sidle closer to Aunt Nkiru and, this time, I rest my head on her shoulder. When she puts her arms around me, I almost jump. Those arms immediately recall Mama's, because they are nothing like hers, too bony, too fragile, and it seems so very wrong, even the smell of Irish Spring rather than eczema cream, and I want to run, to find the same things Helen finds, the gutters and moons and bad friends who break hearts. But my energy is spent. I am tired. I do not move.

I do not want to move.

"Helen will be back," I say, letting my eyelids fall shut, nestling deeper into Aunt Nkiru's shoulder. "She will."

Helen always comes back.

HEY, STOP BLAMING YOUR DEAD MOTHER'S FISTS

There's an unsnoozeable alarm clock in your head. Your room has a lopsided bed and no sheets and unscuffed running shoes near the wilted anthuriums. Sushi Paradise rolls float in mouldy grease. The journal on your nightstand has a shiny golden latch. Its pages are scrawled with *I wills* that never were. You will swim thrice weekly. You will call Adanma. You will run your skin under water. You will find your front door. You will breathe.

If you pull open the curtains, there's a gold ball in the sky. Baby steps take you there. Sweep used condoms and lube-stained wads of tissue into a bag. The bottles too. Dial Adanma's number. Wait for voice mail and hang up when she answers. Call again. Apologize for being a bad sister. Hear her soul rekindle. Ask after her husband. After Aunt Nkiru too. Hear her corny jokes about the Holy Ghost. Laugh like you mean it.

Find a sidewalk. Inhale. Yes, there's a mulchy sort of rot coming from the construction near the lake. But do you feel how the wind makes you more?

Your friends are a relic of the past. There's a room full of them in your head. They're passing around croissants and wine and trading stories about you. *No one is perfect,* they say, *but there's a tolerable kind of badness.* They describe oceans of time between texts, your empty chair at a small cottage wedding, missing necklaces after the night you slept over, a blackened pipe in the trash the morning after you left. Without a word too, nothing until your resurfacing with a *sorry sorry sorry,* but also an *I need ... just until payday.* You were still rambling when they slammed the door.

If you squint through the fog, you'll find that door again. Baby steps take you there. Knock. Even if the hardwood does not budge. Spend a portion of your new grocery store paycheque on a piece of topaz. Mail it with a handwritten apology: "I know it doesn't begin to replace ..." Give them space. Fill this void with the breadth of you. Cross a line off your journal list. Take a pottery class in some woman's home studio. Turn over the matcha mug fashioned from clay, wrinkled but yours. Say thank you when the woman next to you says "good job." Accept her invite for drinks, first at the pub uptown, then at her apartment. Marvel at the alchemy of *strangers* to *friends.*

Rise. Don't despair at the detritus creeping back around your bed. Perhaps it never really leaves. Keep walking. Chase the ice-cream truck. Let yourself giggle. Knock. Watch the hardwood budge. Hand her a bottle of Pinot—from now on, you only add. Talk about old crushes, scraped knees from childhood bike rides, her fear of failure, your fear of raised hands. Gasp when shadows start to form. Is it seven already?

Let the melody of *new friends* loop in your head for weeks. Feel it stutter to static the day you come home to a piece of mail. Shards of shattered topaz in the envelope. Your handwritten apology scrawled over with a Sharpied "fuck you." This is your doing, seven years reduced to two words. This is you—the annihilator, the Great Destroyer—unless it's the filth in your room, which only ever grows: Look around—isn't all the garbage back?

If you peek down, down, down, you'll find a pit without end. Baby steps take you there. Start with the returned mail. Feel how smoothly the creased paper rolls into a cylinder. Stuff it tight and green. Watch clouds of marijuana float against the ceiling. Ignore emails from work. Ignore her texts about missing you in pottery class. About maybe meeting up for a soccer game. About "Are you okay?" Pick up her call a month later. Ask what the fuck's wrong with her. Tell her you ain't a fucking lesbian. Exhale when she hangs up. Good. You won't hear from her again—except up there, in the dark with all the others, her voice slurring between gulps of wine.

Silence her. No, not with the TV. Not the clatter-clank of early-morning tractors. Yes, the old alleyway, with its spray-painted walls, its skulking cats. Its hooded man limping your way, a Ziploc bag of white powder tucked in his fist. Beneath your itchy blanket's cocoon, inhale. Don't stop till it turns your stomach. When the puke backs up your throat, miss the toilet bowl. Splash it all over the tile. Rub your face in its slime. *It's where you belong*. You've heard this before, your mother's words, in that sweltering basement. Drift away now, cold, sweating. Focus on things without faces. Without voices. Like the moon, a prism against the bathroom window. Like the constellation of shadows. Concentrate harder. Fail. Let her voice slither in too, the *I will* that was, the sincerity of "good job" offered so freely that you felt whole and capable, infinite. Like you could believe in you. Let the thought of this newest loss thump your heart into overdrive. Dial her number. Dial again when she doesn't answer. The third time, at the voice mail's beep, leave your message. Your brain is scrambled. Your words are soup. Sound them out. Baby steps take you there. Blame work stress. Blame your hateful friends. Blame your mother's fists. Blame little green aliens from fucking Andromeda. Blame anyone but yourself.

A KEENER EYE

The blond woman orders coffee and doughnuts for her family. While she pays, slowly counting out neat dollar bills, her husband and son stand a few feet back. For a moment, they scowl at each other, and just as quickly, their eyes are on some other thing, the tiled floor, the row of colourful menu screens. It is enough to rouse me out of a half slumber.

Moments later, they exit with their white cups and brown paper bags. Outside, a blizzard rages. I watch them enter a Honda and vanish forever.

For hours, I am unable to dislodge father and son from memory. Questions surface like Whac-A-Moles. Does he scream at his son over slight misdemeanours? Or does the boy resentfully guard the details of his father's lurid affair? And the mother, does she suspect a rift?

Around three a.m., the storm softens into a low wind. I rise and leave. The Tim Hortons graveyard-shift pair behind the counter have not said anything to me; they may not for a while yet, if at all. But it is best not to test these things. Part of having their grace is knowing when to return it.

✦

At midmorning, sleep remains elusive.

After fruitless tossing and turning, I emerge from my tent. Grey clouds scud across the horizon, deceptively calm. The encampment under the Gardiner Expressway is anything but. Two men laugh at a joke and shovel snow away, metal cracking white earth. A teenage girl digs through clothes strewn about from last night's storm. She examines a damp floral blouse and sniffs its hem. Chaos surrounds her: a zigzagging city of tents, blue, white, and red, like nation flags; scuffed shoes; lumpy garbage bags, one of them covered in sticky notes; upturned shopping carts; propane heaters; a bicycle with missing wheels.

Ten feet or so away, a yellow-haired woman squats low, ripping bits of duct tape with her teeth and slowly applying them to torn sections of her black tent. She reminds me of my Njideka, the way she scanned the world around her as if searching for secrets.

"You're too unfocused, dear," Njideka told me the night of my fortieth birthday. "Things escape you."

We were at a restaurant at Harbourfront, waiting on our IPAS and watching boats bob on the lake. When I said nothing, she pulled out a gift-wrapped box from her purse and slid it across the table. I tore through the wrapping with anticipation. Njideka's gifts often functioned as tools for correcting bad behaviour. I expected a dieting book or a mood journal.

It was a camcorder.

"I know you don't love taking photos," she said, as I turned the device over. "But I think you could benefit from stopping every now and then to ... capture the roses."

There was more she wanted to say, I could tell, but she wouldn't if I didn't prod, so I smiled and said, "Thank you." The camcorder stayed in its box until after her sudden aneurysm. The shock of her passing ground the lightspeed pace of my life to a halt. I can barely recall the funeral except that there was an excess of sunlight. Afterward, weeks and weeks in bed. The company's final email used words like *regret to* and *best of luck*. An eviction notice was tacked to my door, and I had no numbers to call, because all my friends had truly been hers. As I decided what my backpack had room for—no to the photo albums, yes to the Donald Duck water bottle—I came across it again. Her last gift.

The yellow-haired woman patches up one more tear and smiles. She clambers inside the tent, zips herself out of sight. My focus lingers on the same spot, the spectre of Njideka shimmering there. Had we been together at the Tim Hortons the previous evening, *she* would have noticed the look, the unspoken hate, the secret moment, gone with the wind. She would have pointed it out to me.

What do you think their deal is?

And I'd have shrugged, my eyes on some other thing.

✦

I'm leaving the new food bank on Queensway, and a voice catches me, floating above the wailing gales. Inside the bank, there's a sorry war going on: bright-pink walls and portraits of sunflower fields clashing with grey soup in ceramic bowls, men and women with grey auras filling every table and chair until they're huddled against the peeling wallpaper.

I stand shivering by the front door, fingers deep in my coat pockets, where balls of cotton lint gather. I hear it.

"The stars burn all night, and the desert rocks sway in gold light."

The singer is across the street, strumming a guitar and wailing into a mic. His eyes are closed. He reminds me of an older Michael Bublé, more grizzled perhaps, his face swallowed by a beard. People walk past him, avoiding his eyes as though he were Medusa. But there's a woman to his right clutching her chest, thoroughly enraptured. She's not on this snowy pavement but in whatever dimension he's pulled her to.

I take the camcorder out of my backpack to start recording, and for the first time since her passing, I hear Njideka. Her voice is disembodied, lilting, slightly amused. It is as though she is standing right next to me, whispering in my ear.

"I love the sadness in his tune," she says. "It is from deep in the belly. From pain."

✦

The Valu-mart cashier flashes his teeth in a way that feels earnest, and I smile back despite myself.

"Will that be all?" he asks, scanning the single pack of beef ramen. I nod, assembling pennies on my palm. He wishes me a lovely day in a way that makes me believe it. The world is bright with sudden possibility. I exit into the mall corridor, a long hallway full of storefronts and steel benches. The benches have armrests in the middle now.

Rising above the chatter of clamouring passersby is a baby's unsettled cry. His mother sits amid a semicircle of grocery bags. She waves a toy rattle, but it hardly placates him. She regards him joylessly. Bags droop beneath her eyes, and her eyes are reddened from tears or lack of sleep, but there is also concern, undeniable. It is this mix of weariness and love that causes me to reach into my backpack.

The picture is taken in a moment, but I stare at it for close to an hour as I sit near a pillar outside, munching on the just-purchased noodle block. I have never been enamoured by babies, nor by the supposed legacy they bequeath—never mind the financial burden they incur. They hadn't appealed to Njideka either, not at first. Years into our marriage, though, we bore witness to friends and neighbours whose lives were constructed around parenthood. Njideka started remarking on adorable toddlers spotted on our date nights. One night in bed, she pressed her skin into mine and asked if I had everything I'd ever wanted.

"Yes," I said, curt and without hesitation. "I do." Seeing all the unpleasant, unuttered things in my eyes, she lowered her gaze.

Staring now at this new picture, I trace circles around the mother's drooping eyes, the baby's round face.

"Cute little one, isn't he?" I say.

Njideka scoffs. "Don't start. Not now."

✦

I amass fifty-three pictures and videos. There are skating rinks, churches beneath blood moons, and boulevards littered by triangular window shards. Njideka cheers the boys chasing after a school bus. She croons at the elderly men wrapping each other in tight hugs—her suspicion is that they are friends reunited after decades apart. When a tourist lags forlornly behind her camera-wielding companions, Njideka calls it a sad old sight. In a parking lot full of old trucks and unmoored boats, a man hobbles around on a walking stick, filling a blue bag with littered cigarette stubs. Njideka imagines the habit is tradition, something his grandfather taught his father.

I flick through my collection on the basement floor of the Eatonville library, where off-white curtains slice the world into a room. Sleepy students shuffle in and out. There's an occasional calculating glance or two at me, but otherwise, I am invisible. When the camcorder is fully charged, I pack up and head toward the door. A lady with pink pigtails sees me and spins around, her pace quickening. Njideka finds it terribly mundane. Were I to capture moments like this, my camcorder would have space for little else.

✦

On the day that Njideka wounds me, I am behind the Mayflower Hotel. Its post-brunch dumpsters contain flaky croissant halves, some of them moistened by discarded bottles of warm orange juice. Two women crouch in front of the nail salon across from me, petting a displeased chihuahua with overgrown fur. When I take out my camcorder, one of them looks right at me.

"She spots my secret eye," Njideka whispers.

"Your secret eye?" I ask, recording.

"Yes. Thank you, by the way, for letting me see this world again. I see you too. How you've changed."

I smile. "Yeah? How?"

"Well, your belly is gone, for one, though you know I never really minded it. And your eye, I think it's keener." The women depart with their leashed and frowning dog. Njideka adds, "I always wanted one of those little fuckers."

"I'm sorry I didn't get you one."

"Sorry doesn't do much for me now, does it? For a self-proclaimed romantic, you really were a miserable fuck sometimes." When I say nothing, she laughs. "Babe. I'm only teasing."

Her jokes were sometimes jokes and sometimes something more. It's harder to tell with her these days, but I know my stack of *sorrys* will only ever grow until it towers over Babel. And I know it's pathetic to keep saying that word, because it wasn't just the chihuahua, and it wasn't just the chubby, brown-eyed toddlers that would never bounce on her lap. There were smaller, crueller hurts. Regardless, the trajectory of our new life can't remain in the shadow of contrition.

I stand for a moment, thinking hard, and it hits me.

"Do you remember that new steakhouse—well, not so new now—on Maple Ridge Drive?"

There is a smile in her voice. "Of course. 'Bastards charge five hundred bucks for a tomahawk.' Wasn't that your excuse? Bad sport. Sometimes it was nice to just pretend."

I grin and turn in her direction. "My dear Njideka, what if we don't have to?"

✦

The snow looks sunlit at night, whirling particles caught in the glare of headlights. Slick, compact cars unroll men in tuxedos and women in glittery dresses. They seem to float on their tiptoes into the castle-like building ahead.

Head bent low, I follow.

Past the front door, the room is warm and awash in soft red hues. Oak and tangy wine colour the air. A small line has formed in front of the hostess, and at the table nearest me, a balding man feeds a much younger woman a forkful of pink steak. She hesitates before every bite.

"His touch," says Njideka. "It's her payment for his opulence."

I reach for the camcorder in my backpack, and a dozen heads turn toward me. It is as if a silent alarm has been triggered. A man in a suit approaches. I do not know if he is a diner or an employee.

"Sir," he says. "You need to leave."

I shift around him, squatting beneath an outstretched hand to steady my lens on the age-disparate couple, but time has erased the moment. The fork is no longer raised. Their faces, directed toward me, reveal nothing I haven't seen a hundred times before. Still, I feel compelled to move quickly, clumsily, my screen's focus a blur. Murmurs ripple through the onlookers as I ready my camcorder a second time.

"Sir," the man repeats, but this is simply preamble. He has taken action, his body obscuring my view, the details of his clean-cut, freckled face forced into magnification. The camcorder is out of my hands and in his. He tosses it to the floor and crunches it beneath his shoe. "*Asshole!*" Njideka says, and I feel her dissipate, no more than empty wind now. The door behind me has opened to let in new patrons, but the cold biting my skin comes from within.

I reach for the man's chest. Half my vision blackens, a sharp pain rippling across my face. I am on my knees, watching dimes of blood dot the carpet. A moment later, I am outside, face down on the concrete.

✦

At first, I walk to shake off the pain. I whip past mist-drenched condos and happy-hour bars. Behind me, a woman says to her companions that there is a conference on Monday with Jamie's teachers; one of them thinks Jamie has Olympiad potential. *Jamie,* of all her kids—can you believe that?

When my heart starts to race, I lean against the window of a used bookstore to catch my breath. Constellations hide in the pattern of dirt dotting the frosted glass. Orion or Aquila or Cygnus. I do not know their shapes, their meanings. But Njideka did.

I could ask her, but I'm afraid.

✦

The weather-beaten warming centre appears in the distance, conjuring memories of bedbugs and needles from the last time. I only enter because my legs are on the verge of collapse. Paint peels from cracked blue walls. The air is mouldy.

A young woman does the intake, such kindness in her voice. She says I've got the last spot for the night and asks one of the men on duty to check my bag. My mat is close to the door, the corner spot of a ten-by-ten-person grid near the toilet. The blanket is scratchy and bare, flattened by all the bodies it's ever held. There is no pillow, but the clothes in my backpack provide enough of a cushion. The woman next to me is curled up like a fetus. She shivers in the heat and mumbles in her sleep. Three rows away, a man suddenly screams a single word: "Turnip!" Then he roars with laughter. There is a brief silence after he stops laughing, the kind of quiet that should be familiar to me but now is eerie without her. My heartbeat flounders in painful staccato bursts. I reach out to Njideka.

"Think his grandfather owned a turnip farm?" I ask, picturing a field of white and purple vegetables plucked in the peak of summer's heat. The silence lingers, so I probe further. "Perhaps he had a little sister by that nickname?" In my head, the farm is replaced by a framed photo of a young girl with braces. Her hair is a lavender curtain. "Or maybe he said something else. Turn up? Tulip?"

All through the night, I ask her questions. The toilet door creaks; a while later, there is the sound of rushing water sucked into a vacuum. Coughs reverberate across the room at regular intervals. There is even a sneezing that lasts several minutes and sounds like death. But nothing from my dear Njideka.

Not a word.

ALL THE FAILURES OF HER BEING

First, the video of Adaeze and the faceless man surfaced online. The days afterward possessed the unreality of a life lived under water, every step hazy and plodding. The original clip amassed twelve thousand views before it was taken down at her request, but by then, mirror copies had appeared all over the web.

Adaeze's phone lit up with messages. From her university friends, with whom she had always shared a shallow approximation of intimacy, so their consolations rang hollow, their questions thinly veiled excursions in gossip farming. From strangers online:

"Hey girl, how are you doing?"

"Took it like a pro—you're a real one."

"Oink oink, fat pig!"

"Ashawo. Satan's maggots will feast on your rotten pussy."

She deleted her social media accounts; still, texts from unfamiliar numbers poured in. An emoji of a cry-laughing face. A detailed essay about all the ways its author would make her his slut skank bitch. A picture of a noose and a bridge.

Occasional knocks pounded her door.

"Ada, are you there? Let us talk."

She did not leave her room, not for classes, not for anything. Her locker was full of canned jalapeno tuna and bottled water, and she held in her bowels, even when this sent waves rumbling across her stomach.

Two days after the incident, a letter typed on her school's letterhead was slipped under her door. The first few lines read, "Dear Adaeze Obilo, we hope this message finds you well. As one of Nigeria's premier Catholic institutions, Concordat University mandates certain standards of character from its students ..."

An hour later, as she stuffed her clothes into a box, the door rattled again. She only opened it because she heard his voice, sombre. "Adaeze, it's me. Let us talk."

His gaze narrowly avoided her eyes, settling somewhere around her neck. It was a wonder, a ludicrous impossibility, that this now docile face had once filled her most blissful dreams. That she had bought a light-up globe so that when it spun, she could stare, entranced, at the white rays emanating from it, imagining him and her jetting across continents, over evergreen trees and snow-sliced tundras.

Limply, he said, "The university put out a statement online. I read that they are letting you go."

Letting you go.

He said it as though her parents had freed her from curfew to attend a night party.

"You recorded us," she said, her voice below a whisper.

"I only sent it to my homeboy, I swear. He wasn't supposed to share it with anyone. I already talked to him."

"Fuck you, Ebuka. Fuck you a thousand times."

"Look, they don't know who the guy in the video is. You're not going to say anything, are you? Because I didn't post it, and you can't prove the guy was me anyway. So it'd be just like lying. You get that, right? It's not like we were official."

She didn't trust what she would say next, what she would do, so she slammed the door in his face.

✦

The turbulent Friday-afternoon flight to Abuja lasted just over an hour, and she spent most of it drafting and redrafting potential emails.

Since you expelled me, you must expel him too. His name is Ebuka Ugwu, and he was my—

Lover.

Fuck buddy.

Accomplice, she decided, the word that best revealed his culpability without divulging the nature of their relationship. Would action against him be more or less likely if Concordat knew all the details? How, on the nights he'd called her over, he'd greeted her with a bag of udaras, the sour fruits plucked under cover of darkness at the faculty quarters, where no students were allowed. Or how, after sex, he'd sometimes dive for her belly button, blowing air into it until she shivered with laughter. How his mere presence had turned his once alien room into a sort of primal laboratory, where she freely experimented with all the capabilities of her body. She'd guided his hands to her throat, and rubbed his spit on her skin, and reddened her back with the claws of his fingernails. As the plane landed, the passengers clapping in frenzied relief, she wondered if she could twist the truth ever so slightly: *He abused me, struck me against my will. I have the marks to prove it.*

She sent no emails.

Outside the airport, taxi drivers swarmed her like vultures, and she chose the oldest-looking one, the man least likely to surf the internet. He asked her how the flight had been and stayed mercifully quiet when she did not respond.

Her parents usually picked her up at the airport, their reception melodramatic. Papa would hug her until the bones of her back cracked; Mama blew kisses all over her face and then pinched her cheeks, lamenting that she wasn't eating enough.

"Why are they starving my tomato jos?" she would say, shaking her head. "I have egusi soup waiting for you at home, my daughter. Don't worry!"

But after Adaeze had activated her new SIM card and called Mama to say that she would be coming home, Mama had murmured, "Take a taxi when you arrive. Bye."

✦

The front door was unlocked.

Papa was likely still working at Zenith Bank, but Adaeze's mother and her younger brother, Chigozie, were in the living room watching a Nollywood movie. On the screen, a young girl turned into a snake, prompting head-clutching screams from the villagers.

"Mama, I am home," Adaeze said. Mama did not move but stared intently at the women rolling in the dust. Chigozie rushed up from the couch, screaming "*Ada!*" but he'd barely taken two steps in her direction before Mama yanked him back down.

"Sit down, joor," she snarled.

Adaeze walked up the stairs and into her room. It was unchanged. Its maroon blinds were lifted high so that too much sun shone on her queen-size bed. Rows of Davido posters covered one wall, his many smiles awash in neon concert lighting. On the other wall, framed certificates sparkled, accolades from primary school spelling bees and secondary school essay contests. The normalcy startled rather than soothed her. This room belonged to the girl who had led soulful teen choirs at Holy Trinity Catholic Church, had cooked egg-filled moi-mois at the Gwarinpa food bank. It revealed nothing of the vampire who'd tasted marijuana in moonlit parks, sometimes from one end of a burning stick, sometimes on a hungry tongue. Who'd filled her mouth with sticks of gum on the return home, tiptoes grazing carpet, who'd breathed a sigh of relief when she slid beneath her blanket, the shadows mercifully still.

Adaeze sat on her bed, lost in memory, and it sank deep beneath her.

✦

Adaeze spent the day in her room. She switched her phone off, even though only Mama and Papa had her new number. Thoughts of the video plagued her. It lived outside of her in a surely still-rising tide of views and comments. How had Mama and Papa even happened upon it in the first place? Perhaps one of Mama's friends had called, barely suppressing their glee at delivering the bombshell. Or perhaps Papa, always active in the political corners of Twitter and perpetually eager to rain abuse on the federal government, had come across the clip as its virality surged. It sickened her that they not only *knew* but perhaps had also played the full video, over and over, unwilling to believe that this wild creature on the screen was their flesh and blood, their tomato jos.

Darkness fell. Insects flapped against her window, their low buzzing briefly subsumed by the approach of Papa's car. There was the slamming of doors, the sound of footsteps, and then Mama's voice, calm and flat: "Come down. Now."

Downstairs, Mama and Papa sat side by side on the black leather sofa. Adaeze took the couch opposite them, fingers twisting the hem of her long skirt. Chigozie was nowhere in sight. They'd likely sent him to his room and told him to play his iPad games with the headphones on. Their approach to household trouble had always been compartmentalization. Even when she'd at one time suspected a rift in their marriage, gleaned it from the way Papa avoided Mama's gaze, from his uncharacteristically profuse praise of her meals, her parents had put on a cadence of affection whenever they saw her watching, their effort strained by its forcefulness.

Mama's face was still blank. Papa, wiry, bespectacled, wore a glare.

"Adaeze," he said. "First of all, welcome home."

"Thank you, Papa—"

"But your mother and I are deeply disappointed in you. We are disappointed, first of all, by your immoral actions. We watched that video more times than we cared to count, unable to understand who it was we were seeing do such dirty things. It is not how we raised you. It is not what our church taught you. It is not who we know you to be. We are disappointed, second of all, by your lack of protection.

Even if you were starving in spirituality, we did not expect that you would also lack common sense. To let the raw genitals of a strange man inside you like that? We do not know what vile diseases you carry, if you have his baby growing in your belly. You will see Doctor Hassan tomorrow afternoon for tests. That is not up for debate."

Adaeze nodded. "Okay, Papa. I—"

"Finally," Papa continued, "we are disappointed in you for disgracing our family name. You have disgraced not just yourself, not just your dear brother Chigozie, who looks up to you—and don't worry, he doesn't know of this, he never will—you have also disgraced us and your grandparents and the proud line of Obilos who have marched before you. After tomorrow's medical exams, you must start applying for transfer to other universities. You will bear every associated expense, including tuition. Indefinite stay under our roof is not an option. You have three months. Good night."

"Papa—"

"Good night, Adaeze."

✦

At midnight, hunger finally struck.

There was a forbidden quality to the world outside of Adaeze's room, and she tiptoed about the kitchen, warming a bowl of yam porridge from the leftovers in the refrigerator. She ate on the veranda. The night's warm wind licked her face. Crickets chirped in the low grass of the neighbouring front lawns. After dinner, she washed her bowl in the sink, the tap's rush like a raging waterfall. A sudden sleepless energy churned inside her, and when she returned upstairs, she turned toward Chigozie's door instead of her own. They had never been especially close, perhaps due to their seven-year age gap, but many long Friday-night sessions of Jenga and Scrabble had bound them. He'd often invented strange four-letter words, invariably with a *Z* or an *X*, and she'd allowed them, the triumphant smile on his face too precious to disrupt.

Even in the darkness of Chigozie's room, she caught his motion as she entered—a clumsy diving under the bedsheets, beneath which a square light glowed.

"Does that ever work on Mama?" Adaeze said.

Chigozie emerged shyly. Then he rushed at her, feet bounding across the bed until he was in her arms, and she lifted him, hugged him more tightly than she ever had. When they parted, she examined him closely. His hairline was thin and crooked, likely a victim of Mama's deluded belief in her own barbering prowess. A wide grin lit his face, so dispossessed of the youthful cynicism that other thirteen-year-olds learned to weaponize.

"You're home early," he said. "It's not June yet."

"I know, Chigo. I just missed everyone so much. I will be around for a while. Is that okay with you?"

Chigozie glanced at the door, his smile fading slightly. "Mama said I shouldn't talk to you."

"Did she tell you why?"

"She said that you had a hard semester at school, that you're very tired. But I know it's because of the video."

Adaeze gaped at him.

He was no longer smiling.

"I heard her yelling," he said, whispering now, as if Mama might be pressing one ear to the other side of his door. "It was late, and she probably thought I was sleeping. But I was on this"—he motioned at his iPad, still aglow under the sheets—"playing sudoku. I remember to check the diagonals now! I bet I'm even faster than you."

"Her yelling—what did she say?"

He mimicked Mama's voice. "'Adaeze has killed me—what kind of video is this?' Papa was trying to hush her. I didn't hear much after that because they started talking so low."

"Chigo, did you see the video?"

"No ... but Kingston at school, him and his stupid friends, they tried to make me watch it. I refused. They said it was a video of you having sex. Like, ew! Ada, who would have sex with you?" His eyes narrowed suspiciously. "Are you pregnant, then? Who's the daddy?"

She draped his blanket over his head and pinned him down until his wild wriggling turned to raucous laughter. When he resurfaced, inhaling deeply, she flicked his nose and said, "No. I'm not pregnant. Won't be till I'm forty and grey-haired and you're taking care of me."

He scoffed. "My friend Chuka says forty-year-old women have cobwebs in their vaginas. And spiders."

"Chuka sounds very wise."

"Mama calls him a charlatan and thinks we don't talk anymore, but he's my best friend."

"Well, I won't mention him," Adaeze replied. They pinky-swore on their promises, and when he showed her what he'd been playing on his iPad, a new game full of lasers and spinning basketballs, she watched him, his gyrating fingers, the focused intensity with which he explained the rules. She marvelled at how easily it bloomed within her, overwhelming, the love she held for him.

✦

While a nurse drew her blood, Doctor Hassan said sternly, "Make better decisions next time, okay? It's a miracle you're not pregnant." Her father watched from a corner of the room, silent as a statue. She wondered if Doctor Hassan had seen the video too or had merely heard about it from Papa. A lurid image arose unbidden of Doctor Hassan masturbating to her silent moans in the privacy of his office.

The ride to the clinic and back was uncomfortably quiet. Adaeze wanted Papa to speak. She wanted to tell him that his words from last night had hurt but not nearly as much as he thought, that she remembered how he'd always chided her softly in Mama's absence and forcefully in her presence. But when they arrived home and he exited his car without a glance at her, a new wound opened in her chest.

It worsened that evening as she showered, running her soapy hands over her skin in a daze. Ebuka's presence loomed against the steamed glass as she remembered the initial coyness of their first time. She'd stayed mostly clothed, her stomach sucked in, while he stripped bare with fervent speed. He was handsome, but his stomach was bloated with flesh and his nipples drooped. The confidence of his easy motion had enticed and boggled her, and she'd found herself reciprocating his swagger on their second encounter. Dancing slowly around the perimeter of his bedroom to the rhythm of his cheers. Teasing the buttons of her top apart until it dropped, coiled by her feet like snakeskin. His face had slackened with such longing, and the delicious high of that look had lingered for days afterward. The thick, pockmarked body she inhabited was *hers*, not some defective, temporary vessel on the slow march to slimness. It was capable of hypnosis.

It felt less capable in the intervals between their encounters, as little as a day or as long as two months. He was a final-year electrical engineering student, and the demands of his projects were volatile. When the days apart became weeks, she turned her bedside mirror around so her reflection no longer startled her, and when she was his again, she took him facing the dust-speckled glass lining the doors of his wardrobe. On the cycle went, his periodic silence stirring loose the voices in her head trained to highlight all the failures of her being.

She wondered if his secret camera had rolled only the one time. Or if he possessed a mosaic of every gasp and moan and position, a collection routinely shared with his closest buddies.

This is us doggy style, and this is my favourite, when she rides me like a horse and I yank her fake brown hair—it's a wig, you know—and she moans like a slut skank bitch.

Perhaps they'd gathered around his phone like children at a campfire, pointing at the misshapen contours of her body, muttering things she already knew to be true. Things now echoed by newly birthed voices whose words slipped into her cereal at breakfast, pressed against her pillows at sundown, followed her into the grey hues of dreamscape.

Adaeze turned the shower valve so the water burned at its hottest. It cooked her skin in vapour clouds.

✦

On Sunday morning, she awoke before the sun.

She changed into her usual church outfit, a droopy formal dress, and waited by the dining room table. Mama came down shortly afterward and jerked in surprise upon seeing Adaeze. Just as quickly, she moved on, boiling water for Papa's favourite green tea. Chigozie followed in a sharp black suit, and Mama asked if he'd slept well. She led him to the living room, where they watched cartoons until Papa appeared.

For the next three hours, Adaeze tested her skill of singular focus—she chose the road's gloomy silver during the drives to and fro and the cross of Jesus Christ during the endless sermon. She no longer believed, hadn't in years, but she found herself drawn to the bronze statue now, its theatre of suffering. His nailed hands. His grotesquely bloody scalp. His mournful face. She considered his saying, *Forgive them, for they know not what they do*. She wouldn't have forgiven—she'd have boiled them until their flesh flayed from the bone.

Once home, Chigozie dashed up the stairs to change into casual clothing. Before Adaeze could follow, Mama said, "Wait."

Adaeze and Papa turned.

"Nwunye mu," Papa said, touching Mama's shoulder. "Is everything okay?"

She ignored him. "Adaeze, did you see them looking at us in church? Even the priests."

"Dear ..." Papa started.

"Next week, find another church. Better yet, stay home. It is not my church you will go to. Do you hear me?"

Without waiting for a response, Mama walked past her, bounding up the stairs, muttering under her breath. Soon, it was just Papa and Adaeze.

"You were her world, you know?" Papa said, a softness in his voice. "She celebrated your intellect and grace with friends and strangers alike, with anything that had ears. Adaeze, you broke my wife's heart. She cries her eyes red every night. Please, please, find a way to fix it, whatever it takes, or her grave will bear your name."

✦

For most of the next week, Adaeze left her room only to use the bathroom and to eat, and then only if the world outside was free of sound.

There was a box in her closet full of Chinua Achebe novels, old notebooks, and *Daily Trust* newspapers from years ago, their pages mottled with soda stains. Before Papa had fully committed to a digital library, "reluctantly relinquishing the past," as he'd said, the paper had been delivered to their front door each morning. Adaeze had collected them, at first to fill out the daily sudoku puzzles, and soon afterward, to marvel at the clean fonts of small letters, the sharp names of strangers beneath looming headlines. There were tales of corrupt politicians and masquerade festivals and dead soldiers, much like the Nigerian works of fiction she loved, except these were steeped in reality and therefore more potent.

"I want to become a journalist," she'd told Mama and Papa the evening of a secondary school career fair.

Mama had grinned. "Journalist, keh? Why not sell bread under the bridge too?"

"Adaeze mu," Papa had said, "it is very respectable, but we thrive by following the smell of opportunity. Nigeria is full of crude oil, you know? It is what God has blessed us with."

Adaeze hoped that the box, with its scent of nostalgia, could fully occupy her. She sat by her desk, absent-mindedly flipping through the pages and looking up whenever she detected motion outside. She watched Papa leave for work in his SUV. Watched Chigozie dash onto the school bus, his friends waving at him from small, square windows. The first morning she saw him run like that, a strange twinge of jealousy took hold. When he'd delightedly leaped into her arms on the night of her return, she'd thought the moment special, but it seemed he was often joyous, always leaping into things. Mama left at noon for long walks but was otherwise home. Adaeze did not know if she had quit her job at the upscale advertising agency in Maitama or if she was merely taking time off.

When Adaeze wasn't half reading words, she was on her laptop, the internet turned off for fear of what might pop up. She knew that she wanted out of this house, with its endlessly humming air conditioners and clanking overhead pipes. She needed to research potential new universities in the country's farthest reaches. Someday, well before her three months were up, Mama's grace would vanish, and she would press against Papa in their shared bedroom and whisper direly, *It is time—she must go*. Worst of all, Adaeze knew that she stayed paralyzed because Ebuka persisted. She relived slamming her door in his face and then the many nights beforehand passed beneath his duvet. Even when its thickness had choked them with sweat, she'd relished the enclosed suffocation, the smell of him, the *I love yous* never said, saved for the right moment.

"What are we?" she'd asked once, immediately hating the infantile sound of the words in her throat, wishing she could take them back.

He'd kissed the bridge of her nose. "You're the only woman I'm fucking, you know that. What's in a name, anyway? It's all in the *doing*."

Her petroleum engineering classes had bored her, and her university friendships were formed by virtue of proximity. Left to their own devices, her thoughts had turned to dark places. Ebuka's presence had always been a fiery sort of peace, the messy calm in subdued storms.

Now she imagined life would always be this: an eternal stretch of languishing in her prison of a room, pathetic and immobilized. Then, on Friday afternoon, precisely one week after her return, Papa came home early, knocked on her door, and entered without waiting.

"Doctor Hassan called me," he said. "Your test results came back."

✦

That evening, Adaeze turned on the Wi-Fi on her laptop. She created a new Facebook profile, its picture a stock photo resulting from an image search for "Black woman," its name an impulsively generated "Missy Davis." In the Facebook search bar, she typed "Ebuka Ugwu." Hovered over the Enter key.

There was a bubbling in her chest, as if the ventricles of her heart were melting into stew. Only hours ago, Papa had said with great relief, "You have no STDS." She'd understood that he clung to the outcome of those results, that in some small way, her lack of disease redeemed her.

The bubbling had started then. Worsened now. Adaeze waited until the feeling in her chest was unbearable before lowering her finger onto the Enter key.

She found his profile easily. He had a post from yesterday, a trite "With God, we command the universe." Beneath that, with hundreds of likes and dozens of comments, was a picture post of him and a stranger, his lips on her cheek. She was smooth faced and beautiful, her radiant dress complementing a figure of perfect proportions. White teeth glimmered in her smile. Sand stretched behind them, its fine edge meeting the frozen rush of deep-blue waves. He'd captioned this photo, "Fellas, I think I found the one: A True Queen."

Adaeze scrolled through the comments.

Heart-eyed emojis.

"Omalicha Nwa!"

"Heavenly God, I am begging you. When will it be my turn?"

The woman, Ifechiluru Okafor, was tagged in the post. Her page was sparse—close-up selfies in nondescript rooms, two-sentence reviews of British TV shows, and a video of her cooking curry chicken three years ago. This video marked the start of her page. Her new relationship status with Ebuka marked the end.

Four days ago.

Adaeze felt a surreal awe. How had Ebuka, with his ungodly gut and oversized front teeth, ended up with someone like her? How had a man who panted like a dog in bed, saliva dripping from the sides of his mouth, and pronounced *baby* like *baybay*, and winked before he left a room like a bad lead in a telenovela, gotten close enough to a woman like Ifechiluru, close enough to taste her skin and smell her strawberry-scented hair and share her with the world as "A True Queen"?

Adaeze inhaled deeply, her body shuddering from the effort. She clicked on the Message button above Ifechiluru's brazen smile. Her fingers flashed across the keyboard, words forming in the milliseconds before each strike.

"I see you're with Ebuka, and sister to sister, I just thought you should know. He gave me herpes and chlamydia. Don't trust him."

She sent the message, and when it did little to calm her rising rage, she slammed the laptop shut and paced around her room, moving in unsteady circles until her knees touched the carpet. Still, she continued, circling the circumference of the same brown patch until friction burned her skin at each point of contact, and then she lay down at the side of her bed, wishing him death. She pictured his head severed from his blood-spurting neck, the rest of him blindly flailing about.

✦

The three weeks that followed were manic. Adaeze committed herself to the constant motion of her body. Whenever Ebuka hovered in the forefront of her thoughts, she strained to concentrate on whatever task lay at hand until his presence was like an armpit sore, a background pain.

She compiled a list of universities currently accepting transfer applications, all of them in the South, away from Abuja. She ranked them by earliest potential start dates. The first, University of Nkanu, Enugu, was in two months. Because the sole printer at home sat in Mama and Papa's room, she went to the nearest cybercafé, a twenty-minute walk turned thirty by her deliberate pace. At the café, she printed out the UNE application form and her West African Examination Council score report. Then, she emailed Student Services at Concordat University for a copy of her transcript. She returned the next day to print an application to the Ebonyi State University, and the following week for more forms to universities in Lagos. She filled out the forms in the café, pausing over "reason for transfer" before scrawling, "More robust petroleum engineering program desired." Where they asked for a university contact number, she wrote her own number instead. Sometimes, the café owner turned in her direction, and she stared back. His look was always one of idle curiosity rather than familiarity, and after a while, she stopped returning his gaze.

She looked up apartments in the cities under consideration, made calls to landlords, refreshed her bank account to verify the presence of her 185,000 naira, and cooked her own meals. Sometimes, Mama drew near while Adaeze stirred the pot. Aside from the occasional dispassionate "Move, I can't reach the kettle" or "Turn down the flame; it's too much," Mama said little else.

Papa was slightly more vocal, especially if Mama was out of earshot. He asked Adaeze to plate him some of her achicha and frowned on the first bite. "Use less salt next time," he said. While she sat on the veranda one night, watching moths fling themselves at the bulbs, he stood over her.

"Which universities are you applying to?"

She told him, and he stared at the clouds. "Take away EBSU," he said. "They have too many strikes. The rest are good." When she went up to the room, she crumpled her EBSU form and tossed it into the wastebasket.

Chigozie also maintained his distance in Mama's presence, but Adaeze snuck into his room late on Friday nights, and he giggled at the exaggerated way she scampered in. They took turns playing his iPad game of lasers—she was quite bad at it, routinely losing in the first forty-five seconds—and talking about the newest girl Chuka had fallen in love with.

"Today, it was Maryam," he said, his head on Adaeze's lap. "He says when we play football, her breasts waggle."

She chuckled. "Waggle, that's his word?"

"Yes. But I don't like Maryam. She's mean. Sometimes she tries to trip me on the grass."

"Who do you like?"

"Miss Kate, our mathematics teacher. She calls me Einstein. I want to marry her."

He fell asleep shortly afterward. She watched him for a bit, listening to his light breathing. She thought of all the things he told her and all the things he didn't. Of how his secrets would grow with time until who he was and who her parents saw were entirely different beings.

✦

On a Saturday morning one month after the return, Student Services responded with a PDF attachment of her transcript. The body of the email simply stated, "Stay blessed."

"Eat shit," Adaeze typed back, and surprised herself by sending it. At the cybercafé, she printed the transcript, then traced her fingers over the unexpected "Dean's Honour List Year 1" annotation at the bottom of the document. As she paid the cybercafé owner, the ordinarily quiet man chuckled.

"You like my café, ehn?" he said, his accent thick.

She granted him a thin smile and looked away as he fished in his register for her change.

"Shy, shy girl," he leered, singing the words. A sudden cold look filled his eyes, and his fingers hooked onto her shoulder. "You were not shy in that video. Not shy at all. I have palm wine in the back. After we finish there today, no need to pay me anymore."

She jammed her elbow into his bony chest. He was a slight man, and the force of her contact sent him staggering backward. Her printed pages scattered on the ground, and she left them there, ran onto the street as he screamed after her.

"*Harlot! Never come back here again!*"

✦

It took her ten minutes to get home, her legs sliced by aching throbs. She grabbed her laptop from her desk and, for the first time since her return, walked into Mama and Papa's room. It was dimly lit and icy with cold air. Mama sat upright on her bed, gaping at the powered-off television and then at Adaeze's entrance.

"I just want to use your printer," Adaeze said. "And then I'll get out, okay?"

The printer was loud and slow, paper crawling from its lip like a white-skinned slug. Adaeze could easily have missed Mama's words, which were whispered gently then, except that Mama's words had never lacked for clarity.

"Why are you breathing so hard? Adaeze, what is wrong?"

The question was wilful in its feigned ignorance, as if all had been right before now. Yet, Adaeze found herself thinking of the time when she, not Chigozie, would sit by Mama's legs watching Nollywood movies. The first time Adaeze had seen a dibia on screen, his bare chest chalk-lined with occult symbols, his calabash of cow's blood offered to the skies, she'd shrunk back in fear. Mama had hugged her then, saying, "God protects us, nwa mu. Don't be afraid." Her hugs had always been of that sort, providing relief to toothless things—make-believe pagans in low-budget flicks or class grades one mark shy of an A. Confronted now with the possibility of a true embrace, Mama's shoulder laid bare for the sinking of tears, Adaeze's anger softened into the deep blue of sadness. Her words trembled.

"I was at the Diamond cybercafé on Bello Way. The man there, the owner, he grabbed me."

"That small idiot who smells like crayfish? Him?"

"Yes. I ran."

Mama sighed, her exhale prolonged. "Adaeze, when you show the world who you are, the world responds in kind."

Adaeze's transcript, fully formed now, hung off the table's edge as if preparing for a dive. In the printer's sudden silence, Mama's words were louder, seemed to echo.

"Did you open your legs for him?" she said. "Tell him to suck the milk from your nipples in exchange for twenty minutes on his computer? It would not surprise me, Adaeze, nothing would surprise me, because I do not know who you are."

Tears stung Adaeze's cheeks, and they drained her—their heat, the tickle of their crawl down her face. She tore the paper off the printer and headed toward the door. She almost made it out. It was her mother's defeated muttering—"My daughter is a harlot"—that made her spin around. It was that word at the very end, and her mother's effortless dispatching of it, and the way it unfurled from her tongue.

Adaeze took long strides across the room. She bent over her mother's face, and her mother flinched, shifting backward.

"Adaeze, do you want to fight me? Is that what this is? Will you slap your mother for speaking the truth?"

"Fuck you."

Mama laughed, raised her hands to the ceiling. "Father God, see the kind of daughter you have given me. Have I not served you well? Have I not given you my heart?" She turned to Adaeze, and her age showed on her face in brutal transparency, the carved wrinkles like lines on a map next to the whites of her ruffled hair. "I bore you for nine months and wiped your dirty anus when you shit and kept your belly full. When the milky pap upset your tummy and you poured your vomit all over my skin, I said, 'This is it. This is the dress of motherhood. I will wear it proudly.' And for what? For *what*, Adaeze? I am a failure."

"Do you want to know all the ways you have failed?" Adaeze snarled, waving the paper in the air, brandishing it like a weapon. "Do you want to know the names of all the boys I kissed in secondary school, and all the girls too, and which ones put their fingers inside me? Or should I stand here and tell you that the devil made me do it, and I can be your tomato jos again? For once, I will be honest with you. I will let you know. Not just this month. Not just this year. You have always been the mother of a dick-sucking harlot. That is your dress."

Mama smiled bitterly. She sounded tired, on the verge of sleep, when she spoke. "You will burn in hell, Adaeze, at the Lord's appointed time, and I will not waste my spit on you to put the fire out." She looked at her watch. "Chigozie's father will be back from his morning jog in less than fifteen minutes. By then, I want you out of this house. Do you hear me, Adaeze? You will never come back."

But Adaeze had already left the room.

✦

It took her all of two minutes to pack. From her closet, she grabbed a random assortment of clothes, the running sneakers that never ran, all the old newspapers. She ignored the filled-out application forms in the drawers, reached beneath a tangle of old cables and half-working earphones for an envelope of naira notes.

Mama watched from nearby, impassive, and when Adaeze reached for Chigozie's door, Mama ran toward her.

"Where do you think you're going? Leave my son alone."

Adaeze pushed in.

Chigozie was deep asleep. Drool oozed out the side of his mouth. She bent low and kissed his forehead while Mama watched pensively from the doorway. Adaeze thought of parting words, something to whisper in his ear and leave buried in his subconscious, something to bind them until the next time, but nothing emerged, so she kissed him again and hoped it was enough.

✦

At the nearest major intersection, she flagged a taxi.

The driver rolled down his window, his car reeking of excess cologne. "Where are you going?" he asked with brusque impatience, and when for a moment she failed to speak, he sucked his teeth and drove off, cursing. The next taxi pulled up only a minute later, and quickly she said, "Wuse Motel."

It was a three-storey building with zinc awnings and a large central fountain that hadn't worked in years. She knew next to nothing about it except that Papa sometimes drove past it on their Christmas-week visits to his parents in Lagos.

The receptionist smacked gum bubbles and tapped away on his phone until she cleared her throat. Upon looking up, he smiled apologetically.

"Welcome, madam. How many nights are you staying?"

"Just one. But I may extend it by a few days if that's okay."

When he offered to help with her bag, she shook her head. "No, thank you."

He stepped around the front desk. "It's no problem, ma, plenty of stairs to your room."

"I said *no*."

He raised his hands, annoyed. "Okay, ma. Calm down."

Room 304 smelled like stale soup. The sunlight that slanted in through its windows was a dull and dusty kind. She fell on the bed, which creaked beneath her weight, closed her eyes, and prayed to the pillows for relief. But there was none. No sadness either, nor anger. It was as if all the emotion had been wrung out of her body, leaving behind a numb shell.

She had lunch at a nearby kiosk, cold garri with milk and sugar, then returned to the motel. All day, there was an odd sense of waiting for something. Only when her phone buzzed with an automatic text from her telecom network about weekend bonus rates did she realize what it was.

Papa.

She was waiting for his call. He would say, *Mama is angry, but please, come home.*

When midnight passed and her phone remained silent, she wondered if he had begun to call upon his return from jogging, if Mama had put her hand over his in disapproval. But Papa was a wilful man, wasn't he? He had never really done anything he didn't want to. She pictured Mama and Papa tangled in their bed at that very moment, sound asleep.

✦

Adaeze connected her laptop to the motel's Wi-Fi. First, she logged into the Missy Davis Facebook account, untouched since the night of its creation. There were no new notifications, no indication that Ifechiluru had even read her message. Next, she moved on to Twitter, created a new account, and typed in the search bar.

Dozens of results loaded. In some, the clip was even grainier, so that her pixellated face was nearly unrecognizable. Others had been edited in various ways. An upbeat circus-clown tune played over the last ten seconds of one. In another, the moment before Ebuka—only visible from the waist down—ejaculated, he morphed into an image of a muscular and disapproving Jesus Christ.

Most of the associated comments were from two weeks ago or earlier, but the most recent was only a half-hour old: "I just know his dick tastes nasty." She found lustful fantasies, commentary on the generation's failed women, half-baked jokes, size comparisons to Ebuka's penis, disgust at the video's very existence, the assurance of hell's unbearable temperatures, remarks about the unflattering excess of her various body parts.

"My ex did this shit after we broke up," said a user named Eniola Akande in a video response. She was short and thin, her hair laid in a field of cornrows. "And I slit my wrists with broken glass. Y'all are foul."

There was only one reply to Eniola, its account owner faceless: "Sounds like sex ain't the only thing you're whack at. Cut harder next time."

A linked thread led to Concordat's official statement on her expulsion, and the replies there varied too: support, confusion, anger, amusement. Dawn tore holes in the sky, lifting shadows from Room 304. Adaeze kept scrolling. A weight pulled at her eyes. Her neck hurt from the angle of its bend. But even when there were no comments left, even after she'd processed and discarded the latest entries of the night, she returned to the video, played it on a loop, waited for oversaturation to yield some kindling of solace. But there was none to be found, not in the relentless watching, not in her distance from home. She longed for her room, with its oversized posters and her sea-soft bed, and for Mama's familiar silence. She would do anything to get it back, would prostrate herself before Mama, would lick the floor clean beneath her feet. And once inside, she would dash upstairs, press Chigozie into her chest. He would ask where she had gone yesterday, and she would smile and say, *Nowhere, Chigo, I am here to stay, remember?*

It was a simple knowing, the impossibility of it all.

She returned to the Facebook tab, clicked around. She began typing a new message.

✦

Adaeze checked out of the motel before noon, stopped at the kiosk to buy an assortment of drinks, and took a second taxi to Gwagwalada Transit. On a plain of dusty road, buses arrived and departed, and hawkers wove through the open gaps with their sun-relieving yogurt and bags of shelled groundnuts. The bus Adaeze took managed to fit fifty into its thirty seats. She sat in the back row, squashed between a toothless elderly woman and a loudly snoring man whose head lolled like a rag doll's.

It was just past two when she arrived at Lafia stop, outside which a bevy of taxis waited. She got in the nearest one and lapsed into an unsettled half-hour nap. Her destination loomed ahead when she woke up. Cracked and brittle grass flanked the entrance of the Nasarawa State University, Keffi.

The campus's central quad was chaotic with life. Students chased after battered footballs. Others leaned against tree trunks, lost in the clamour of conversation or flipping through textbooks. In one corner, a caftan-draped man wrapped sticks of beef suya in folded paper cones, selling them to the line growing before him. It was on the other side of the line's tail that Adaeze spotted Eniola Akande.

They approached each other with the awkwardness of strangers, and when Adaeze stretched out her hand, Eniola backed away slightly.

"Jesus, you look like shit," Eniola said.

Adaeze chuckled. "Yeah, I don't know the last time I had a good night's sleep."

A prickly silence lingered as Eniola led them into a row of peeling buildings. She unlocked a door at the end of one corridor. Her room was tiny and stuffy, its twin-size bed overflowing with rumpled clothes. In a corner sink, oily paper plates were stacked.

"Pardon me if I didn't feel like cleaning up," Eniola said. She sat on the edge of her bed while Adaeze settled into a low chair, its metal back hard against her spine.

"It's fine," she said, and when Eniola didn't reply, Adaeze reached into her bag and pulled out bottles of water, zobo juice, Sprite, and vodka. "They're all warm now, but I hope there's something here you—"

Eniola reached for the Sprite. "I'm trying to cut down on my sugar, but fuck it, I've been good." She took a steady chug, closing her eyes as she swallowed. "So, I'm still not sure what to make of you, Adaeze. Being here, I mean. Wanting to meet."

Adaeze drank from the vodka bottle, grimacing at the taste. "I'm not here for money or anything like that. To be honest, I don't even know why I came. I know I need to find a job soon and figure out where I'm staying and what I'm doing with my wretched life. I'm a smart girl, I know I'll figure it all out. I'll be okay. But it's hard to even breathe when there's so much *tired* trapped in my chest. I'm tired, Eniola. I'm tired of the hate, I'm tired of the anger, I'm tired of the tears, I'm tired of remembering—every bone in my body is just tired."

Eniola finished the rest of the Sprite and tossed the crushed bottle. It landed near one leg of the metal chair. She raised her right arm—it was pockmarked from wrist to elbow with scabs of different sizes.

"I used to feel like my blood was dirty," Eniola said slowly, "so I cut my skin to let it out. Wore long-sleeved shirts on the days I left my room. Came back trembling and sat right here on this bed. Pen, blade, glass from a shattered mirror, it didn't matter. It was all about seeing the dark red leak out. Like if I did it enough times, I'd be clean again. Till I cut too deep one day, and a good friend found me passed out on the sheets. Some days, my blood still feels like mud, and there's this itch that festers in my head. Some nights, there are nightmares. Vivid." She ran her fingers over the ridges on her arm where the scarred flesh was a different colour. "There's been none of this, though, not for a while. I'd like to think that's something. I guess we'll see."

Adaeze looked down at her thumbs on the straps of her suitcase. She didn't want Eniola to see her face, which was too sleep deprived to properly mask her disappointment. For what exactly, she did not know, but there it was anyway, the feeling that Eniola and her messy room and her sterile words and her unconquered pain had let Adaeze down.

"I checked his profile last night," Adaeze said. "Ebuka Ugwu. He's been with this girl for a while now. Pretty thing. They seem happy."

"Think she knows? About the video."

"Probably. Not sure it matters much." She rose. "I'll get going before I pass out on your floor."

Eniola leaned over her bed, made a hesitant motion across the small space separating them. She placed a hand on Adaeze's side. "This should have never happened to you. I'm sorry that it did."

Adaeze stared at her, sat back down. "Oh. Yeah. Thank you." She shifted on the chair, scratched her neck. "Thank you, Eniola."

EKENEDILICHUKWU HATED GOD

For the Smallness of Hatred's Origin

Because months after the gunmen's bullets tore through eighteen youth choristers in nearby Akpor, Reverend Ejike said that endless mourning disrespected the Most High's design—they were reunited with Him, after all. The Communion wafer tasted strange that morning, a brittle, melting thing. Still, Ekene rose with the congregation on every piano note, singing and clapping.

Because when Pa passed away, Ma tore through her clothes at the midday funeral and sullied her hair with fresh-rain mud. She knelt long enough for the stones to draw blood and begged the unrelenting skies for Pa's return. Ekene did not miss Pa, not the worsened temper that had plagued his final months, nor his unshowered, bedridden musk. But for the cessation of Ma's tears, he crouched beside her long enough for his thighs to burn, imploring the heavens too.

Because he did not recognize the long-standing simmering in his chest until the night of his fourteenth birthday. Despite his pleading, Ma had not excused him from working the overheated kitchen at Crunchies, Uncle Ikenna's café. Either in defiance or self-celebration, Ekene had reached for the smallest piece of a customer's gizzard on the sizzling pan. Uncle Ikenna caught him, made him spit it out. "God hates thieves," Uncle Ikenna said, not unkindly. A thought burned clear and sharp in Ekene's mind, freed at last: *I hate Him too.*

For the Rays of His Light

Which shone down on Mr. and Mrs. Ezilo, their neighbours since time immemorial, until they weren't. Years ago, their brilliant Kosisochukwu had won a government scholarship to a university in oyibo land. At *fifteen*! Ekene's age today, as Ma liked to remind him, never mind that Ekene had not been alive during that era of apparently free-flowing funds. (And where exactly had he been? How did one access memories of a preceding void?) Now, by His grace, Kosisochukwu had finally secured her parents' entry into a better world.

The night before their departure, the Ezilos invited Ma and Ekene over for dinner. There was sweet red wine, which Ma let Ekene indulge in just that one time, and semovita with beef-laden soup. While the adults traded stories in the candlelight, Ekene stared at them and considered the falseness of this gathering, which suggested that they dined together often, year-round. Often offered each other more than a yawning kedu on the mornings their paths briefly crossed. He considered the unusual shrillness of his mother's praise when dinner ended, her hands arched to the ceiling: "Ka anyi kene Chukwu." Kene Him for the enterprising daughter, even if her efforts had taken a decade to bear fruit, and wasn't that all right, because His time was the best?

The morning after, Ekene helped the Ezilos pack their things into the airport-bound van Kosisochukwu had arranged. He moved blackened pots, gele wrappers, Maggi-cube pouches, and yellowed photo albums, sections of entire lives sifting through his fingers in twenty minutes. Mr. Ezilo lamented the mattress of a thousand memories he could not bring along. Mrs. Ezilo fussed over the contents of a thick file folder, double-checking for passports and stamped letters. As they hugged Ma a final time, Mrs. Ezilo let loose a disbelieving laugh. The sound lingered even after their van disappeared in a cloud of dust. A joy so light, its taste was elusive on Ekene's tongue.

For the Two Bonnyfaces

Bonnyface, the grey rabbit half-hidden by a thicket of shrubs, spotted on the usual evening walk from Abuloma Road to Crunchies. Ekene's legs were numb from a day spent dashing between traffic-stalled cars and soaping their windscreens. While squatting to rest for a moment, he'd spotted the rabbit's visible half, its stomach cleaved open and wetly red. Its fur was warm to the touch and pulsing. Whatever had torn into it was long gone, but its front legs still twitched, manic, almost musical. The marbles of its black eyes caught and reflected the setting sun, shimmering even after motion ceased. A name was the only dignity Ekene could offer it.

A month later, that unplaceable instinct to label another surfaced again. Was this a sort of resurrection? No, not quite. Yet, here was a second Bonnyface, the name granted to a five-year-old girl who started wandering Abuloma alongside her mother, pleading for spare change. One vertical half of the girl's body was severely burned, while the other half was almost shocking in its smoothness.

The cooks Ekene assisted at Crunchies, older boys prone to constant gossip, identified the mother from his descriptions of the daughter. Evidently, while the woman's husband had toiled away at a communal maize plantation, she had toiled away beneath various men in their marital bedroom. When he found out a year ago, the husband retaliated by tossing Bonnyface into a cooking flame. After her mother pulled her out, screaming for all the neighbours to hear, he warned her to leave with the dirty little bastard or face the fullness of his wrath. Now, mother and daughter roamed the streets, their hands perpetually outstretched.

The boys narrated all this with excitable jubilance, as though Bonnyface's tribulation was karmic. How could it be? Her face was so gaunt it resembled a skull. She pulled loose, rattling coughs from deep in her rib cage, which was visible through her tattered brown dress. A rank odour followed her too, painfully reminiscent of Pa's last days, and Ekene learned to move in the opposite direction upon her approach.

One afternoon, the smell announced itself before the sight of her. Ekene turned around to see Bonnyface looking right at him. Her mother was twenty steps away, pleading on bent knees with an impassive Dangote trucker. Ekene started to move away, but Bonnyface waved at him. He paused, waved back. She smiled, revealing two missing incisors. Her sheer fragility struck his chest with a familiar lurching.

For the Shape of His Insides, All Black and Squirming

Especially at Crunchies, where the day's attempts at ducking fast-swerving okadas gave way to the night's reduction in stimuli. His inner gaze was sharpened by the easy routine of cleaving fish heads and dicing okra. The arm's consistent motion, even when it ached. The smell of blood that so easily camouflaged its tang unless you went sniffing for it. The older boys' circuitous conversations, their grating laughter at stale jokes. All that sameness a blank canvas for the mind's painting. A mirror for things like:

Why was he so short? Even twelve-year-old Musa, who rinsed the windscreens after Ekene's soaping and dried them with a long-handled sponge, stood three heads taller. A bass in his voice too. A hint of facial hair.

And why did his insides feel like a living thing, a separate entity cohabitating with Ekene, so feverishly restless? Jumping, bouncing, rising in intensity, a slight waltz at sun-up, a hundred-man tango at sunset.

And why, sometimes, did everything provoke such rage? How Uncle Ikenna smiled on the Fridays he handed Ekene a slim envelope of cash. Ma's narration after their pre-bed showers about all the big men with BMWs whose children she babysat, and how they never finished their lunch, and how their portside homes glistened—wallpaper, chandeliers, stainless steel, floor-to-ceiling windows. And all the what-ifs: what if they moved closer to the city, prayed harder, switched churches, what if she were eighteen again and (her voice falling, as though Pa could hear her from the great beyond) she decided this time that she would not marry for love, what if, what if, *what if*? What if this was all life would ever be?

And why did guilt follow the rage? Especially when he considered all he *did* have. A roof over his head, the absence of Pa's screaming, clothes without holes in them, dinner before sleep, a mother who sang him gently awake at the rooster's cry. Did Bonnyface's mother ever sing to her? Ever kiss her forehead? Had Bonnyface ever known how it felt to hunt a firefly's flaming tail in the sanctity of darkness?

And all that constant squirming, inner winds begetting tornadoes, would not matter if Ekene's body brimmed with even a molecule of energy. Why was sleep so brief, a blink in the night? Was it so impossible to linger in the dreamless quiet for an hour or two longer? For forever? Wasn't there a melody to that idea? A sleep from which you never woke.

For All the Friends, Foes, Strangers Who Croon His Name

Did He soak it in with boundless joy? Or perhaps a deep anxiety, fearful that something would change someday, that a collective knowing would settle in their hearts, and their well of exuberant exaltations would dry up. "Ka anyi kene Chukwu" from Ma's lips. "Alhamdulillah" from Musa's when he and Ekene counted the day's meagre gains. "Praise Be" at Saint Mary's Catholic Church: homily, Holy Communion, a dozen testimonies before Reverend Ejike's final words. Professions from newlyweds, from teenage mothers cradling frayed and weeping bundles, from passers of higher-institution entrance exams, from the newest reverend sisters of the Oro-Igwe convent. Chief Ojukwu went last, a towering man who slow-walked toward the altar in his purple agbada overflowing at the shoulders and the ankles, followed by his entourage of gospel-swaying bodyguards, their hands bearing silent praises: cartons of Indomie, baskets filled with garden eggs, jangling car keys to new pastoral fleets, money turned to goods turned to Him because "He replenishes threefold, do you not see the proof in Chief?" And in the bygone days of Divine Love Primary School, before Ma and Pa had decided it cost too much, there had been morning assemblies full of children's songs—"Under the Canopy," "What Can I Say," "Since I Was Born," "Joy Joy Joy," "Lift Him Up," "Everybody Blow Your Trumpet." Lowered knees and lowered heads everywhere, all the time, all eyes closed except for Ekene's. He studied the faces around him, so steadfast and serious, vibrating intensely, even the faces of students who stabbed juniors with sharpened pencils and stole cash from the purses of distracted teachers. What a person He had to be, to be sung to all the time, praised endlessly for merely existing, worshipped even on that scorching road—Abuloma with its endless hawkers and throbbing feet, its buckets of Gala meat balanced on tiny heads, its black-smoking cars, their radios blaring that He was the Most High, Ancient of Days, Unchangeable Changer, I Am That I Am, Alpha and Omega, the Beginning and the End, the Lily of the Valley. Ekene had never seen lilies in valleys, but he had seen both lilies and valleys separately, and he couldn't surmise how their combination amounted to infinite power. More perplexing now were those folks behind steering wheels who bobbed along to their radio tunes, white rosaries dangling in front of them, and how they turned their heads or wrinkled their noses or wound their windows up when Bonnyface's mother staggered toward them. How sometimes, before looking away, they turned a dial in their car and the song's volume increased, loud enough to make out the lyrics in crystal clarity: "*All His blessings, my parents cannot offer / All His blessings, my teachers cannot offer / All His blessings, even my president cannot offer.*"

And the Place Down Below for Those Without Song

First, though, Ma taught him about Up Above, where bliss was eternal and the springs ran with honey. In Up Above, every believer sang His praises day and night. When Ekene asked if that would not get boring, her eyes narrowed, and she told him that blasphemers belonged to the Down Below. Infinite as the ocean, flaming yellow, and filled with wailing bodies. She never described the smell, but Ekene imagined the frying fatty beef of Crunchies mixed with the fetid, unyielding stench of Pa. No sweat because each bead vaporized off the skin as quickly as it formed. Was there even skin in the great beyond? And what exactly determined who went where?

Surely, Up Above belonged to Ma, Musa (never mind that his bible was written in Arabic), Bonnyface, Kosisochukwu Ezilo. Every choir boy, every Christian Knowledge teacher, every pastor, even the stupid one he'd heard about on Ma's radio. He'd tasked his followers with burying him alive and digging him out three days later. Despite their discovery of his corpse, they'd rejoiced: "Our Lord has called Mbaka home early."

A trillion kilometres below: murderers, blasphemers, and boys his age who tricked girls into lifting their skirts. Bonnyface's father, whom Ekene pictured as a hunchbacked giant with completely black eyes and raised fists. But even for such a man, Ekene could not mathematically compute the balance of a cruel act, vicious as it was, against permanent burning. Forever and ever and ever. Once, while Ekene boiled water for Ma's Sunday morning tea, he jabbed his finger over the spout of the steaming kettle and just as quickly removed it. A fraction of hell, a fraction of a second, and its pain defied tolerance.

There had to be other places in the great beyond. If miserly Earth contained Port Harcourt and Abuja and Ghana and Europe and sawtoothed mountains and arid deserts, then surely His domain had a plethora of realms beyond Up Above and Down Below. A Purgatory for in-betweeners. A Resting Place where angels took off their wings and stretched their feet. A Garden of Youth where girls like Bonnyface could chase marigold butterflies for a thousand years and never tire, where her steps would not lag as they had started to recently, those heaving coughs crumpling her to the ground and sending her mother dashing frantically to her side. A Court of Souls where Eternity Lawyers argued before Him over who went where. Clearest in Ekene's mind was the Factory of Spirits in which He birthed all life. Mechanical and moon sized, its interconnected tubes, spinning gears, and perpendicularly oriented conveyor belts combined to churn out new spirits at a breathless pace. Some spirits became angels, others demons. Some spirits became Eternity Lawyers. Others fell from great heights into the bellies of pain-wracked women and produced within them tiny, toothless things.

Ekene knew all of this the same way one knows the sky's colour before a storm: it was a knowing baked into the pores of skin. Yet, no matter which new world he contemplated, week after week, month after month, his mind invariably returned to Down Below. To the unshakable thought that it was his ultimate destiny.

For the Thief Who Shimmered Beneath the Dogonyaro Tree

Burned a bright orange in the evening, almost angelic in appearance but for his guttural screaming. How his arms flailed. How strange to reconcile the charred, motionless husk afterward with any sort of former life. Before the shimmer, this husk had patrolled the city roads in a one-man protest, his bullhorn proclaiming Chief Ojukwu to be a wicked man, a glutton whose bribery-fuelled housing projects had rendered a dozen families homeless. The thief spoke of children who excavated flooded gutters in search of scraps, sucking banana remnants from discarded skins. The "thief"—even though it was never quite clear what he stole, only that his accuser drew the mob, poured the kerosene, and lit the match. The same accuser danced down Saint Mary's halls the following Sunday morning, just behind Chief Ojukwu. What lodged itself in Ekene's mind: Chief Ojukwu's teeth-flashing grin, his unburdened swagger. A man deemed fit for a lifetime of enjoyment.

For the Big Woman with Too Much Pomade

Who beckoned at Ekene and Musa with snapping fingers from behind the already shiny windscreen of her Mercedes-Benz. At first, they thought she was calling for the boy behind them selling satchels of chin chin. Most drivers turned away when he and Musa approached, after all; most drivers refused to offer a single kobo even after they were done. Not her, with the head full of pomade, the lips smacking on cherry gum, her "well done, unu, well done o" after they had soaped and rinsed the glass.

She dug in her purse for one, two, *three*, FOUR thousand naira. Ekene took it and stared at her, expecting her to snatch it back with laughter, but she said instead, "Buy something sweet, inugo." The words that left Ekene's lips surprised him. "Thank you, ma. God will bless you and your children and your children's children."

"Amen," she said, nodding. "Amen."

The lightness that bloomed in Ekene's chest brought to mind other days. Ma making her egusi soup with cubes of peppered goat. Musa jumping onto a passing truck's long bed and making away, undetected, with a six-pack of Malta Guinness. Oh, how they drank that night, bellies bulging, Ekene's joy untainted even by the earful Uncle Ikenna gave him for arriving late to Crunchies. There was also the week he'd gotten a 99 percent on a mathematics test. Ma had pressed all of him into her, humming a proud hum that seemed to emanate from deep within his own chest. Life gained a sheen in her grasp, seemed connected to something larger and kinder than itself. Until the following week, at least, when she and Pa sat him down and explained why he couldn't go back to Divine Love. Ekene learned what days were the rule and what days were the exception.

For the Factory of Spirits Above the Clouds, Which Changed Everything

Two Sundays before his sixteenth birthday, awash in the usual late-night musings that preceded sleep, Ekene lay in bed, turned toward his mother's shadow. He listened for the sound of her breathing. If her spit gurgled suddenly in her throat and robbed her of oxygen, if she thrashed and kicked and begged, He whom she constantly *ka anyi kene*'d would not lift a finger to clear her respiratory tract. Because that was His ... *nature*. Reverend Ejike had discussed this just hours earlier in sermon, explaining God's nature as a triplicate: Father, Son, Holy Spirit.

Recalling those words in the pensive dark, Ekene was struck by a question, which quickly morphed into undeniable fact: What if He had not created the Factory of Spirits? What if, instead, God the Spirit was *of* the Factory? Birthed by a natural universe, bound to its laws and limits.

Ekene sat up sweating, and Ma stirred. Had she awoken to see his half-bent shadow, had she put her hand over his heart and felt the pace of its beating, he could never have found the words to explain himself. How infinitely more breakable life seemed in the face of his new understanding. He thought of OG Bonnyface. Its roving black eyes in those moments before death, eyes that might have glimpsed Ekene's much larger stature against the fading sun's glint. Which might have triggered within Bonnyface a desperate unheard imploration—*save me*.

And he would have. He would have.

If only he'd known how.

For the Sequences of the Cosmos

Ekene's sixteenth birthday began, as usual, with a slice of Ma's chalky homemade cake. Her cooking far surpassed her baking, but Ekene had learned to swallow each bite without a wince. Life's routine offered little compromise, even on special days, which meant that an hour later, Ekene and Musa had already started to prowl Abuloma together. Accidents on the road had a regularity too, especially in the morning, when traffic was not quite gridlocked. The day's first: a Toyota on an adjacent lane striking an okada driver. There was an algorithmic inevitability to what followed. The Toyota's windscreen bloomed into a spiderweb of cracked glass. The okada driver flew backward in a pirouette Ekene wished he could permanently freeze, for the driver's sake. A man in the air in the shape of a spiral. Like something from a painting. Something beautiful.

There was no art in the cracked neck, in the pooling blood, in how quickly Abuloma resumed its operations after the body was peeled away. There were none of Ekene's usual questions either, which now seemed stunning in their childishness (Why had He not spawned a mattress beneath the flailing body? Or turned the ground to foam?). He was useless, perhaps by the Factory's design rather than by choice, but useless all the same, chained to the unflappable natural cycles one learned simply by observing.

Everything died.

Moonlight tugged the tides upward.

Roaches scattered beneath the glare of a swinging lantern.

Ma's late-night tongue found its way from the spoiled children of corrupt senators to the secondary school production where she had once played a famined kingdom's queen. Queen was sometimes huntress, huntress sometimes witch, but there always existed that play, and such applause afterward, and her subsequent knowing: "In another life, but for Pa, rest his soul, I could have been Patience Ozokwor."

Children in school uniforms briefly flanked Abuloma just as the sun was rising, many of whom would find their way to various universities, here or in oyibo land, many of whom would join Ekene on the road, perhaps with their own buckets and sponges, or with chin chin baskets, or with voices booming destinations from the roofs of danfo buses. All of it happening independently of their will.

If mere willing could alter the world's path, a grey rabbit would be napping restfully beneath a mahogany tree's shade. And one week after Ekene's sixteenth birthday, a nameless mother would not have shrieked his world asunder. Her scream briefly redirected every eye on Abuloma. She was crouched over Bonnyface, who was slumped by the roadside, unconscious. Ekene dropped his bucket and wiped his soap-wrinkled hands against his jeans. Musa thundered questions at his back, but Ekene kept moving until he was right beside Bonnyface. Her mother ran her hand against the unburned part of Bonnyface's neck, taking deep breaths in tandem with her movement, as if to suppress an outpouring of sobs. Bonnyface wore frayed white slippers, both of which had come undone. A pink floral sock—new from the looks of it—was peeling off the heel of one leg. Ekene snapped it back into place. Next, he placed each slipper back onto her feet.

"Madam, make I drive una to hospital?" asked a nearby okada driver, walking his motorbike slowly closer. Without a word to Ekene, the woman carried her daughter over and took to the back seat. The okada sped off at once, pushing farther and farther until it was no larger than a speck. Ekene remained rooted to the spot, unable to move even when Musa shook his shoulder.

In the days afterward, neither mother nor child returned to Abuloma. They lingered in Ekene's mind all the same, their background presence increasingly unbearable. On the sixth evening following their disappearance, Ekene broke his usual near-silence at Crunchies and asked if any of the older boys had seen or heard anything.

One of them, Tochukwu, had.

His family attended Yaba Ministries, a Pentecostal church twenty kilometres away. Hundreds gathered daily beneath its cavernous roof, drawn to pastors they said turned battle-crippled men into mountain climbers. According to Tochukwu, Bonnyface's mother had arrived there on the day of the incident with such frenzy. A physical altercation had almost broken out between her and one of the security guards, resulting in a ban. Undeterred, she returned often, day and night, her daughter curled motionless against her chest. She screamed at the incoming parishioners to intercede on her behalf, but whenever she drew too close to them, security intervened again.

"Why isn't she at a hospital?" Ekene asked limply, to which Tochukwu chuckled.

"You think say she get even a single naira? I swear I think say her baby don die o, cuz the body no dey move at all. Maybe na why momsy don craze finish."

Ekene stared at his hands, one holding a fish cleaver, the other curling and uncurling. In his mind's eye, the wails of Bonnyface's mother were wispy red jets rising past her throat and up toward the treetops, the starless clouds, velvet space.

Toward a Being up above powerless against the cosmos and its sequences.

For Needing Him, Despite Everything

To rise with morning light.

To slow the desiccation of his mother's aging skin.

To survive the roads where death hid in hungry wait.

And even now, to rid his legs of their godlike paralysis. Ekene needed Him to gather a defiant resolve and push past Uncle Ikenna, who was taking customer orders in the adjoining dining area. Uncle Ikenna asked why Ekene was leaving so soon and then, when Ekene continued wordlessly out the door, snarled that Ma would hear about his insolence.

Ekene moved with no destination in mind. He crossed embankments, drifted against highways. The sun was long gone, but these darkened roads were not desolate enough. There were women selling MTN recharge cards under yellow umbrellas. Bicycles racing bicycles. Boys and girls dancing in a yellowed soccer field to bassy highlife melodies.

When, finally, he found the street empty of souls but for a couple walking hand in hand, Ekene pulled the cleaver out of his backpack and pointed it shakily toward the man's chest. He didn't know he would be able to do it until he did, and even then, his body felt like another's, its motion puppeteered. He tried to fill his voice with all the gravity he could muster, but it squeaked as he spoke, diminishing his courage. The man might rush him if he felt brave. Despite the man's frightened face, he was bigger and taller, with triceps muscular enough to crush Ekene's rib cage with the right downward force, and if he charged, would Ekene strike? Would he plunge the blade of the cleaver into the man's body like it were fish skin?

In Ekene's head, two words looped: *Lord please, Lord please, Lord please.*

The man's legs trembled as he lowered his phone and wallet to the ground. His girlfriend's jaw clenched and hardened. She did not comply until Ekene pointed the cleaver at her too. Ekene transferred their possessions to his backpack. He backed away until they were out of sight, then broke into a run so fast that his breath turned ragged and fiery, his heart seemingly on the verge of failure. Unable to bring himself to turn around, he primed his ears for the sound of pursuit, for police sirens, for the end. When he was certain that he was alone, he collapsed in a heap near an expanse of waist-high brambles. Within the prickly shrubs, he tried to hold back what was coming, but his tears burst out with force, as though they had been building steadily inside him since his first gasp of air. The man's fearful, wide eyes surfaced in Ekene's mind. The man's prayers to the same God, too, which had been unspoken but sensed. Was it the case that a prayer could indeed be answered, but only at the expense of another's? Ekene did not know. All these questions, their weights coalescing, and not a single answer.

Ekene gathered himself when he saw flashlights fluttering in the distance from a side road ahead. As calmly as he could, he walked in the opposite direction for minutes, until he was standing outside a closed bank at the end of an unfamiliar street. He stank of sweat, and his legs shivered from exertion, but the night was only just starting. The phones he'd taken could be sold at GSM Village but likely for very little. No cash in the wallets either, although one had a debit card. He inserted the card into the ATM beside the bank's entrance. The machine's blue screen lit up with four tiny squares.

Ekene's still-racing mind unfurled from the present moment and sped ahead. He knew the general direction of Yaba Ministries, but he didn't want to take a bus or a taxi there. Especially if this worked and his backpack was filled to bulging. Especially if his arrival there had to depend on the will of another. At this point, surely, Uncle Ikenna had contacted Ma. She was likely pacing the room, thin lipped with anger, which would morph into unbearable anxiety in the hours it would take Ekene to walk twenty kilometres and back. There was also the chill to worry about, a damp in the night air that promised to give way to skin-soaking rain. Perhaps if he ran, he could minimize exposure. Yet, none of these concerns would matter if this part didn't work.

For Bonnyface, it had to.

Ekene pressed the ATM's keypad.

1111 failed, the screen flaring maroon.

So did 9999.

Ekene swallowed and wiped at his runny nose. He rummaged through the wallet a second time and fished out a driver's licence. The man's birthday: December 10. He folded the licence in his palm and closed his eyes. He felt exposed, so utterly naked. Despite his shivering, the words were steady on his lips, a singular communion from Ekene to Him:

"Help me. Please."

Ekene typed 1210. For a few seconds, his finger hovered above the Enter key. Then he pushed. His clattering heart slowed. Paused. The ATM screen beeped and flared a vivid green.

MAMA'S LULLABIES

Autumn had just begun when Onyedikachi kicked her fiancé, Maduka, out of their jointly owned condo. For hours afterward, she curled beside a window, a mug of unsipped black tea cooling on her lap. It seemed grievously disrespectful—this idyllic day, Toronto's treetops and gentle waters coated in gold sun. Her phone buzzed sporadically: TELUS receipt, bridesmaids' group chatter on WhatsApp, yoga class reminder. It was the text from Maduka ("I'm sorry, please let us talk") that undid her, sagged her stoic shoulders, contorted her face. The sky turned foggy.

✦

For two weeks, Onyedikachi ignored Maduka's daily pleas to talk. She deflected questions from loved ones about their postponed wedding. The hardest of these conversations was with Mama, Maduka's loving mother. Onyedikachi worked overtime at her software engineering start-up and drifted to sleep on glasses of Merlot. One evening, a panic attack spiked her chest with needles, lasting until dawn.

So she agreed. She and Maduka would meet on Friday night for exactly one hour at Fufu House, the Nigerian restaurant in Lawrence Heights where they'd indulged on special occasions.

"This is not an attempt at reconciliation," she warned him over the phone. "I just want closure." The lie tasted sour on her tongue. Her only craving was for the blissful ignorance of their former lives, her body warming his backside.

For the Fufu House meeting, she arrived ten minutes early. The restaurant smelled like overcooked suya. Old Pete Edochie movies played on the blurry wall-mounted television. Physically, nothing had changed. But there was no flicker of warm nostalgia anymore, only the chill of upturned memories.

✦

In the haze of those memories, one recurred: JSS1, some two decades ago, the first time she had ever experienced betrayal. A janitor had caught prepubescent Onyedikachi in the stall of a non-operational school bathroom, reaching into a boy's underwear. She struggled to explain that she was merely curious about their differing body parts, not that any set of words would have stopped the janitor from reporting them to the principal, nor the principal from contacting Mother. When she arrived, Mother drew a fist and struck Onyedikachi's left eye in front of watchful classmates.

"Next time, ashawo," said Mother, "you will know where your hands belong."

Years later, with hardly a goodbye, Onyedikachi chased a scholarship out of Nigeria to the University of Toronto. Still, Mother's shadow cast itself on Onyedikachi's solitary nights with beautiful men. Come sunrise, those men disappeared. Except for Maduka. They met while taking the same third-year elective, Modern Bioethics. Joint study sessions became midnight walks near Trinity Bellwoods Park, his fingers gently pinching her palm's flesh beneath snow-frosted gloves. During their first few months of dating, Maduka obliged her desire for limited sexual activity. But scared that his patience would vanish, Onyedikachi finally pushed them toward trying. They went slow. The union of skin on skin was a new language, an awkward dance, a thing rendered familiar by patience and practice. In the afterglow of their post-sex cuddles, she often listened to him snoring on her chest. Often thought the same wild thought: *You are mine, forever.*

✦

At Fufu House, Onyedikachi first asked Maduka about Kennedy, the man who'd somehow found her number and sent her an essay's worth of messages with phrases like *never knew* and *burdened conscience.* Kennedy had followed it up with a photo of Maduka asleep on his white, sunburned chest, Maduka's spit-specked mouth open. She must have stared at that photo for hours. Had she been at work then? Or had Kennedy taken it on one of those early weekend mornings when Maduka had supposedly stepped out for a run?

"I met him in January," said Maduka, all low register and downcast eyes. "There's been no one else except him. I swear, on Mama's head."

Onyedikachi stabbed a piece of plantain. She dropped her fork. "Where did you two meet?"

At GoodLife, evidently. Small talk between barbell sets morphed into coffee chats at a nearby Starbucks, which morphed into cocktails at Kennedy's place in Etobicoke. Maduka said same-sex attraction had plagued him since he was a boy; he'd been too ashamed to tell anyone but God.

"Remember in February, when I started going to church again? Even during the weekdays. I don't know what it was about Kennedy, but I could feel my impure thoughts moving closer to action. I begged God for control. And I still fucked up. Nwunye mu, I'm so sorry."

Fucked up, as if the act had lasted minutes instead of months.

Onyedikachi shook her head. "How could I have been so blind?"

"You never suspected because it is not who I am. Not with you."

For so long, Onyedikachi had drawn a powerful comfort from her knowledge of Maduka's layers. The days his fluorescent smile belied a sadness on the verge of revelation. Lingering scars across his toes from a boiling kettle dropped in childhood. His ever-listening ears, whether she was rambling about toxic work managers or the funny weirdness of belly buttons. Even the depths of his rage when a drunk fool squeezed her ass in a sweaty club near Keating Channel. Now, all she saw across the table was an anxious little child. The barbed edges of unkind words gathered near her tongue. She raised her fork instead and swallowed the plantain whole.

✦

They met again the following Friday night.

Onyedikachi asked Maduka when he'd last seen Kennedy.

"The month before I proposed," Maduka replied, picking at a napkin. "I couldn't ask you to marry me until he was out of the picture.

Breaking it off hurt him. He reached out to you so that he could hurt me too. He's a petty man."

Onyedikachi thought of the photo, how comfortably Maduka had clung to a petty man's chest. She asked him what he liked most about Kennedy. Beneath the table, she scratched at her palm with nail-chewed fingers, preparing to hear about the depths within Maduka that Kennedy had excavated, depths forever unknowable to her.

Maduka floundered and stuttered. After some prodding, however, he shyly admitted to Kennedy's love of '80s R & B, how they'd eyes-closed-danced to Luther Vandross in the bedroom. Onyedikachi stopped scratching. Maduka's swaying hips were not some foreign domain. She and he had swirled together many times beneath grey thunderstorms and on the white sands of Caribbean resorts. The week an infection had shackled Onyedikachi to a hospital bed, Maduka called in sick to work and refused to go home, instead sleeping on a chair next to her. To cheer her up that miserable first night, he'd hooked his thumb with hers, sung a Latin tune, and pantomimed a salsa show on the pillow, using their fingers as the dancers' legs. Onyedikachi had laughed so hard, grateful for the gift of him.

✦

The following week, more questions. Had he ever experimented in Nigeria, perhaps at his all-boys secondary boarding school? Would he ever see a therapist? Had Kennedy ever come over on the weekends when she was travelling for work?

Some questions, though, she could not voice except to herself in the sleepless loops of dusk. Who had fucked whom? Had it hurt, or had Maduka discovered an indescribable pleasure, the kind her body could never offer? Had they used a condom? Had he thought of her at all?

One morning, Onyedikachi picked up the phone to call their family doctor and arrange STI testing. But Dr. Chidolue would likely ask too many questions, and even if he didn't, the results might provide the sort of weighty answers she wasn't ready for. What was it, this idiotic bit of hope that they could somehow survive Kennedy's existence? She put down the phone. Heard Mother's cruel voice in the silence: *Next time, ashawo, you will know where your hands belong.*

✦

At the fourth meeting, Onyedikachi brought up Mama.

"She's been calling non-stop, asking if all is well. Maybe we should talk to her."

Maduka jerked against his chair as if doused in cold water.

"No."

His sudden panic was incongruent with Onyedikachi's knowledge of Mama, a woman who had sold her ancestral home and moved into a flat to ensure Maduka could chase his dreams abroad. Who, on meeting Onyedikachi for the first time in Lagos, had kissed her forehead and soaped her feet in a warm calabash, crooning, "My daughter, you are home—nno."

"Why not?" asked Onyedikachi.

Maduka collected himself in a series of long exhales. Picking at his napkin more urgently, he spoke of days Onyedikachi had never known about. How his six-year-old self had sometimes awoken in the dark to Mama rubbing olive oil on his forehead and singing Igbo gospel lullabies. "Nothing else in this life matters," Mama often said. "Heaven is the goal."

When the browser history on her laptop exposed a dropdown of gay porn sites, she'd confronted twelve-year-old Maduka. At first, he blamed it on a computer virus ("My friend's desktop had the same problem!"), but Mama's death glare quickly compelled him to confess. She sank to the floor. "Sodom and Gomorrah have claimed my son," she wept.

Mama sent Maduka to live and serve as an altar boy at a local parish for twelve weeks. Minister Gordon taught him to fear hell, not as an abstract biblical fable but as a visceral reality. Gordon often soaked the tips of Maduka's toes in boiling water and asked him to imagine that flesh-peeling heat all over his body.

"Are your perverse fantasies worth God's eternal rage?" Gordon asked, his voice always soft, always kind.

When Maduka returned from the parish, Mama hugged him tight enough to crack his spine. "This satanic phase is over now," she said. Maduka vowed then to prove her right.

"You are not the only one I've failed," he told Onyedikachi. "If Mama finds out now, after everything she's sacrificed for me, it will destroy her. Nwunye mu, please."

Onyedikachi's throat held a blob of spit, but she could not swallow. She reached for Maduka's hand.

✦

Outside Fufu House, Onyedikachi tried to carry on with life as usual, but the usual was inseparable from Maduka. Most of his things were still at their condo. On aimless drives around the city, she heard his disembodied voice in the passenger seat wisecracking about careless pedestrians. She still bought his favourite orange juice and saltine crackers at Sobeys, lined them in rows in the pantry.

Heavy snowfall carpeted the soccer field next to their condo on a Thursday morning. Onyedikachi grabbed Maduka's old jacket, ripped at the armpits and spilling down, and walked to the field. She pressed her back into the snow, flapped her arms like wings, traced horns atop the head imprinted in the ground. A perfect snow devil, just like Maduka had shown her. Staring at it, she understood that she would never again brave dating apps and liquored breath in downtown bars. She could not memorize the shapes of new bodies.

She called Maduka. He answered on the first ring.

"Tomorrow," she said, "let's meet at our home instead." She paused. "You could even spend the night."

✦

That Friday evening started out like all their old ones. They cooked jollof rice together, Onyedikachi incrementally dosing the pot with cayenne pepper while Maduka taste-tested. They polished off the bottle of Taittinger champagne he'd brought over. Their IKEA sectional, assembled three Christmases ago, still snugly held their weight, his back to her chest. There was need in how she held him, need in how he pushed his spine so that it compressed her sternum.

"You're bisexual," she said. As if it were not a question, not a final prayer. "I think what you felt for Kennedy is real. But so are we. Our years together didn't come from nothing."

"Bisexual," Maduka said slowly, tasting the word.

"Yes. You've always been there for me. Always. And sex with us was good, right? Did ... did you think of men when we made love?"

Maduka sat up. He sighed. "When we started dating, I worried all the time that my affliction would get in the way of my sexual obligations to you. So I got a prescription for Viagra. It helped me get out of my head. Allowed me to focus on giving your body the attention it deserved."

Maduka went on about how he'd popped the pill even on the days without action, just in case, how nothing else had mattered beyond her pleasure. Whatever he said next, Onyedikachi did not hear. She pictured him locked in their bathroom. The shower running cold. Her, eagerly tossing in bed, in silk lingerie, sea green. She pictured her hunger for him matched by the secret workings of tiny blue capsules. Every single time? He was committed, truly. Not to her, but to something grander. A God-ordained vow made long ago and an intention to follow through, no matter the cost or missteps.

The coloured threads of their living room rug swam into numbed focus. A rug patterned with masquerade faces. A rug purchased in Abuja to adorn their newly bought condo, which had followed their graduations and their acquisition of dream jobs and should have been followed by marriage and children, the first boy to be named Emeka, after Maduka's deceased father. The past and the future crashed upon her at once, and Onyedikachi felt as though she were finally waking from a long, fuzzy dream.

"I think you need to go back to your hotel."

"Nwunye mu." Maduka reached for her shoulder. "I didn't want to upset you. I only meant to be honest. To hide nothing else."

"Please, Maduka."

Just before she closed the door on him, he clasped his hands, prayerlike. "You cannot tell Mama. I beg you."

The calm with which Onyedikachi moved afterward seemed fragile, as if the lightest breeze could fling it aside, revealing something ugly and unknowable, something she could not survive. Slowly, she took photographs off walls, snapshots of lies captured atop Montreal summits and forest-flanked zip lines. She pulled cologne-scented sheets off their mattress, emptied closets into suitcases. She tore from their frames matching paintings of snowmen crafted in hot-cocoa winter classes. Throughout the night, she whittled down the evidence of their shared existence. Phone calls followed in the morning, starting with Dr. Chidolue and ending with Mama.

"My sweet daughter," Mama crooned. "Is all well?"

Onyedikachi regarded the condo's graveyard: crumpled birthday cards, empty juice bottles, heaped shirts, a single jewelled ring, things that had once held a quiet comfort. She saw the futility of her efforts too—her skin could not be ripped from its bones. Wearing her most regretful voice, she told Mama that she and Maduka had decided to part ways. The wedding was cancelled. Mama gasped and started to cry and spluttered, "Why, my daughter, why?"

Your son is a homosexual, Onyedikachi almost said. *And you are a horrible mother*. But her lips possessed their own volition and would not form the words. So she stood silent instead, in this room she no longer recognized, listening to Mama's sobs.

THE ALCHEMY OF HIS MIRROR

It took our second encounter for me to guess and the third to be sure, but his hair was alive. It breathed its own breath, as sentient beings do, and revealed its fearlessness in the wild swings it took, the delicately combed dreadlocks, the oily Afro, the knotted braids that cascaded past his neck like a waterfall, stopping just short of the tip of his spine, from which wings would sprout if man could fly.

He never brought it up. I didn't either. I suppose it became one of those axioms that settles into the background, even as it continuously shifts, like the clothes we wear or the meals we eat. No, when we communed about hair, it was always about mine. How did I want it today? Number 1 or Number 2? Skin faded or slightly taller? And for the beard, he could leave it dark and full but sculpted, or remove it entirely, or settle somewhere in the middle with a stubble. I always got the same thing, but he always asked, and I liked that he always asked.

The scissors snipped. The clipper whistled in a low drone. Hair fell like cashews shaken from a tree: bunches of it at first, pieces big enough to fill your fist, then smaller bits, soft stone-sized clumps landing on my cloth-covered lap, on the floor of his living room, the quartered-off section of it near the front door, where he set up the pillow-topped chair and the slanted body-length mirror and wrapped the black fabric around my neck, never too tight.

He asked how Calculus 101 was going, and I said I wasn't sure. It wasn't too hard yet. At seven weeks in, it wasn't supposed to be, but I could tell I would struggle when integrals and derivative equations popped up. I had them highlighted in green marker on sheaves of paper Professor Markham had handed out on the first day of class. A thick filled-in line over the narrow typeface of "Week 11" and "Week 12," when they would jump from the confines of the page to populate my nightmares.

"Or maybe a good dream," he said, blowing on bee-buzzing blades. Particles of hair and dust fell to the ground. In the glow of the tall lamp beside me, they looked like snow. "You haven't failed yet. You probably won't. Be confident."

I could not respond because the clipper was moving around my moustache now, dancing along the terrain of my upper lip. At his direction, I turned my lips inward, helping him to expose and excavate any stray follicles in hiding.

"How's your girlfriend doing?" I asked, when his focus shifted to under my neck, where the shrubbery knotted like interlocked fingers. He raked through the bow-tie tufts with a metal comb, and I felt them resist at first, reluctant and slightly ashamed, and then part. The initial wave of… not pain exactly simmered into an almost-ticklish comfort.

"She's good, good," he said. "I finally met her parents at their brownstone cottage near Woodson Lake. You know where that is, right?"

I shook my head, at least as much as I could with his fingers fanned over the top of my scalp, holding it in place to unleash a second wave on my thinning sideburns.

"It's not far from here—a ninety-minute drive, maybe two hours with traffic on the 401. Well, I don't want to say they're racist, but I don't think they like me. She made them sound like golden retrievers, all sunny and energetic, but they were cold."

"Frosty the Snowmen."

He chuckled. "Exactly. I hope it's something else. Maybe they were tired that day, cuz it was pretty late. I don't know."

I thought he did. In these lands, where snowfall was not just fiction plumbed from the movies, a young truth was taking shape, gleaned from thinly pressed smiles and hastened footsteps, from the evanescent glances of passersby on winter streets. It wasn't malice, not particularly, but it wasn't home either, where a stranger's approach bore no weight. There was an ever-present guardedness, taut in the air like an unspoken rule. In its recognition, I curled beside dew-tainted windows on twilit mornings. I watched droplets form on glass panes, tiny, contorted mirrors. Tears traced snake paths on my face until my eyes reddened and the hiccups started. I'd travelled a thousand miles to seek the future; instead, I'd found faces that turned away in proximity to mine. I found all the ways my tongue buried words in a silent graveyard.

The first time we met, I found necromancy.

Back then, he still worked at the student centre barbershop, which was tragically named Stylez for All. Four different chairs were available, but I took his without hesitation. His fingers probed my skin. His questions probed my mind. I wondered about his alien energy, vivid, curious, slightly unnerving. Even back home, I often lingered in the shadows, the back corners of large crowds, the places where the sun couldn't reach. In the sight of too many eyes, my voice had a way of crumbling, like beach sand tugged by waves. It crumbled even faster in this world, where on my first day, I learned from a garrulous taxi driver that I had an accent.

So my responses emerged slowly. They arrived in bursts of one or two words at a time, the air of a customer intent on keeping a transaction a transaction. But he laughed easily, and his questions never ceased. That day, a snapping turtle let loose its shell, released it to the faltering sand dunes, the crashing waters, and stepped into the light, slowly but moving ever onward.

He left Stylez shortly after. When I asked why, he simply shrugged. Later, he said he wanted to run his own salon. Another day, he said he would determine and then return to his ancestral roots; he would live on the warm shores of Cameroon or Ivory Coast. Then he talked about managing a designer clothing store in the Caribbean. In any case, this city, which had thus far circumscribed the entirety of his life and his parents' lives, would not be where his story ended. He said the world was too small for that.

He promised not to surrender my fate to the three remaining "incompetents" of Stylez. Only if I were willing. It was strange at first, watching my hair collect on his carpeted floor, while muffled conversation and a whiff of stew wafted from the apartment next door. But strange had a way of dissipating when a thing became two and then more.

Stranger yet was hearing my voice say, unwavering, "If Mr. and Mrs. Frosty don't fuck with you, that's their loss. Hers too."

"Amen. So tell me, who has your heart these days?"

"Nobody. I'm going to be a monk for the next six months."

"Right." He scrubbed the back of my head with a wood-backed brush. "That's what all the players say."

Words didn't always fill the din. Sometimes, there was silence, the kind that shapes itself like a high-backed chair, one you can sink into and close your eyes and feel the breeze of an overhead fan on your scalp.

In the last month of my past life, my ex-girlfriend and I had discovered that *forever and always* had an expiry date, that the flames of twinned hearts couldn't burn across vast blue oceans. She cried on my shoulder, and I held her tightly, wishing I could summon words from the stew of them frothing in my mind, wishing I could twist and turn them into a small gift, offered to her.

Here. This takes the pain away.

But I was no alchemist.

All she and I had left was the silence of that lingering moment, and I realized, when I stopped fighting so much, that it wasn't so bad. Soft voices whispered beneath her tears, light on my cheek; they murmured in the grazing brush of her perfumed hair.

There was nothing so grand now, not with him, or perhaps it was grander; perhaps the tranquility was communion, the kind of covenant that allowed one to grant his bare throat to the bladed hand of another.

"Get ready," he said, turning a bottle of liquor-scented aftershave onto several cotton balls. I used to be a churchgoer. Liberated from the watchful eyes of devout parents, I hadn't gone in weeks, but I recalled how, at the end of Mass, the priest would dip his gold-tinted aspergillum in a goblet of holy water and sprinkle sanctified droplets on the faithful, purging us of our sins. Mother and Father closed their eyes so tight when the mist descended on their faces, their supplicating hands raised to the arched ceiling. On my skin, the drizzle felt like the javelin pricks of an unwanted sneeze.

I found true penance in these damp cotton balls, as he massaged them into the pores of my neck and scalp, stinging fire trailing his motion. I closed my eyes and released a low stream of air through gritted teeth.

"So dramatic," he said, unhooking the barber cloth from my neck and shaking it with a magician's flourish. "You're all set, boss."

This was the covenant's conclusion, the promise fulfilled. In front of his mirror, my head turned left and right, this time at my behest. It lifted in the direction of his tiled ceiling, where speckled stains browned the plaster, so that the otherwise hidden parts of my jaw glistened in the reflection.

Last night, I had surveilled myself similarly, running two fingers through the untidy forage that framed my face. I had pinched my cheeks, twisting them in the nip between my thumbs and index fingers, wondering if it was the jowls, or the melanin, or the tricks of a paranoid mind that robbed me so profoundly of solidity.

"Hello," I said then, dragging out each syllable, listening to the way the words bent and twisted as they left my throat, my ears seeking the accent, what they called it when you sounded like an other.

The alchemy of his mirror was in seeing how my newly cut hair sat on my skin. How it breathed its own life, birthing a smile I could not hide even if I tried. To communicate the extent of it all was hard, and possibly strange, and would take forever anyway, so I simply said, "Thank you. It looks really good."

I counted three neat tens from my wallet. He bunched them inside a fist and slid them into his pocket. "You look ready to roam the streets. Right now, mothers are hiding their daughters."

I chuckled. "Nah. I'm probably going straight to bed."

As I worked my feet into my shoes, a small puddle forming from the thaw of their snow-covered soles, he picked up a broom and swept all the liberated hair into a dustpan.

He said, "I'm a night owl, so I'll probably be up watching TV. I don't like horror movies because I believe in all of it, the ghosts, the demons, the trapped souls, but I rented this one online."

I grabbed my jacket from the cherrywood shoe bench by the front door. The bench was filled with his many pairs of red sneakers and flanked by two potted plants, their brownish-green fronds bending. "What's it about?"

"A serial killer hunting two mute buddies at their cottage. My friend already told me they win at the end, so I think I'll be okay to watch it."

Clad in my jacket, I was ready to leave, to step out into the world again, with its solemn rules and steady march of new deadlines. Except I wasn't.

"Hey," I said. Drums banged to life in my chest. "I don't have anything planned for the rest of the night. Do you mind if I watch it with you?"

He went still for a moment, long enough for me to ponder how well received it might be if the ground parted beneath my feet and a void swallowed me whole. Then he beamed, that wide smile of his that revealed shiny teeth.

"Sure, bro, come on. Get your ass on the couch. I'll grab us drinks from the fridge." I reversed the last thirty seconds, shaking off my jacket and then my right shoe and then my left shoe. I walked past the little corner of the living room that had always defined the extent of my reach here, the entryway portion of it with the indented chair and the swept-up hair and the slanted mirror. I moved on to new territory, where his mahogany-brown couch, aged by grey lines and bits of leaking foam, faced the television. Beside it, a coffee table sparkled with half-full bottles of bourbon and dog-eared books about Commonwealth nations. A mini-fridge sat in the corner, and he squatted before it, rummaging within.

I sank onto the couch and accepted a bottle from him. It was an unfamiliar double IPA, its green surface polka-dotted with flaming skulls. The tang was bitter in my throat.

"That's strong," I said.

He plopped beside me, taking several steady chugs from his own bottle. "That's nothing."

I scoffed. "Let's see how tough you are when the killer shows up waving a giant machete." I hadn't eaten much today, and already I could feel a heady buzz, liberating my anchored thoughts so that they floated like clouds. He chuckled and raised his arm. Our bottles clinked. The sound was a single dulcet note, stolen from an orchestra's symphony, lingering overhead.

On the screen, over brooding synths, a masked man approached a cottage in the middle of the woods.

PERFECT LITTLE ANGELS

Wednesday, June 30

We meet for the first time in the realm of 1s and 0s.

A warm Lagos rain pelts the bedroom windows and leaks through the ceiling into a bucket near my brother Ndubisi's bed. The sound keeps him turning until he settles into an open-mouthed snore. I pull out my phone, its brightness at the lowest setting, and log in to the app disguised as a calculator.

The square grid has a few dozen picturesque profile photos—mountaintops, Black movie stars, sunbathed fields of wheat. Your exposed chest stands out as unfamiliar. At first, I suspect treachery, that your image is pulled from the web like all the others ... like mine, the grinning Cheshire cat. But it bears no glamour or fantasy. Stretch marks spread like fingers across your sternum. Your neck, where the photo begins, is dotted with acne.

I glance at Ndubisi's bed and think of my cardinal rule: *only look, never engage*. The words ring hollow from repetition.

My thumb taps on your chest.

I type.

"Hi."

A second passes.

Another.

You reply.

"Hey."

We talk about the rain. I hate the way it muddies the streets, turns potholes on the path to work into sand-coloured pools. You like how crickets chirp against its patter in a sort of orchestra. We talk about the upcoming election (neither of us plans to vote), the newest Nollywood movie, which you saw alone at Genesis Cinema two weeks ago. Surprisingly decent, you say.

We do not talk about family. How many brothers, how many sisters. Whether our fathers are around or distant, dead or alive. We skirt any mention of where we live. We especially do not talk about why men like us are on an app like this in the middle of the night. But for hours, we do talk. When morning light starts to break the sky, the horse hoofs of rain dulling to tiptoes, I am taken by surprise at time's passing.

Your next message makes me slowly sit up: "Is it possible for you and me to meet?"

For the first time on this app, a *you and me*.

Shivers graze my neck. I stare at the ceiling, thinking of the two men caught in a hotel room last year. They were marched out onto the streets, beaten with tree branches, pelted with stones. Ndubisi and I had sat in our sweltering living room, watching the droop of their faces on the television as police officers carted them into a van. Ndubisi cleared his throat and spat on a wall.

"Abomination," he said, not referring to the mob still trying to reach into the police van with their fists and twigs. Nor to the thick films of red covering the men's eyes, the dripping welts tattooing their bare stomachs.

I am thinking of the two men, and all the other men before them, flashes of faces in newspapers or obituaries or nowhere at all, when you send a second message: "Still there?"

You follow it with a picture of your face: one eye winking, tongue sticking out, dazzling smile.

I do not send one back.

My fingers seem to move of their own accord: "On Friday evenings, Salamander Hill is desolate."

Friday, July 2

When the half sun sinks, I shutter my tailor shop and walk seven streets over to the library-in-progress. It is mostly a hole in the ground flanked by fences, yellow tape, and bulldozers. Despite the day's waning light, all motion seems magnified. A blue-feathered swallow surveys the street from atop a broken light. Teenagers on the edge of the construction ground lean against cranes, passing cigarettes around. You, broader and taller than I expected, stand at the intersection and watch me approach.

Against every instinct, I do not turn around and flee. I nod slightly and walk past you, watching in my periphery as you follow. We cut through the market and past the backyard of a small church concluding evening Mass. Passersby dwindle as we approach a gravelly dirt road; it stretches for a kilometre into Salamander Hill. Then it is just us. Our dulled footsteps.

You and me.

The hill's humid base is surrounded by a circle of dense detritus: muddied sneakers, wilted nylon bags, crumpled soda cans, discarded fruit rinds. A home for all that our town rejects. You stand next to me. I don't look at your face, but I know your body is tensing up at the stench. I fold the cuffs of my trousers. You mirror me. We wade through the slime.

The hill slopes gently upward. At the top, we fill our lungs with a sticky wind. Beneath us is the duplex-studded sprawl of our town. The treetops burn orange. Trawlers bob atop the grey surface of Aye River. On our left, bumper-to-bumper cars honk on portside roads. But for the black smoke oozing out of their exhaust pipes, they'd almost look playful. Like children's toys.

I want to tell you about all the Friday nights I've spent up here alone. How I inhaled. Took in the week's stress, the tailor shop's monotony, Ndubisi's beer-scented rants, the dwindling customers, my flashes of fury, until they sat in my lungs like stone. How I exhaled them onto the breeze shifting across town.

Instead, I turn toward the ring of summit boulders that shields us from the world below. We sit in its centre and wipe the muck off our ankles. Our legs almost touch.

I look up at your face, but you stare straight ahead. Your beard is ruffled, untamed. Your jeans are covered in dust. Your lips are dark stained. If I leaned in close enough, pressed mine to yours, would I taste cigarettes? Red wine?

I comb through our long chat, seeking something to jump-start a conversation. Your favourite novel is none because you hate reading. You were obsessed with a local artist called Princess Ife in your secondary school days. And you don't feel like a real Nigerian because you can't handle alligator pepper. These tidbits of trivia find their way to my tongue only to disappear.

You're a beautiful man. And I am not. My stomach is skeletal. Pimples line my cheeks. Perhaps that's all our silence is—your disappointment in my form, and my recognition of that.

Suddenly, you turn toward the sky, where many stars bloom.

"This is nice," you say.

I am surprised by your voice, its softness.

"It is," I reply.

So we stare at the clouds. We watch them cradle the moon.

Friday, July 9

You've been offline since our first meeting.

Every second since has been as stretched and taut as rubber. I make my way to the construction zone, wondering if my hope is illogical. I recall the months when Ndubisi bought nearly a hundred lottery tickets. He spent nights by the television squeezing an empty bottle, the seventh or eighth of the hour, as winning numbers were rattled out, none ever his.

The hole in the ground is wider now. There are no twilit birds or teens. But at the intersection, there you are in a tank top and shorts, not fidgeting, looking my way. You don't grimace at the stench of Salamander Hill as we make our way to the top.

I start for the ring of boulders, but you grab my shoulder and point toward the town. Strobe lights from an ambulance dance on a bridge. The hoods of two cars are tangled in a metal kiss.

"There's been an accident," you say, and already, it is more than you have ever uttered to me.

"I see that. There's ten a day now, it feels like."

"Do you do this often?" you ask. "Bring men up here."

"No. You're the first I've met from ... the app. First I've brought up here."

You chuckle without smiling.

"It's *true*," I say. A swish of anger flares in the word.

"Why me, then?" You sound almost accusing. "Why now?"

"I don't know."

"Ever fucked a man?"

"No. Never done anything with anyone. Well, a girl kissed me once back in secondary school. And I've watched porn ... that kind ... a few times."

"And you're really twenty-two."

"Yes. Are you really twenty-three?"

Your lips curl in amusement. "Haven't been twenty-three for three years now. But I'm told I look it. How did you find this place?"

"Oh, my older brother did. Ndubisi. Long ago. Ma and Pa moved us here from Apapa and started a sewing business. Our superstitious neighbour got this idea in Ndubisi's head that having a small reptile in our home would mean good luck for their work."

Your smile reaches your eyes. "So your brother came here to find one?"

"For many nights, yeah. Dragged me with him too. It was before all the trash, so there were usually others around. We found rodents and centipedes and one time a dead hawk. But no reptiles. Not until after months of searching."

Something in my voice makes you shift closer. "Are you okay?"

I want to tell you that there is a ghost in my memory, mostly conquered but for the occasional haunt: a small and beardless Ndubisi dashing across Salamander Hill, easy to laughter from his own stupid jokes, even on the days we returned home empty-handed. I laughed too because I liked the sound of it and how his happiness promised mine. I lead you a quarter of the way down the hill. Here, I say, is where we found a slumbering leaf-toed gecko.

"It was the most excited I ever saw Ndubisi. He danced all the way home. Ma was less pleased though. She asked him to get rid of it, but Ndubisi swore God had sent us Meso."

"He named it Meso?"

"Short for Nmesomachi, yeah. He almost got in trouble at school because he kept picking insects out of the Primary Six garden to feed his little pet. Sang to it every night, told it all kinds of stories about his day, massaged its little neck with his thumb."

You chuckle. "Meso lived like a king."

"Sure did. After Ndubisi found Meso, he didn't really have a reason to come back to Salamander Hill. I didn't either, until the last couple of years, when it turned into a dump. I realized I could shake off a rough day here by myself."

"Well, you and the shit and the flies."

"There's none of that *up here.* Just a good view and some quiet. I know we can hear the cars and the danfos, but they're down there. It's like there's thick glass between us."

You don't reply. It's as if you're listening for it the way I do, beyond the whoop of distant sirens, beyond the sound of breath leaving our nostrils.

"How about you?" I ask.

You frown. "How about me what?"

"You been with any guys?"

"Yeah. Plenty. I've fucked guys. Guys have fucked me."

"Oh."

"Most of it was back in Abia. Before that, though, I had a girlfriend. Loved her. We were together for six years. Had plans to get married someday."

"Why didn't you?"

The question causes your eyes to lose focus. You stare at me without seeing me. After a moment, you head up the hill toward the ring of boulders. I join you there, sitting far enough away this time that our legs can't touch. My stomach is strange, turning, twisting.

"Do your parents know?" you ask. "Your brother?"

"My parents died eight years ago. Not long after we found Meso, funny enough. Lorry driver fell asleep one night and cleared their car off the road. And no, Ndubisi does not know."

"I'm sorry," you say.

"It's fine. Happened a long time ago."

"Doesn't matter. That must have been hard."

I shrug. "Sure, but not because of grief. Ma and Pa were hustlers, the never-home type. Ndubisi looked after me far more than they ever did. Everything he cooked tasted like charcoal, but he always made sure I ate and got enough sun and did my assignments. After they died, he changed. I had to grow up fast. Dropped out of secondary school to take over their business. Been looking after us ever since."

"Jesus." An overdramatic sadness contorts your face. "All by yourself?"

"Who else would do it?"

"Right. Well, my parents are around, thankfully. And I've got a younger sister. Esther. None of them know. They never will. But something possessed me to tell Vanessa. I'd have died for that woman, probably still would today, but it didn't make me right for her, not in the way she deserved. I knew from the start too—that's the fucked up part. There's a whole silent conversation that goes on the first time you kiss someone, you know?"

I want to tell you that I don't know; you know I don't. But you're sliding over slowly, leaning forward to close the oblong patch of pebbled dirt between us. I want to stop you. I want to tell you that my heart is beating so fast I'm certain I will die, that my stomach still feels all kinds of twisted. I want to tell you that being this afraid tastes like metal, that we should go our separate ways and never speak again, that I will delete the app tonight and return to real life. But your cold hands cup my face, and your tongue parts my lips. The taste of you is cracked and salty and laced with cashews, and I chart the skin of your mouth, and your hand presses against my back, and your eyes are closed, so I close mine too, and in the darkness, a thousand stars explode.

Friday, July 16

This time, when your tongue moves lower than my neck, I don't push your head away. You unbuckle my belt, and I learn how another's touch can cause my back to fold in shivers. Afterward, you direct me downward, and I focus only on the dark and how it is all skin, nothing but skin, I focus on your words—*go deeper, not so much teeth, breathe, faster, slower, yes, yes, just like that*—until your words aren't words at all, but moans blending into a single sound.

Until you're shivering too.

Friday, July 23

We sit on the edge of Salamander Hill. The night is a black paper-thin wall slashed beneath shadowy buildings and an uneven sea of lights. Orange spots cluster near a large petrol station and a quietly thumping club. On either side of this dense shimmer, red vehicle lights cut through pockets of darkness. Your focus is on the centre of our view, where green sodium arcs from a park bazaar reflect on the water. The neighbourhood of your previous life was all brown plains and wiry trees. Now that you've learned to look closely, I think you appreciate this view the way I do, for all the multitudes that it holds.

You scan below with an outstretched finger.

"Where's your shop?" you ask.

I guide your finger to one of the dark patches. "Right there. Tiny street. Ndubisi once mentioned moving us somewhere closer to the main markets, near the action, but you know how he is."

"All talk."

"All talk and drink and sleep and TV. He's always watching old sports games, like Pa used to on Sundays. Stuck. Sometimes I wonder if dropping out of school was the biggest mistake I've ever made. Friends I grew up with keep packing their bags and disappearing from here. They're actually starting their lives."

"School honestly doesn't always help," you reply. "Only reason I got a job at Shell after undergrad was because of Dad's connections. And he's the only reason I'm bothering with my master's now. After I'm done with Ikeja Tech, I don't know what comes next." You look around. "Couldn't even tell you where it is from here."

I smile. "Guess."

"Ugh. I don't know. It's next to a small church with a zinc roof—Holy Ghost something."

"There are thirty churches like that."

You place a palm over your eyes and zigzag your outstretched index finger, stopping at a shadowy water tank towering over an orphanage. "That it?"

"Not even close."

You drop your hand on my knee. "Fuck."

"Why didn't you do your master's in Abia?"

"Oh, I just needed to be far away from Vanessa for a while."

"Because she hates you?"

You shake your head as if such a thing is impossible. "Vanessa's made of pure love. When I told her the truth, she didn't speak to me for weeks. She came around eventually though. Forgave me, even, after days of talking and asking questions. But our families went to the same church. They shopped at the same markets. She didn't complain or anything, but I could tell it was hard on her. Seeing me.

Remembering what we'd lost. So I left. I know I can't stay away forever. I'll have to see her again someday. And Dad. Mom. All my nosy aunties asking when I'll come to my senses and marry her."

"Vanessa took it okay. Maybe ... maybe your parents will too."

Your laugh is bitter. "Papa's a nobody here, but back home, he's practically a celebrity in all our churches. He'd rather die than have a single soul think his son is a faggot. One time, years back, he caught Esther masturbating. He burned her hands with a hot iron and locked her in our basement all weekend. He'll choose God over us any day."

"That's our dear Nigeria."

Your grip on my fingers tightens. "It always fucked with me how Dad could say he loved us more than anything. How he could make us feel it too. But what he really loved was his idea of who we needed to be, some biblical fantasy. The moment we weren't God's perfect little angels, he became the devil. I never got it."

A memory rises from the ether: a squeal and a blood spatter. "It's not so strange," I reply, staring at the intersection of our knuckles. "The day after Ma and Pa's funeral, Ndubisi took his dear Meso outside. He picked up a rock and crushed it. Chucked the corpse in the trash. His face was blank the whole time. It was scary seeing him like that, but I understood what he was thinking. Meso's job was to protect Ma and Pa. Meso failed."

"Ever worry he'd do anything like that to you? If he knew. Could you tell him one day?"

In my mind's eye, a jet of spit strikes a studded wall and hangs there. Long ago, a bad day was Reverend Sister Kate, my primary school headmistress, flogging my entire class for noisemaking. It was falling off the branch of a mango tree near the lagoons and scraping my knees bloody. On those days, Ndubisi shelved his playful barbed words. He ruffled my hair with his hands and walked us to the market for sachets of frozen yogurt. But he died with Ma and Pa. The mud-streaked man I pull out of the gutter every month is a stranger.

"I won't tell him. And he's blood, so I can't ever leave him." I pause. "There are days I wish he were dead."

You drop my hand. "Do you mean that?"

I look you right in the eyes so that you know I do. "Alcohol poisoning probably, the way bottles pile up around our bedroom. Or a heart attack. If I told him, I'm sure he'd do worse to me than he did to Meso, like I betrayed a promise I never made. But he's the traitor."

I don't tell you that I sometimes spit in Ndubisi's food, that I sometimes imagine his death at my own hands, my palms clasped around a dinner knife's hilt. My trembling shoulders say enough. You pull me toward your chest. We are beyond the ring of boulders, conjoined pixels exposed to the dark world below.

I bury my nostrils in the smell of you and let the tears fall.

Thursday, July 29

I love you in the morning when I scrub my skin with a soapy sponge. I trace circles on the nipples that you will taste tomorrow.

I hate you in the afternoon when my phone stays silent, its screen frozen on the text message I sent you yesterday. The app has been uninstalled from my phone for a month now, and I wish you texted as much as you did that first night.

My measuring tape runs halfway up a green cloth patterned with snarling lion heads. I fold the fabric and sew along the sides, keeping my fingers left of the needle, just like I pretend Ma taught me. I prick myself when my phone buzzes and barely notice the drops of blood striking the ground. It is only a text from Ndubisi. He saw a purple dragonfly on the window.

Mrs. Adebayo stops by in the evening to pick up her twin daughters' slippers. Her husband waits outside by their car. He opens the passenger door for her and kisses her square on the lips in front of all the passersby. I know what his touch stirs inside her chest.

At home, I make a stew out of tomato paste and sliced potatoes. On the first bite, Ndubisi says that it tastes like heaven. He says he loves me. When the power goes out, the old soccer game on the television fades to black. He screams and flings his bowl against the wall.

When he falls asleep, I take my phone out. You still have not replied. I memorize your number again. I swipe through the sparse photos on your Facebook account. You're five years younger and on a horse with Esther. A dirty-green lake eats up the background. You're ten years younger, perched on the shoulders of your father. His smile is warm. He's commented on every picture: "My handsome boy."

My phone buzzes.

This time, it's you.

"Busy day! Can't wait to see you tomorrow."

I sigh.

Ndubisi rises from bed, muttering. He stumbles in the dark to the door and pushes instead of pulls. He lowers his pants and urinates all over the wall, then returns to his dreams. I get a rag from the bathroom, mop up the liquid, then head outside to the apartment building's stony backyard. The moon is a sickle. I wash the rag in a metal bucket and hang it on a clothesline. A plane flies overhead.

Its dulled roar stirs a vision: Ndubisi waking up to an empty apartment. Before he turns the cable of his phone charger into a noose and swings from the bedroom ceiling fan, he checks the living room, then the bedroom, then the bathroom, then he calls my phone. But it is switched off. We are bound to Canada, you and me. Remember when you said you could never leave? Your eyes are glued to the window. My palm is on your lap. From all the way up here, the clouds look bigger than the mountains.

Friday, July 30

In the centre of our shield, we rebuckle our belts. I graze the stubble of your newly shaven jaw. I don't tell you I miss your beard's thickness, how it swallowed the cuticles of my fingers.

"It's our monthiversary," you say, and I hate that you follow it up with a laugh.

"I want you to fuck me," I reply.

"What?"

"We kiss and suck every time. I think I'm ready for the main course."

"Not here."

"Where, then?"

"Where's this coming from?"

"Do you not want to?"

You stare at me. "Since you brought it up, you want to hear a secret?"

"Sure."

"My salary from the university library—I decided to start saving a bit of it each payday. Enough for a hotel room soon. Salamander Hill is cute, but I think our real first time deserves something a little more proper."

I sit up. My smile is impossible to hide. "I'll start saving too."

"You don't have to. It's my treat."

"No, I will. And we'll have to be really careful. Can't check in together, you know? But yes, yes, let's do it."

You kiss the bridge of my nose. "It might take a few weeks, but it'll happen. We'll have a good time, you and me. We always do."

You and me.

On your lips, a song.

I lean in to kiss you, but you quickly pull away. Behind us, there is the sound of rustling stones, a patter of feet drawing nearer. You pull an index finger against your mouth, whisper, "*Shh.*"

A shadow passes, briefly visible through a slit between two boulders. It is a stray dog. It continues past us and down the other side of the hill until its steps are hushed.

"Fuck," you say, wiping sweat off your forehead. "Where the hell did it come from?"

Slowly, my breath comes back to me.

Friday, August 6

The rain hammers all around us, matting our clothes against our skin.

"I have something to show you," I say. From my pocket, I withdraw a pair of earphones plugged into my phone. I give you the right ear and take the left.

"What is this?" you ask.

"I got curious about your teenage crush. Princess Ife."

"Okay, she wasn't exactly a crush."

"Her old music's way too hard to find, by the way, and it doesn't look like she's made any new stuff. But this Nairaland forum led me to a super-sketchy website with a billion ads and two STDs. It had the download link for her first album."

Your lips curl into an O shape. "You're lying."

"Took all night to download it, but it's legit, I think. Wouldn't let myself hear past the first thirty seconds of track one. I imagine you've heard it all before."

"Are you joking? Heard it, memorized it, doodled it on all my school notebooks. It's been years since my last listen, though."

"Good. Are you ready?"

You nod fervently and kiss my forehead.

The first track, "Egwu Nwa," is bombastic but muddled. Drums soar above a woman's sultry crooning. Eyes closed, you squeeze my kneecap and move your head to the beat. During the song's outro, you explain that she's singing from the perspective of a newborn child excited about life's undiscovered prospects.

The remaining tracks have the same bubbly low-res sound. Although I find little to appreciate in her voice or the instrumentals, I am enraptured by your response, how her voice rattles the past out of you.

"I used to imagine this song playing at my wedding," you say, after the last track disappears beneath the softening storm. I am wrapped between your legs, my back to your stomach.

"Your wedding with Vanessa?"

"Oh no. This was before her. My bride was a groom. Big muscled man named Seyi."

"Ah, a Yoruba fuckboy?"

"Seyi was an angel, thank you very much. Literally. He had these feathery white wings coming out of his back. We flew to space every night and napped on different stars."

I snuggle deeper against you. My pressed weight must hurt a little, but you don't protest.

"Never imagined a wedding for myself," I say. "Expensive. Too many eyes. Plus, it'd have to be in a church."

"You know there are other kinds of weddings, right?"

"Not that I've seen. It's always a church. You know I still go every Sunday? It's not like I believe. A lot of my customers knew Ma and Pa from church, and they're the kind of judgy folks who'd take their business elsewhere if I ever stopped showing up. So I'm there in my Sunday best every morning. I swear Mass is getting longer for no reason."

"I hear you. And there's a new offering every week."

"Right? Donate to the motherless babies. Donate to the babyless mothers. It'd help if the priest was hot, but yeesh, let's just say that Princess Ife won't be making a tune about their faces anytime soon."

Laughter makes your chest rumble. "I go too," you say. "Habit mostly. But I think I still believe. Not in the church and its hell gospel, but in something bigger than us. A powerful thing that loves me the way I am, makes life worth living."

A thought surfaces, the kind I know to keep to myself. This time, I let it out.

"You don't need some made-up entity to love you the way you are. I love you the way you are."

You scoff. "Shut up before my dark ass starts blushing."

"Listen. I'm serious. Feels like I've been waiting to die these past few years. That's it. Just live to die and become nothing forever. Maybe that's why I never bothered to talk to anyone online before you. It couldn't go anywhere in a place like this; it couldn't mean anything. But I was wrong."

"Oh, wow," you say. Your voice falters slightly on the *wow*. "Yeah. Well, I appreciate that. I guess I'm used to other guys just wanting to fuck from the get-go. With us, you took the lead to chat about stuff that actually mattered."

"Exactly! It sounds corny, but I cherish our conversations with all my heart."

"They're nice for sure. Like a few days ago, this guy was online. His roommate was out, some weed party in Ikoyi, so he had me come over, we fucked, it was over in five minutes. Don't get me wrong, it was fun. Hot sex with hot guys always is. But I didn't even get his name. It got me to appreciate how different our vibe is. I think the past few weeks will make our first time at the hotel feel amazing."

You continue talking. There's a strip of cheap hotels near your barbershop, and you think we might be able to book a junior deluxe room in one of them by September. I lose track of what follows. The rain has stopped falling now, and a light breeze billows in its aftermath. On my skin, it is an icicle's stab, burrowing past flesh, past vein and blood, sinking deeper.

"I thought you deleted the app," I say, cutting you off midsentence.

Your brows crinkle in a frown. "Oh no, I didn't. I mean, I'm not online all the time, but if I'm done with class or work and get a random craving, it's there, right?"

"Right."

I stand, wipe the water off my face.

"Are you okay?" you ask.

"Yes."

"You sure?"

"Absolutely."

"I know we don't really talk about other men. Just figured our business is our business."

"Of course. I get that."

"Especially because I'm probably heading home after school next year. At least for a little bit while I figure out what comes after."

"Yep, yep." I almost glance at my wrist for a watch I don't have. "It's getting a bit late, no?"

"Oh, damn, it is. Time flew by with Princess Ife. Thank you again for that. The nostalgia hit hard tonight." You kiss me. It seems so unsanitary now, the exchange of saliva and bacteria, the bruise of your lips, the wet stench of you. "Same time next week?"

I manage a nod.

You say you'll text me soon.

As always, you descend Salamander Hill first. But I don't follow five minutes later. Gravity pulls me right back down, and hours pass before I'm moving. I stop at the base of the hill, its many smells ripened by rainwater, the penance briefly paid for something better—a beautiful view, a warm touch.

Questions rise. How many? How often? For how long? Right after our moments together, or many days later? They gather until I'm on my knees again, until I'm one with the buzzing flies.

Saturday, August 7

It is an hour after midnight, and the bucket near Ndubisi's bed is almost full. It catches stray droplets from the bygone rain, their plops like sirens in the silence.

We meet in the realm of 1s and 0s.

Your exposed chest stands out as familiar.

I type.

"Hi."

A second passes.

Another.

You reply.

"Hey. New to the area?"

"Wanna fuck?"

"I have roommates," you reply. "Can you host?"

"Yes. Got any pics?"

You send eight. Each one, faceless but undeniably you, plunges my stomach down further until I'm struggling for air. There are front and back body shots, a zoomed-in picture of your fist around your penis, a bent-over picture of your ass bared open with your hands. From this angle, you couldn't have taken it by yourself. One photo shows your condom-wrapped penis halfway inside another's ass.

"Got any?" you ask.

I send you the nude pictures I pulled from the internet only minutes ago. Across the room, Ndubisi stirs and mumbles in his sleep.

"Hot as fuck," you reply. "Where are you?"

"Surulere. Face pic?"

"I don't send that."

Liar.

"Good night."

Seconds become minutes. I worry that you will not respond anymore, but there it is, a darkened selfie of you in bed. You are shirtless. There is just enough light to make out your fresh stubble, your winking eye, your stuck-out tongue. My vision blurs behind a liquid wall. The ache is unbearable.

"Where in Surulere?" you ask.

Every motion afterward seems disjointed. My fingers seem to move of their own accord. I take screenshots and navigate to the aliased Facebook account I created thirty minutes ago. I click on your father's profile and introduce myself as an old secondary school classmate from Abia, concerned about evidence of his son's wayward behaviour. I send him all the pictures.

On the app, you send a second message: "Still there?"

Sunday, August 8

I know what kind of day it is from the early morning smell of eggs and sardines. A lumpy garbage bag sits in a bedroom corner. The ends of many empty bottles protrude from its sides. Ndubisi has a plate of sandwiches ready for me in the kitchen.

He asks if I slept well.

He asks if he can accompany me to church.

He squeezes a fifty-naira note into the first offering's collection bowl.

On the walk back to the apartment, he breathes in the sunny air and wipes forehead sweat on his wrinkled but clean-smelling long sleeve.

"Inspiring sermon," he says.

"Very," I reply.

When we arrive, I help him dump the garbage bags in the overflowing bin behind our building. Later that afternoon, power returns, and he asks if I want to watch a rerun of an old Super Eagles game. My phone buzzes with a text from you.

"Go ahead, bro," I tell Ndubisi. "I'll join you soon."

"Heading to the cybercafé this evening," he replies. "Going to have them format my CV so I can send out some job applications this week."

"You've got this, bro."

He smiles like he's just won the lottery and pulls me into a brief sideways hug. From beneath the kitchen sink, I pull out a fresh bag and leave it in the same corner of our bedroom. In a few weeks, it will bloat enough to rip in several tiny places.

I close the door behind me and push my back against it and inhale. There is not enough oxygen to restore calm. "Yes," I text you. "Now is good."

You call immediately. Crackling engines and a hundred conversations mingle in the distance, forcing you to raise your voice. I hold my breath, uncertain of what you're about to say.

"Hey!" There is a smile in your voice. "How are you?"

"I'm okay. Ndubisi and I just got back from church. Everything okay? Where are you?"

"I'm at a motor park. It's so crowded here. I keep checking my pockets every ten seconds to make sure my wallet hasn't disappeared. Hold on. Yep, still got it."

I wonder if my chuckle sounds just the tiniest bit different to you. "Are you going somewhere?"

"Dad called. He's fallen sick. Very sick, it sounds like. Never heard him so shaken before. He needs to see me for a few days."

For the last thirty-six hours, I've struggled to ignore my body's silent war: chills pricking my arms, abdominal cramps, fragments of us on Salamander Hill circling my mind's edge, struggling to break in. For a few seconds longer, I keep them at bay.

"Oh no," I say. "I'm sorry to hear that."

"It means we won't be able to meet this Friday."

"That's fine! I appreciate the heads-up."

"Yeah." You pause for long enough that I have to rely on the background roar of bus conductors to know you're still there. "I realized something this weekend."

"What's that?"

"Dad is a strong man. Extremely proud. When I heard how afraid he sounded on the phone, it scared me. The first thing I wanted to do was see you. I feel so calm when you hug me. Just hearing your voice is comforting. I'm sad we won't meet on Friday."

Strained images, circling faster and faster. "Me too. You know I'm always here for you."

"I know. And I know our last conversation was a bit weird. That's a hundred percent on me. Stuff you said reminded me of Vanessa. All the feelings I struggled to feel for her, I kept trying to pretend they didn't exist for you. Truth is, all I ever wanted was a nice distraction. It scares me that you've become so much more than that." Your voice drops. "But I'd be a fool not to say this. I think you're a beautiful man. I love when you play with my beard. I could listen to you talk for hours and kiss you for days. As soon as I get back, I'm booking that hotel room for you and me."

My shaking phone is pressed against my ear hard enough to leave a mark. I almost say the words.

Don't go home.

Never go home again.

But you would ask why, as if I knew why I'd done it, and my silence would resound against Ndubisi's chants reverberating from the living room. Years-old games animate him like this. First comes his pitchy ode to the players: "Who sabi fight Super Eagles; who fit pass Okocha!" Then the celebratory thumps of his fists against walls, enough to whiten our frayed carpet with a layer of plaster. Our carpet is the age of memory. It pools at the edges with ceiling water when a storm descends, with the drip of Ndubisi's clothes after another post-bar rescue from rancid gutters. It seems cosmic now, the sound of his voice, me and him entwined ever since drink or lust turned Pa toward Ma's legs.

I'm so sorry, I want to tell you. Instead, I say, "Have a safe trip, Kelechi."

There is a beep when the call ends, the remnant of you and me. A final mocking melody.

RAT CARCASSES, WINE SHEETS, AND THE COLOUR OF FOREVER

The abandoned book in Room 1, like everything, reminds Kesandu of her baby girl, Chiazakam. The pose-stuck ballerina on the cover has Chiazakam's long limbs, and the book's spine is as thick as her favourite historical novels. There was a time Kesandu obsessed over old truths too—Lord Lugard and the amalgamation of Nigeria's protectorates, Mary Slessor and all the twin babies she plucked from the bushes, July 1967, Sani Abacha's destruction. Smaller, newer messes occupy Kesandu now, removed from the grand concerns of historians but cyclic all the same. Here, it is tame: the book and a windowside box of peeled clementines warmed by the late-morning sun. Wilder things find Kesandu in other rooms of Christ the Redeemer Hotel, though they don't faze her at this point. Room 4 is a museum to sexual obsession—there are used condoms in the dustbin and on the desk, a shit-stained thong beneath the duvet, towels bunched up and sopping wet beside the bathtub, which contains long strands of black hair, streaks of gelatinous lube, and pleather handcuffs. Room 7 at one end of the hallway shows evidence of a party, the saddest party in the world for having happened here. Green balloons bob from chair arms. Confetti dots the floor and the square enclosure outside that passes for a patio. Glitter too, which the sticky roller that Ifeanyi finally sprung for—out of pocket, of course—does not pick up, so Kesandu has to go down on her knees, creaking back be damned. She sweeps the yellow, green, and red bits of silk paper into a dustpan, thinking that if her ever-considerate Chiazakam had thrown this party, she would have cleaned up thoroughly after herself. In the age-worn cabinet, amid empty bottles of Jose Cuervo and Heineken, Kesandu finds a potent clue. A wet-stained shirt with the words "If you see this bride-to-be, buy her TWO shots!" printed above a deceivingly elegant face. Room 8, on the hallway's right side, has a plugged-in iron burning a hole into the ironing board.

Kesandu expects no less from Ebo District. She has developed a method for taming the madness. She starts each shift by wolfing down a Toblerone bar, hating and loving the decadent, sugary goodness, its burst of energy. Next, the rooms in sequence. Once through each door, she moves counter-clockwise, from desk to bed to patio to bathroom, emptying leftover trash into dustbins and dustbins into black garbage bags. It's easy to spot what does not belong. Food and empty wrappings are invariant. Sometimes, there are wallets or keys, which go to Ifeanyi. Kesandu takes the fantasy novels. Occasionally, there is something in a category all its own. Two headless rat carcasses in the bin, likely the work of budding ritualists or a novice serial killer. A fat roll of marijuana, which, against her better judgment—it's precisely the kind of nonsense she used to warn Chiazakam against—Kesandu later smoked at home. A tiny gift from a job that mostly takes.

After the picking is the stripping—old bed linens exchanged for new. Then comes mopping, unless the stain is stubborn and adhesive, in which case she gets on her hands and knees with a rough sponge, feels her spine chip away some more. She used to worry about mirrors until she realized that most people don't care about them, even if they're fairly smudged. She moves on to the bathroom, the spraying and the rag-drying, and the bathtub, which she blasts with a dose of scorching hot water. After restocking tea bags, sweeteners, and new rolls of toilet paper, she finishes with a cursory inspection of her work, lifting toilet lids and opening drawers to check for anything one might complain about. Ifeanyi insulates her from customer rage as best he can. "So sorry, madam," and "I'll look into that, sir," and "How about 50 percent off your last night?" Not that it stops an overzealous guest from knocking against her cart and pointing at their open room door, saying the water makes their skin itchy or the AC doesn't run cold enough, and what is she going to do about that?

It's surprising that only one guest has ever complained—to Kesandu's knowledge, anyway—about their things moving about. They suspected theft even though nothing was missing. Ifeanyi dismissed it (once the woman was out of earshot) as a cheap attempt at a discount (which he granted anyway). In truth, while the stayover guests are out and about in the city, Kesandu does riffle through their things, seeking secrets in their luggage. Most times, she finds mundanity. Extra pairs of underwear, or shaving razors flecked with dried blood. The rare thrill comes from a folded test result with sombre implications. White powder in a Ziploc. A vibrator whose length terrifies and amuses. She never takes, only looks, every probing peek adding some colour to an otherwise monotonous shift. 2Face Idibia and Wande Cole had once enlivened the day's slow passing from her MP3 player, but those wild stirrings of emotion have now simmered into placid waves.

The stayover guest in Room 11 holds no secrets in their backpack. Their top drawer contains Shoprite receipts and a worn King James Bible. A surprising tidiness orders the rest of the room, all things in place. They have even left a five-thousand-naira tip in a rubber-banded wad on the dresser. Kesandu leaves the kind stranger an extra towel and an extra bottle of shampoo (the sulfate-free type, because Ifeanyi does listen to guest feedback, bless his soul). The long day is almost over. She's just about to walk past Room 12, which has the "Do Not Disturb" sign hanging on its doorknob, when she notices that water is starting to leak out of the room into the hallway. There's music coming from in there too, a sort of ballad, but no other sound.

Kesandu frowns and bangs on the door. When no one replies, she swipes her key and walks inside. There are three naked people asleep on the bed. Bare bodies are no surprise. Many times, guests walk around their rooms unclothed, having left the "Housekeeping Wanted" sign on their door (mostly) by accident. They rise rapidly from the toilet, retreat beneath bedsheets, or freeze in shock when Kesandu enters. And she, mildly amused by the theatrics, says "sorry" in the same breath she uses to walk back out. But this time, she ventures farther in, surveying the desk, which has at least thirty mini bottles of vodka on it, some empty, and a stack of identical CDs. She turns back to the naked bodies—the women are in their twenties, the man in his thirties. Their plump copper bodies are stark against his thinness. His groin is a forest of hair.

The sound of running water invites Kesandu deeper inward, to the ajar bathroom door, the source of the flood, and a song: "*Sand bed, low sun, she's licking ice cream / Horse rides, ocean breeze, she's smelling freedom / He's gone, gone, gone, and she's tasting freedom.*" Inside the bathroom, there's another woman, also in her thirties, thin and bare. The woman has her back to the wall and her shaking, sobbing head buried in her knees. Kesandu eyes her for bruises, finds none. A rugged speaker perched on the toilet tank drowns out the woman's voice. The toilet is clogged but mercifully churns out clear water. There is an overflow from the bathroom sink too. The confluence of streams runs past Kesandu's feet and into the main room, where all things aground are soaking—a blue purse, high heels and flats, the base of the bed, a phone with a cracked screen.

Kesandu almost speaks, but she's startled, intrigued even, by this woman's lack of reaction to her presence. She's too lost in herself, in her own barely audible weeping. It is easy to imagine that the force of her tears is what submerges Room 12, a powerful hurt unnamed, and Kesandu thinks of Chiazakam and the final weeks before Amawbia Grounds claimed the unimportant bits of her. Springtails in dirt and a worn headstone and disintegrating bones—these mattered little anyway, since the bulk of Chiazakam, the important bit, lives on somewhere high above, somewhere Kesandu knows she is going to someday, forever. Still, she doesn't let such thoughts linger for too long, so she forces herself to move, first to turn off the sink, then to touch the strange woman's shoulder. The woman flinches. Kesandu suspects that the scarlet around her dilated irises is not entirely from sadness; there's a soupy haze to her eyes. But the breach of skin against skin initiates a dawning, a soul returning to itself. The woman rises wordlessly. She wipes her eyes and runny nose, takes stock of Kesandu and the flood and her own existence. She whips past Kesandu into the bedroom and shakes the man, begging him to wake up.

The women flanking him stir before he does, but soon he's mumbling too, asking what is wrong. Kesandu is already exiting when the bedside trio spot her. She promises to get the manager, apologizes for the intrusion, and closes the door behind her. Once outside, she collects herself for a moment, then starts toward the lobby, her cart momentarily abandoned. She walks slowly to grant the guests enough time to comport themselves, and she wonders if Chiazakam ever cried that way, so lost in her own pain that the whole wide world disappeared. Once Chiazakam passed ten, she never cried in front of Kesandu. And the month after she turned fifteen, Amawbia Grounds laid claim to that inconsequential physical portion of her. Otherwise, she'd be thirty-six now, not frozen in Kesandu's mind. The possibilities always whirl: lawyer or doctor or engineer. More likely: teacher, writer, architect. And how many hearts would she have broken or mended? Or bound herself to? Maybe someone with a good soul like Ifeanyi, not that Kesandu would ever have mandated sweet Chiazakam being with anyone she didn't want to be with. Or with anyone at all. No, Chiazakam would have enjoyed the small amount of freedom that Kesandu herself had been denied. Of course, now, Chiazakam enjoys the kind of freedom that earthly offerings cannot begin to scratch.

Behind Kesandu, the music coming from Room 12 turns off, lending the cracked walls flanking the hallway a ghostly quality. Ifeanyi has been pushing the owners of Christ the Redeemer Hotel for a renovation, but they're not having it. The owners are twin brothers who live somewhere abroad—Belgium, Kesandu thinks—although once a year they visit the hotel as part of their annual pilgrimage back to Nigeria, eager to see the staff who "keep their money engine running." They like to announce themselves in tacky multicoloured suits, bearing gift baskets of bad perfume and European dark chocolate for Kesandu and Ifeanyi, supposedly valuable for having come from a foreign land. Ifeanyi's devotion to them feels like a waste of his talents. Their frugality renders him manager, receptionist, post-housekeeping inspector, and, on unusually busy days, co-housekeeper, all for the pay of one. Nevertheless, he takes on each required role with enthusiasm, going above and beyond as often as he can, from recompensing bitter guests with his own funds to buying and hanging massive red bouquets on the lobby walls to offer a semblance of atmosphere. Before Ifeanyi, there was Gozie, and Gozie would have merrily napped on that lobby desk while the hotel burned. Kesandu considers herself somewhere between Gozie and Ifeanyi, neither slacker nor overachiever, content to fill the precise expectations of her job and no more. Before the call of Amawbia Grounds, she lived a much busier life on Chiazakam's behalf, with night school and weekend shifts and second jobs, but afterward, her existence acquired a sedate hue. Her only real end goal is reunion with Chiazakam, and she is content to walk slowly there. Just like this. Step by step. Breath. By. Breath.

In the lobby, Ifeanyi is sitting straight and tall, laser-focused on the hotel's entrance—until Kesandu's interruption. His face knits when she narrates the Great Flooding of Room 12, skipping the details about nakedness and crying and miniature liquor bottles.

Ifeanyi consults a ledger. "Four guests, you say? There should be only two guests in that room. Mr. and Mrs. Anyanwu. Here till tomorrow."

That the man is wedded to any of those women surprises Kesandu. She does not recall seeing rings. As she heads back to Room 12 with Ifeanyi, the two women who had flanked Mr. Anyanwu in bed scurry past like rats, now dressed in crop tops and miniskirts, their heads bent low. Mr. Anyanwu and the bathroom knee-hugger, who must be Mrs. Anyanwu, are standing outside the room in bathrobes and furry white sandals, a patterned hard-shell suitcase beside them. Mr. Anyanwu shoots Kesandu a look of derision and then, before Ifeanyi can speak, says in a supercilious baritone that their toilet is broken. Ifeanyi, ever the diplomat, apologizes profusely and offers them a no-added-cost move to Room 14, plus late checkout for tomorrow. Kesandu mentions that she hasn't cleaned Room 14 yet, but Mr. Anyanwu says they will take it as is.

After the Anyanwus are resettled, Kesandu mops up the bit of water that leaked into the hallway and then joins Ifeanyi in examining the damage to Room 12. It seems thankfully minimal. He's turned off the water valve and tried to unclog the toilet with a plunger, to no avail. At least the wet floor is tiled rather than carpeted, but it's gained a stink despite the flood water's clarity. The trash is easy stuff: greasy to-go containers, empty coffee packets, those small vodka bottles, and cans of Red Bull. Ifeanyi strips the linens and the soaked curtains for the laundry room's morning spin tomorrow. With the curtains gone, a red-burning sky gleams behind the dirty window glass.

"I know it's getting late," Ifeanyi says apologetically, "but can you handle this room before calling it a day? I'll call someone for the toilet tomorrow ... maybe Chidi, if he's back from Cameroon."

Kesandu nods. "Of course." She motions at the wall separating Rooms 12 and 14. Her voice dropping, she says, "Did you see those two women fleeing like frightened children when we were coming?"

Ifeanyi smiles and draws a shushing finger to his lips. After he's gone, Kesandu sighs and starts on the room. As she cleans, she abandons Wande Cole to focus intently on any sounds emanating from Room 14. There's nothing for a while, then a hushed conversation between the Anyanwus, then music again, even louder this time. Giggles and gasps. A sound of pleasure that starts high, then goes low, as if trying to control itself, then back to high. A thing so primal and animalistic it reminds Kesandu that humanity descended from apes. She has never understood or desired the delirium of sexual ecstasy, how it makes you lose your mind. Henry, the man Grandma all but forced her to marry (and to be fair, his grandmother had pushed him too) hadn't really asked for sex—except during their scheduled Friday-night sessions, which happened mostly because they were trying for children. In the moments their bodies united, the physical sensation wasn't unpleasant, just unfussworthy.

One of the Anyanwus is snoring by the time Kesandu finishes cleaning. Room 12 smells like lemons. She contemplates washing the curtain-free window too but hears her tired bones laugh at the thought. No, it is time for the twenty-minute walk back home. Time to microwave the plantain and beef stew left from last night's cooking, then to read the night away until morning comes. New beginning. New cycle. But …

Chiazakam's voice rises inside Kesandu as it sometimes does when she senses herself getting foolhardy: *Mama, go home.*

"Hush, girl," she replies. "Go play tennis with Jesus, and don't worry about little old me." After Kesandu drops off her cart at the supply closet and locks it down, she returns to Room 12. Sits on the edge of the newly made bed, then slowly lies across it. Sinks into it. She thinks of all the bodies this mattress has ever held, here and before it belonged to here, all the lives and joys and hurts and little boredoms. All the midnight musings. She thinks of all the stories that cannot be gleaned from the messes guests leave behind.

The singular snore from Room 14 is unrelenting. Deep enough that Kesandu's first instinct is to assign it to Mr. Anyanwu, but her Chiazakam had struggled with sleep apnea, and the worst of her snores sounded like a middle-aged man's. Kesandu's intent listening goes on for minutes and turns into sleep itself. Into dreams of Chiazakam, just like always. Memories lived and unlived and imagined. Next thing Kesandu knows, she's waking up.

Those first few groggy seconds are a struggle to untangle the interlocking of sight and sound and time. Room 12 is thick with shadows, and as Kesandu sits up, wiping drool off her lips, she hears Mr. Anyanwu's voice, strong and clear, drifting across from the wall they share.

"Part of me still thinks where we're going is nowhere at all. But a bigger part thinks, hopes, there's more to ... all this. And either way, it matters that we're doing it together. I know it does. Are you ready?"

Mrs. Anyanwu: "I am. I love you."

"I love you more."

There is a pause, another, then an explosion of sound. Kesandu jumps. Mrs. Anyanwu makes a low scraping noise—something between a moan and a cry—and Kesandu finds instinct driving her legs into the hallway. Room 14 has the "Do Not Disturb" sign on the door, but she ignores it and charges in. As she registers what she's seeing, the door closing behind her, regret follows. The feeble hope that she's still sleeping. But Chiazakam is not here. This is no dream.

Mr. Anyanwu, naked again, is splayed on his back, his left hand curled in a grip around a pistol aimed at his skull. His face is a pasty blob, not quite a face, and Kesandu doesn't let herself look long enough to discern the intricacies of his unbecoming. She does take in the dark red-wine ooze that blooms across his pillow and down the side of the bed. Mrs. Anyanwu is lying bare next to him, chest up, a second gun aimed neckward, but she has not pulled the trigger, even though her finger is on it. The gun trembles in her hand. Her eyes are closed and twitching. *It is not too late,* Kesandu thinks. She can still flee this madness. Instead, she steps forward, palms raised, all kinds of heat spiking her neck. She says, "Madam, please. Mrs. Anyanwu. Please. Stop."

Mrs. Anyanwu opens her eyes and looks at Kesandu. Then the sight of her husband distracts her. Her whole body trembles. She punches his shoulder lightly and leans over to kiss his neck, then she puts one arm around his waist, the other slinking past the bed's edge to point the gun downward.

"Soon, babe," she murmurs. "Soon. I promise. Just need a little time, that's all."

"He killed himself," Kesandu says. It's an obvious thing, and her lips are forming those words, but she notices an alien taste in her mouth. For all of the hotel's vices, Kesandu has seen death here only once before. Years ago, an elderly woman checked in alone for four nights but died on the first, her varicose-veined skin stiff and putrescent by the time Kesandu walked in for housekeeping. Amid the horror, a clear thought had surged: the abject loneliness of the woman's passing, along with the small comfort that Chiazakam had not left this world by herself.

"He killed himself," Kesandu repeats.

Mrs. Anyanwu is humming atop her husband, like he's nearly asleep and she wants to take him all the way to dreamland. After a few more seconds, she slowly rises from her husband's body, half her face, her hair, and her left shoulder all caked with his blood. She trudges from bed to desk, where she takes another small bottle of vodka from a row of them and drains it in one unflinching gulp. She moves to the hard-shell suitcase by the curtain, prompting Kesandu to take a few steps back. Kesandu wonders if Ifeanyi heard the gunshot. No, he'd have come knocking by now. And how late is it anyway? Hakim, the night clerk, might have taken over already.

From a side compartment, Mrs. Anyanwu pulls out a CD case, the same kind Kesandu had glimpsed when first entering Room 12, then drops to her knees, her back against the curtain. She cradles the disc in one hand, gazing at it. The other still clutches that pistol, and though Kesandu's stare cannot keep from returning to it, she has a feeling Mrs. Anyanwu will not shoot her. So Kesandu moves closer and sits alongside her, both of them facing the bed where a man is now a corpse.

Kesandu regards the CD case more closely. It appears to be a musical album: *The Wondrous Wahalas of Auntie Kosi*. A woman of about seventy in an emerald asoebi dress stands grinning beneath the curving text. Mrs. Anyanwu seems to vanish into the picture, as if it tethers her to a place she cannot yet abandon, and Kesandu dares to hope. She can leave this room alive, Mrs. Anyanwu in tow.

"Who is Auntie Kosi?" Kesandu starts, cautious.

Mrs. Anyanwu looks up, registering surprise at Kesandu's presence, as if she materialized out of the ether. Managing something of a smile, Mrs. Anyanwu turns back to the CD. The blood on her face looks like a melting mask under the fluorescent lighting, eerie with the smile, but when she speaks, her voice is tender.

It all rattles in her head day and night, she says, everything, all the time. But if memory is a photo reel, her aunties are the starting edge. They sweltered in a smoky kitchen while her raucous uncles and their rogue sons sat in the parlour, hollering over DStv. Mrs. Anyanwu stood next to the stove, no older than six, not a Mrs. yet, watching how the women peeled the potatoes and pounded yams in a mortar. How they tended to their specialties. Auntie Vero made the rice and soups. Bitter, crusty Susanna handled all the meats: chicken, goat, fresh tilapia. Kosi, her tongue prone to jokes but not tastes, handled the salads. It was real communal living. A big house that was yet too small for their numbers and never dull with silence. It smelled of beer from all the cans cracked open at breakfast, lunch, and dinner. Mrs. Anyanwu would even receive a few cool sips from Vero and Susanna, if she was on her best behaviour. Yes, a good drink loosened the tongue, they said, left no room for pretense. It was the way of their grandparents, and their great-grands, and their great-great-grands, all the way back to Adam and Eve.

Mrs. Anyanwu says it was divinity that crossed her path with her husband's; his childhood was so starkly different. Smaller. Quieter. Rooms that smelled of tea with honey, and brothers he battled over the pot's last salmon by whispering "Fishy fish fish!" and televisions with channels ruled by his own little hands. His favourite cartoon featured red-tailed mice dancing to keep the sun from crashing into Micetown. It was never clear how their song staved off the apocalypse, but it did, and he came to associate music with salvation.

Mrs. Anyanwu starts to tremble again like she's cold. She strings together Igbo-sounding words, but Kesandu cannot parse their meaning. She motions at the CD, which by now is sitting to the side of Mrs. Anyanwu's legs—though not the gun, no, the gun is still firmly in her clutch, its aim in Kesandu's general direction. The morbid thought crosses Kesandu's mind that a bullet to the throat would simply mean a quicker reunion with Chiazakam.

"Auntie Kosi," Kesandu says. "Was she a singer?"

Mrs. Anyanwu chuckles. "God, no. Auntie Kosi and harmonies were like cement and Fanta. But her speaking voice could make you forget every nightmare you ever had. I thought she could sweet-talk even death away. If only."

"What was it? Old age?"

No, Kosi had gotten to the point where dying in her sleep was more likely than not, the bedrest age, but she was a defiant old widow. When her legs started to fail, necessitating a walking stick, she increased her daily motion. One afternoon, on a solitary stroll to the market, some boys surrounded her. They took her purse, then her life. Kosi's mouth could lash pepper-laced insults for days. Consensus among the other aunties was that she must have stayed a stubborn fighter till the end.

Fighter. Coleslaw prepper. Those words didn't suffice for Mrs. Anyanwu's knowledge of her oldest aunt, so after graduating from UniLag, she spearheaded a musical project in Kosi's honour.

"*The Wondrous Wahalas of Auntie Kosi*," Kesandu says.

"Yes." Mrs. Anyanwu runs a thumb across Kosi's cheek on the CD case. "It wasn't just me though. These songs are my voice. Auntie Kosi's beautiful history. But it was *his* melodies and *his* heart that brought it to life."

Mrs. Anyanwu had interviewed aunties and uncles and cousins for every scrap of Kosi lore she could find, putting them all online on her blog, *Ifesinachi's Number 1 Person*. She'd uncovered reckless teenage trysts with no-good boys. Stints at various convents. And, till Kosi's dying day, a hidden world passed in the houses of troubled marriages, fixing what needed fixing. If a man roughed up his woman, she found Kosi, and Kosi found his penis with a knife's edge, threatening to slice it off if he so much as forgot to say "good morning." And the unions she deemed beyond repair, she split. She was mediator and battleaxe.

"See," Ifesinachi says, pointing at track four on the CD, "Warrior Heart." As Kesandu surveys the track list, she can't help but wonder what Chiazakam's life would look like ordered as an album. Would the first track detail the despair of fruitless trying, those solitary years with Henry? Or the ecstatic disbelief when finally, Chiazakam fizzed to life on a sonogram? All the names Kesandu had played with vanished in favour of a new one: Chi a za kam, "God has answered me well." Would the last track bemoan the car crash, how Chiazakam and a much older boy Kesandu didn't know had wrapped their delicate bodies around an indelicate tree? The things formerly unimaginable that were found in the wrecked car: condoms and liquor and pill-sized hallucinogens? Or the Chiazakam-shaped hole that lingered forever afterward? The random outbursts of tears in the middle of the day. The panic attacks that yanked Kesandu out of sleep. And worst of all, the feeling that she had not really known her sweet baby Chiazakam, and if she hadn't known her, then who could she claim to know in this life? Was she not an island adrift? Or would the album end on the bit of sunny hope she'd come to caress like a second child in the many years since? That this world was the dream before you awoke to real life. The temporary stage. That she and Chiazakam were fated for an eternal reunion.

Ifesinachi is still going on about "Warrior Heart." Apparently Mr. Anyanwu had penned every line, translating into lyrics, melodies, and verdant instrumentation all the notes Ifesinachi had gathered. They had worked out of a small studio, where Ifesinachi initially interviewed potential collaborators. At first, she was doubtful of Mr. Anyanwu's quiet demeanour, mistaking his shyness for a creative void. However, it quickly became clear that he was the only responder to her online ads who had bothered reading her blog.

"My name is Chibuike Anyanwu," he said, "and I see your vision."

Ifesinachi scoffed. "Is that so?"

"Yes."

Chibuike saw the powerful aunt for what she represented. It wasn't enough to reckon with her life. Her absence was a story too. He envisioned an album that spoke to the kind of town where young boys murdered their elders. "Why do we consume our brightest lights? Our generational knowledge, which teaches us manners of survival you can't read in a book. Why?"

His questions widened Ifesinachi's vision. They decided that each song on the album would be accompanied by a distinct video: a chronological collage of Auntie Kosi's best pictures; snapshots of domestic life from marriages saved; the bliss of dissolved relationships too, a former wife freed from abuse and enjoying a day at the beach;

footage from Kosi's well-attended funeral interspersed with recent local headlines about unending violence. Yes, this project would be their rallying cry. It would save a town on the verge of moral collapse.

"Can songs do all that?" Kesandu asks, unable to help herself.

"Of course. It's in us, you know, to transform and be transformed. You have earphones dangling out of your pocket, which means you like music. Something about it changes you."

"It makes the day go faster, that's all. The things that transform me, I think they're more tangible. Every breath of air in my lungs, for example. And my daughter. Chiazakam. She passed on, but I try to live my life in her honour every day."

"See? If I gave you a pen and paper right now, I bet you could write a million songs about her."

"Maybe. Nothing that could change anything though. Or do her life justice. The size of it, and how I see her. All the colour she brought."

"The grey before the colour, or the black and white—that's art too. Chibuike taught me that. How to linger in that space before the most magical moments. Like before your daughter, there was her father, yes? And a love there, no matter if it was brief or everlasting. Now, think of the love that had to exist to get *him* to exist—that's art too."

Ifesinachi continues on a rambling loop, iterating over the expansive tree of ancestral loving that started in the Garden of Eden, and isn't that the purest art, the kind that endures till today? Kesandu almost replies that a forced marriage is not art. That love is not the machination of unbending grandmothers. It is not the absence of choice. And isn't it funny, in the way cruel things often are, that shortly after Chiazakam's birth, Henry followed the siren call of a big-bosomed woman? Although *followed* is not quite right, because he took this woman *in* and tossed Kesandu *out*, doing his best to sob on that humid evening. It was very difficult, he said. But also right. And how pathetic to have listened to his nonsense with a care for him still surging within her. While Kesandu can never imagine herself sitting down to pen a song in Henry's honour, she can admit to that care in this crazed space, with an armed woman who sings about transformation while her husband rots mere steps away. Already he has started to smell—no, not yet, it's not his stink in the air but the stench of sweat and fear. Yes, Kesandu had felt something for Henry, a care approximating love, built from the ground up by the thousand Friday nights before Chiazakam, all of them so identical and relentless that she'd been convinced they would last forever.

Friday Nights Forever had begun with the end of her shift as an optometrist's assistant, a time well before Christ the Redeemer Hotel. Her patients were mostly on the wrong side of fifty; their milky cataracts, fading vision, and ocular melanomas lingered as Kesandu stepped outside the clinic, then broke into a run. She fled, fled, fled from the gods of decomposition, not resting until the sky was bruised and purple. She'd catch her breath on the edge of a gated estate, where slick, multi-storeyed homes glimmered behind barbed wire. Her heart always took a long while to settle. Too long, which she told herself she would check with the doctor about soon. A self-evident lie promised on all the Fridays before. But the past is beautiful because it wraps the future in glitter, makes it nice and shiny and full of potential, the kind all her teachers had said she possessed.

Every Friday Night Forever, Kesandu watched the security guard at the gate's outbuilding, his unsettled side eye tracking her. She stretched her legs all the way and then some. She smelled the strange mix of food in the air: corn, oranges, spicy stew, and something other. The sound of distant gunfire carried from one of the houses farther down, some video game, and she imagined that she and Henry and their imaginary son, who had arrived when they first started trying for sons—Chekwube, five now—were passing around controllers and turning two-dimensional aliens into high scores. She imagined AK-47S, which made her think of the first gang movie she'd watched with Grandma—*Issakaba,* with its sullen, scary men—and then she thought of Grandma, how love could coexist with hate. Every week, the night took her here, and if she continued down that path, she would never leave, so she turned around for a second run, this time to Henry. She imagined the guard checking out her buttocks as she departed, but it was one of those thoughts she never shared with Henry. Otherwise, he would ask why her mind was so vulgar. His favourite word, alongside *order,* as in, there is an order to things, a preordained manner of composition, so why not change into running gear after work instead of turning heads with your work blouse and flat shoes? *Vulgar* and *order* coming from a man who scratched his balls and sniffed his fingers when he thought she wasn't looking. Said the things he said in bed because to him, sex life was distinct from real life.

There it was, the rusting metal post on the corner that led to the door that led to Henry that would lead to Chiazakam, even though on those Friday Nights Forever, Kesandu couldn't have guessed that she would gain such a wonderful gift only to lose it one and a half decades later, and the house too, for a narrow flat on Ebo District. Or that somehow, after all that, she would be okay. She *could* guess—because it was the past and the future of Friday Nights Forever—that

Henry was inside scratching and sniffing as he set up their weekly game of Monopoly on the dining table. A birchwood table last year but a glass one today, because only the stupid little things changed while the big things stayed the same. And wasn't that Henry, always swapping little old things for little new things? Always promising he'd see the doctor about that sporadic wet cough that wracked his chest when they dined on ogbono soup before playing their game, moving pieces along the board. Her, the dog. Henry, the thimble. Her, the winner. Him, making his stupid little joke about being the real victor because he got to fuck her afterward. And wasn't *that* word vulgar? *Fuck, bitch, that's my pussy* loosed between grunts, phrases no doubt picked up from the secret porn videos he still imagined she was clueless about. His bedroom vocabulary irking her even though his hypocrisy was the least of his vices. An irk that, anyway, lessened slightly after he kissed her forehead and neck, then turned off the lights and fell asleep. His snores followed. A thousand snores for a thousand nights, and somewhere along the way, the guttural sound of his troubled breathing went from keeping her up to soothing her. After all, if she listened, the vibrating motor of his throat said, *You do not have Chekwube, but you are not alone. You will live forever in nights with sunset trails and gunfire and leery guards and companionship.* He came to symbolize this permanence in her heart even after he became old news, a death of sorts, pure memory, and she forged new Friday Nights Forever with Chiazakam until she too became a relic—except high above and down here, deep inside and immortal, and how could any one song ever convey the weight of that?

But Ifesinachi is insisting on it, family trees and the billion billion souls who walked the earth, and it's all love, all art, all transformative on a cellular level, even if her own folk were too blind to see it. Like Aunt Susanna, who could smile at you while digging a knife into your ribs. Refused to donate a single naira to crowdfunding the project, unlike the others. Said she wouldn't bother telling her friends at the Mother Teresa Garden Club about it, because worldly songs did not compel them. When the album failed to generate sales or conversation, Ifesinachi knew that Susanna was in part to blame. Bad energy like hers—especially of kin—spoils the core of one's longings.

But by then, it was almost okay, because she had Chibuike and his healing force. That was their beautiful paradox, how each felt that the other only gave. See, he'd moved from Port Harcourt by himself because staying there would have destroyed him. A boy wielding a cleaver had robbed him of all his money. His girl had ended things afterward. So he'd passed the subsequent months with any bottle that could numb his brain. Had left the city seeking salvation. Something new and good to own his soul.

"Serendipity." Ifesinachi almost sings the word. "That's what it was. Our demons were mirrors. Vero and Susanna made sure I only ever had sips of their good-good here and there, but by ten, I was hiding away in the garage while everyone slept, downing entire beer cans. I was eighteen when it almost killed me at a campus party. After I got out of the hospital, I quit. Not for the first time. Shit like this, you're always taking off and on like an ugly blouse. Always fighting your brain. Doesn't help that this particular demon's everywhere. Saying no once takes everything. And I mean everything. But I had to make that same choice a thousand times. A thousand more. At hangouts with friends. Alone in bed. Before graduation. Every time I visited home. 'Why?' they would ask. And I just kept it at: 'I don't want to today.' Couldn't really explain that it was always calling my name, that answering would mean the end of me." Ifesinachi stares down at the gun in her hand. Turns it over slowly. "Guess I did answer. In the end. But when I met Chibuike, I was fighting hard. Been off it for two years. Him too, a few months. Felt good having someone who understood. Someone I could be accountable to and keep safe. We needed our minds clean for the project that would change our world."

But when the album failed, her old cravings flared up more than ever. She and Chibuike were lovers now, their post-work evenings spent in the studio, their nights in the same bed, in a cozy new flat. He met her family. To no one's surprise, he and Susanna did not get along. Chibuike resented her lack of support for their album, and she was happy to return his ice. All the others loved him though, his wit and musical ear and fervent, open adoration of Ifesinachi.

"You have no idea how much it meant to him," Ifesinachi says, her free hand taking Kesandu's, her head—the non-bloody side, thankfully—reclining onto Kesandu's shoulder. Kesandu pats the hand that holds hers, squeezes it, hoping Ifesinachi can feel what she's sending: *You're not alone.*

"What did it mean to him?" Kesandu asks.

"Well, that beautiful man, he'd never known a love that doesn't bruise. His mother loved him only on the days he didn't upset his father. And his brothers called him only when she made them. He found something different with me. We prayed together, he and I, and he always ended with this ... refrain. 'God, please protect that which is mine and ours. Fill our love with the shape of you. Let it honour you.' So tell me, how could I go and ruin us by falling back into old ways?"

Ifesinachi and Chibuike brainstormed in the studio for their next artistic project. They both had day jobs—him helping to manage a cybercafé, her teaching at a primary school—but his ambition was still to create an album with the potential for social transformation. Secretly, though, Ifesinachi was tired. Done. Drinking again. The first break happened at a sports bar across from a post office she'd visited to mail some letters. Then a palm wine stall at Ogbe Oye Market. Both times, she put a finger down her throat to force out whatever hadn't been digested, then swirled her tongue with mouthwash. A third time followed. A fourth. Soon, she was hiding Jack Daniel's in an opaque water bottle. She got home before Chibuike, took a few sips, then stowed the bottle in an empty box for sneakers that Auntie Vero's husband had gifted Chibuike. The sneaker box sat inside old bins in their pantry—not the best hiding spot, but few options were good when you lived with your partner. Still, a thorough shock had paralyzed Ifesinachi the day she came home to find Chibuike perched on their bed, the water bottle in his hand. She spluttered her apologies, diminished and ashamed. She was a failure. She would have understood if he'd decided to leave her for his own sake.

"Some days, I think you know me more than I know myself," he replied, shaking his head. "And other days, I wonder. Ife, I could never do anything but love you." The bottle was half-full, and he chugged the rest of it like water. "There," he said, smiling at her stunned face. "We're back at the bottom together. And together, we'll climb out."

That night, they made love in a different way. Soul to soul. She felt the collision of their histories, a whole universe within her, and there he shone, the face of every galaxy. Within weeks, they were drinking with lunch and dinner, before sex and after. Beer, wine, tequila, milk and rum blends, vodka in skull bottles. She took a swig of Hennessy and breathed it into his mouth. He trapped it beneath his tongue. Swallowed. "We are two heartbeats," he said, his eyes molten brown as they found hers. "One soul."

On some workdays, they called in sick. Enjoyed takeout from Drumstix and five seasons of true crime. Played Uno, Scrabble, and Battleship. When they were feeling especially risqué, they invited other women from online pages into their bed. Once or twice, a man too. There were boundaries with the strangers—no kissing or bareback—but Ifesinachi loved watching Chibuike conquer another woman, loved watching her moan and reach for his lips only to be met with his turned neck.

The day Chibuike's boss called to terminate his employment, that loss cut through their haze a bit. He'd liked teaching older folk who had never used a keyboard before how to type and search the internet. He drank harder that evening, and after their usual lovemaking, he almost fell while reaching for the towel to wipe Ifesinachi with.

"I'll get it," she replied, but he surprised her by screaming, "Fishy fish fish!" and surging forward anyway. His jelly legs buckled, and she fell upon him with the towel, wiping his groin.

"Fishy fish fish," she said, laughing. "Really?"

The phrase entered their secret lexicon.

"You know, the one every couple has," Ifesinachi says. Kesandu doesn't know if it's the lighting or something else, but Ifesinachi's left eye is starting to look more bloodshot than the right one.

Kesandu nods. "I do. With me and Henry, it was 'nwoke oma' or 'nwanyi oma' when we met irritating guests at a get-together. If they overheard us and understood Igbo, they'd think it was a compliment."

"Ha. Well, we started saying 'fishy fish fish' everywhere."

Its utterance relied on three things: their well-developed telepathy, liquor surging in their veins, and a perfectly spontaneous moment. While shopping, they came across a woman's full cart. Her back was turned as she hunted for sardines. "Fishy fish fish," Ifesinachi said, motioning at the cart, which prompted Chibuike to grab it and push it all the way out of the store. No one stopped them.

Fishy fish fish, and they prank-called random numbers, pretending to be the responder's long-lost billionaire relative. They swiped naira notes out of a threesome partner's wallet while she cleaned up in the bathroom. Fishy fish fish was the song of them versus all the world's things.

"I wanted it to last forever," Ifesinachi says. "Living for two. But then ... I got sick. It took us five different tests to accept what we were seeing on those sticks. I was pregnant. Me. A baby. New life. Something that was of us and yet more than us. We had enough sense to know that we were not ready to be parents. We weren't right. But you know, actually saying those words—'We have to get rid of this child'—it felt like the worst thing I'd ever done. Do you know what that feels like?"

Kesandu thinks of Chiazakam, the weightless, pawpaw-yellow version of her that had curled up in her arms in the hospital room. She cannot imagine having given her up for anything. Yet, a thought lingers beneath the surface, the regret of trading more time with Chiazakam for extra pay slips. Sure, she can find all the evidence of proper motherhood. Holistic life lessons, like when Chiazakam was caught copying answers to a Hausa exam off her deskmate, and Kesandu expressed her disappointment but also said mistakes were okay. *We all mess up. And don't fear failure—a bad grade is better than a guilty heart.* Stories about family narrated over late-night suppers so that Chiazakam could feel rooted to her past. Questions answered about what it meant when blood surged between her thighs, and why Daddy no longer called since getting a son with that other woman, and what to do when a boy in class said he liked her. But the truth is, there were birthdays remembered a day late, drama club performances missed, and nights Kesandu got home to Chiazakam already self-tucked in bed, her back to the bedroom door. These days, she thinks of her daughter and sees a lover of history, but it had been one book, Kesandu's own suggestion, and Chiazakam had been eight. In fact, if Kesandu really thinks about it, she can't recall whether Chiazakam actually said she loved the historical novel or said it was just okay, and she hadn't really tracked what Chiazakam liked to read outside of class requirements, if she even liked to read at all. But what could Kesandu have done differently while striving to put good food into her daughter's mouth? She supposes that question has a million different answers, but different does not mean better. There would always have been some other thing slipping.

"I don't know exactly what that feels like," Kesandu replies. "But there's no evil in stopping yourself from having a baby you weren't ready for. It's a battle even when everything's working right."

"Nonso," Ifesinachi says. Their baby's name.

It was Chibuike's choosing, and Ifesinachi remembers her rare anger at him. Why name a soul that would never be? She made all the arrangements, got a date booked. Before the day of excision, however, Susanna called, as she did every few weeks. She asked if Ifesinachi was still with "that funny man." When Ifesinachi replied that the funny man would someday be her husband and the future father of her children, Susanna laughed.

"My sweet, sweet Ife. The good Lord gifted you a brain fit for your fancy book thoughts. And a strong ear for songs of this new age. But your hands are not a mother's hands. We have always known this, and it is okay."

Ifesinachi's voice deepens, even now, with the rage she felt in that moment, her blood rushing upward, her nails clawing into the phone. After the call, she marched into the toilet, where Chibuike sat pooping, and kissed him. She said they would raise Nonso. No, she wasn't joking. Nowhere near here, though, where Susanna's ill will could taint him, not at first. After Chibuike was convinced of her certainty, he pledged himself all in, the work ahead theirs to surmount.

Together, they emptied all their temptations into the sink, sold all the things they didn't need, and moved into an even smaller space one state over, their jobs abandoned. That initial period of cold turkey was the worst, familiar yet no less painful. Conjoined night sweats and nightmares, tremors in the bathtub, heated arguments over dumb little nothings, struggling through the haze of it all to clutch on to their love. But then it got easier. They wedded in private to sanctify the depths of their commitment. Chibuike got a decent job working construction for a luxury condo, and Ifesinachi tutored part-time at an after-school remedial math centre. She embraced the swell of her body, bigger skirts, bras one size up, then another. They substituted greasy takeout for homemade veggies. Chibuike cleaned up after her when her bile missed the toilet bowl. He bought her antacids and almond milk for the heartburn, sliced fresh grapefruit for her morning sickness, and replaced the double-cream cookies she'd stocked up on for her binge-eating sessions with juicy green apples. He took her on walks around the city, even when her body ached and her belly itched and her bones wanted no motion, insisting that the fresh air was good for Nonso. Before bed, she clasped her hand over her stomach, and he clasped his hand over hers, and they sang songs they'd invented for their baby. She gasped at the first kick. Cried at the second. Cried some more when he didn't kick for a while, wondering if a sickness in her body had swallowed him whole. They hung his ultrasound photo on the refrigerator, marvelled at his skull, his curving stomach, his tiny hands seemingly clasped in prayer. Each passing week, they tracked Nonso's ever-changing size by units of healthy food: sesame seed, blueberry, bell pepper, lettuce, watermelon. And then there he was, in her arms. One of the easiest children, the midwife said. Barely any tearing, minimal stitches, and he had big, healthy lungs.

Kesandu thinks of her own Chiazakam, who came into this world to a backdrop of wartime violence: dual screams, bad bleeding, fecal matter, and the slow, slow recovery, where it felt like her insides had been pierced through and rearranged. She feels light-headed now. She glances at the gun still in Ifesinachi's hand, then at the door, wondering what time it is.

"Where is Nonso?" she asks Ifesinachi, who does not seem to hear her. Ifesinachi says Auntie Vero had once mentioned the identical paths of her three children: God's worst trial in her belly; afterward, God's purest magic. Once they were out in the world, it only got better. The first day Ifesinachi held Nonso, that magical love had mixed with disbelief at the inception of this impossibly small, impossibly perfect being. This was Chibuike, all him; she saw it in Nonso's sharp, roving eyes, and she'd love him just as easily.

What followed instead was the burping, peeing, and shitting, the endless feeding, the bewilderment when his back's smooth skin broke into a flaky rash—she threw out all his old creams for new ones, but the rash only spread. Nonso's gums flared wide every few minutes to suckle, and she started to see their violent pink even with her eyes closed. There was an absolute lack of pattern to Nonso's demand for more, more, more and his refusal to sleep long, even when he'd had his fill and was put down. Whenever Ifesinachi was awake, which was always, she wanted Chibuike up, fearful of where high-stress solitude would lead. They napped together too. Synced as usual, him and her, diaper-changing, blanket-swaddling, back-patting zombies, the days bleeding together so that four days felt like four weeks, and four weeks felt like forever. She worried about all the ways this world could claim Nonso. Drowning in the bathtub. Choking on milk and ceiling-blown dust. At her own hands. She worried that the air-poisoning taint had never been Susanna's but in fact had always been hers. One afternoon, she dropped Nonso, and he shattered into a dozen triangular pieces—she jerked, realized that she had been holding a plate and that he was still in his crib, wailing at the sound of broken ceramic. He wailed while she showered and on their groggy runs for bottles and fresh Pampers. He turned the heads of strangers, deflated Ifesinachi's desire for anything, including Chibuike. Once, while Ifesinachi clipped Nonso's nails with the special clippers, Chibuike, red-eyed, suggested that they clue her family in on Nonso's existence, they could use the help, and Ifesinachi got so upset at the insinuation—*we are not enough, not good enough, Susanna was right*—that she clipped into Nonso's skin, and Nonso cried so hard that she screamed in his tiny face and walked into the bathroom and slammed the door, not coming out even when Chibuike banged and banged.

"It must have been his fifth week when he started sleeping a little better," Ifesinachi says. "I was drinking juice, and Chibuike was on his soda cleanse, so he was sipping on mineral water. And I said we deserved it. A nice glass of wine, just this once. Vero and Susanna had drunk way worse when their final children came along, and those ruffians are doing okay. One even works at NNPC. I said I'd freeze a few bottles of milk so Nonso's food was good. Chibuike looked at me like I'd suggested we swallow bleach. He said one was never just one. But I said it was different this time. We had Nonso to keep ourselves in check."

They agreed: one bottle, no larger than 750 millilitres, but even as they picked the Moscato out of a wine fridge at the store, Ifesinachi felt the beckoning of stronger liquors from shelves all around her. Their throat-burning heat and sweetness. Their eager scratching at the portion of her brain where they would always live. Kesandu, her stomach in knots, knows what she imagines is a lesser version of the feeling from her Friday Nights these days, her running of old replaced by picking Toblerone bars from an aisle full of assorted candies—balls of caramel chocolate, coconut-vanilla swirls, family-sized packs of Mars bars. The body aches to surrender to all poisons, and sometimes, control is choosing the tiniest evil.

"When we got up front to pay though," Ifesinachi continues, "the cashier pointed at the whiskey bottles near the checkout. Said they were doing a two-for-one special if we wanted it."

And you said no, Kesandu thinks. *Took your tiniest-evil wine bottle and went home and had a glass and that was it. I had a glass or two myself on those hard nights. Those long, long nights.*

They didn't say yes. They didn't say no. Chibuike and Ifesinachi stared wordlessly at each other like they'd been asked an unexpected math question. Like they were each waiting for their better half to make the better choice. The cashier took that for an answer, added the bottles to their order, and then they were back home with three items instead of one. It was almost midnight.

Chibuike poured them half glasses of Moscato. When they finished, he poured them some more, and when the wine was done, he glanced at one of the whiskey bottles. Ifesinachi screwed its top loose, filled their cups to the quarter mark. They drank in silence now, more slowly, slinking into a soothing and familiar headspace. Ifesinachi looked around. Their parlour was dimly lit by a lava lamp. The DStv bill hadn't been paid, and their TV screen was stuck on a hissing channel of static, a million criss-crossing black and white ants. In the bid to satisfy all of Nonso's needs, housekeeping had taken a nosedive too. Clothes everywhere, Chibuike's sneakers tracking mud on the carpet, light-up toys for Nonso next to empty cartons of mineral water next to cartoon-printed mats with raised surfaces fit for eventual crawling. Ifesinachi looked at Chibuike, really looked, and saw the mess of their home reflected in his wild eyes, his chewed-up lips, his untamed scruff and wizened face. Nonso was sucking their life force. Their love force too.

As if triggered by his mother's thoughts, Nonso started crying in the next room. Chibuike sighed, and Ifesinachi said she would let him tire himself out just this once. Minutes passed with only signs of intensification, so she went in there, clinging to the wall for support. Nonso refused to latch onto her nipple.

What about the bottles of milk? Kesandu thinks but does not say.

Ifesinachi transferred him from crib to bassinet and walked him to the parlour. She'd thought of using the maroon shawl for transport instead, because it worked better sometimes, bound her and Nonso chest to chest, but his tears had already provoked such a headache, and she didn't want his touch.

"I don't know if it would have changed anything," she says. "Feeling his skin on mine. And yet, I can't stop picturing the shawl hanging over the window ledge beside the crib. Just there."

While Chibuike sang, she rocked the bassinet, but Nonso wasn't having it. At his worst, nothing calmed him, not dimmed lights, not a flood of sunlight, not white noise, not his pacifier, not food or music or anything at all.

Chibuike said, on the verge of tears himself, "Jesus fucking Christ, what does he want?" And as Ifesinachi picked up her glass for another swig, the funny thought crossed her weary mind.

"Fishy fish fish," she said, motioning at the whiskey bottle that stood on the table's edge. Chibuike turned toward it. Ifesinachi's memory struggles now with what came after. If they fed Nonso by dipping their fingers in the bottle and then letting the droplets seep onto his lips. Or if they poured it over his mouth for a direct intake.

"But it was quick, I swear on Auntie Kosi's soul." Ifesinachi is rocking back and forth, the back of her head banging in a rapid rhythm against the curtained wall. "Five seconds. We fell asleep right there in our chairs. I woke up in the morning, picked him up to change his diaper, but he ... he wasn't ... and Chibuike tried too, he did. Shook him so gently and then hard and clapped in his face and ... it was five seconds. I swear."

Afterward, they sat next to him for a long time, waiting for the relief of Nonso's tears, even if they came like a storm.

Rain rain, go away, Kesandu thinks, recalling songs of old in the days before walking. When thunder's deep growl had driven Chiazakam to tears, Kesandu had thought of riding the next white streak of lightning up to God's gates himself. She'd puff her chest and ask him who the hell he thought he was, scaring her baby like that. She thinks that maybe it's raining in this room too, and that's why she's so cold, unable to move for fear of snapping a frosted bone. She thinks of Chiazakam before the long limbs, her angel loving the waters and how they wetted the soil. She thinks of her marching into the kitchen, her white dress for first Communion ruined with mud streaks, earthworms wriggling in her eager fist.

Kesandu pictures herself walking out of Room 14, not another word heard.

They waited till darkness fell, Ifesinachi and Chibuike, and when Nonso didn't stir, they buried him in a field only they knew. A field only they would ever know. They moved again afterward, tried to restart their lives, just like always, but it was only two days before wine wet their lips again. This time, Ifesinachi wanted to drink until the blood bubbled out of her skin. When she popped a pill for the hangover headache, she imagined emptying the rest of the bottle into her stomach. Imagined crossing busy roads with Chibuike, not looking for what was coming. In every corner, she glimpsed the possibility of death's relief.

"He was the only thing that kept me going," she says. "But we'd worked together on so many tracks. In our heart of hearts, we knew when a song was done. No new melodies to be had. We were lying on the dirty floor in our new room with no bed, and my stomach was hurting. My kidney and my liver and my heart. It hurt to breathe. So, I made the joke. He laughed like always and said why not. He'd been there too, for a while. He was ready. One last party, like from the good old days. Then me and him off to sleep. And he did it. Found his peace, finally, and I'll be meeting him soon. I promised."

Kesandu clears her throat before she can get the words out. "Your aunties. Your uncles. Susanna. No one knows about Nonso?"

"No. Not a soul. It's been only me and him for a while now. I'm sure they've been calling and trying to bang down all our old doors. But we stopped checking a long time ago. And I can see your face, you know? I can feel your judgment like you're God himself. So, go ahead. I won't stop you." Past the curtain, dawn is starting to make its way into Room 14, dappling the frayed edges of Ifesinachi's hair. It doesn't take much work for Kesandu to picture this woman on fire.

Ifesinachi raises the small piece of black metal she's clung to all night. She puts the gun's barrel in her mouth and tightens her lips around it. Kesandu does not know how a day that started with the familiar smell of Dettol and bleached towels has led to this half-bloodied face before her, one eye redder than the other, and the sweaty grip that pulls Kesandu's palm toward her own demise. One second to pull the trigger. Quick as the thought Kesandu had once had while crossing a bridge, her arms hovering over the railing. Amawbia Grounds mere metres behind her, the green waters below so calm.

Even then, Kesandu had long ago learned to let thoughts stay thoughts, except for the ones you needed. Now, she pulls the gun out of Ifesinachi's mouth and tosses it to the side. Ifesinachi stares where it lands but doesn't dive for it. Doesn't flee for the other gun cooling next to her husband either, the sheets around him stained a colour no machine in this building can clean. Her face crinkles, and she goes on all fours, but the tears or vomit Kesandu thinks are coming emerge as dry heaves and hiccups. Ifesinachi, quivering, lets out all she can at this moment, in this room, even though it's not enough, and how could it ever be? She's murmuring her apologies. Or maybe staking a small claim in the here and now to the dust motes: "I can't join you. I can't. Not yet. I'm sorry. I can't."

If he hasn't already, Ifeanyi will clock in for the new day soon. He deserves better than dealing with the decay of an existence too heavy for its body, but Kesandu knows that she has already cleaned her last room in this hotel, and he will have to find someone else. The soul before her is clinging to life, despite not knowing how to live. Where to start. And Kesandu is thinking, despite all her inner voices wondering whether she's gone mad, that maybe she has some answers. A long talk with Ifeanyi. A story for lazy police officers about a man who killed himself next to his sleeping wife for unknown reasons. Phone calls to bereft aunts. But first, the hiding of her new roommate's gun.

Kesandu rises. The stretch of her cramped legs should offer relief. Instead, she feels the night's weight on every pore of her skin, slowing her pace. Ifesinachi is still hugging the floor on bent knees, her lowered voice releasing all the words that might allow her to stand. To hear the things Kesandu needs to say. For now, Kesandu picks up the tossed pistol and stows it in the hard-shell suitcase, which opens to reveal more CDs, unmarked pill bottles, flaking leather belts, two wallets, and a wood-framed photo: black and grey swirls in the shape of a newborn. There are odd things too: sharp blades of golden-brown grass scattered all over, pink quartz stones, a can opener next to empty sardine cans, bits of leftover tuna, and crinkled slices of paper towel covered with paragraphs of red ink, the words barely legible. More items loom beneath the surface, a hint of green fabric peeking out, but Kesandu zips up the suitcase and slides it into a corner of the room. She parts the curtains to let the sun all the way in, then walks over to where Chibuike lies, the second gun still in his clutch. Careful to avoid looking at his face, she pinches at a white portion of the bloodied sheet and pulls the linen over most of his body's length. His right leg still sticks out. Thin hair spirals around a birthmark on his ankle and spreads like vines into the darkness beneath the sheets. His bluish toes look recently pedicured, and Kesandu wonders if Ifesinachi had managed that one small thing even on the verge of their demise, if she lifted his feet onto her lap and clipped slowly at each nail, careful to avoid the skin. She wonders if he's truly at peace now, Chibuike in the same place as Chiazakam, both maybe even trading stories with Auntie Kosi.

Kesandu has always left questions of what one deserves to powers greater than herself. She is better equipped to speak on eternities, having encountered so many, all of them guarding their surprises. The life before Henry, full of village streams fit for swimming and Grandma's delicious water gourds. The slow, steady stretch beyond Chiazakam, when the sight of tree bark no longer unravelled Kesandu. And now, another day after forever.

Wherever it may lead.

ACKNOWLEDGMENTS

I am deeply thankful to every literary journal editor who took a chance on publishing and promoting my work, always with such kindness and enthusiasm. I learned much about resilience and refinement from you all.

Major gratitude to Carolyn Forde, my tireless and supportive agent, for championing *Perfect Little Angels*. Likewise to the incredible Brian Lam and the entire Arsenal Pulp Press team for diligently bringing these stories to life. Catharine Chen's careful edits taught me much and strengthened my work, and Jazmin Welch's sharp eye for design bestowed it with aesthetic warmth. I am also thankful to the skilled Julian Adon Alexander for his gorgeous, affecting art, which graces the cover.

Immeasurable love and thanks to Professor Helen Elaine Lee, who helped me clarify early on the kind of writer I wanted to be and granted me such hospitality in my early days at MIT. I was a teenage boy far away from Nigeria, separated from my family, and you often felt like a second home. Your lessons about craft and life will linger forever.

The earliest drafts of a few stories here passed through the meticulous minds of Chelsea Barabas, Chloe Yang, Daniel Guberek, and Nailah Smith. I am grateful for your judicious insights during our many online workshop sessions. To my friends who read a number of these stories with much hype—Benjamin Kwashigah, Brenda and Gary Doyle, Deborah Sedem, Devon Clarke, Korede Ogunyinka, Kosi Nwagbara, Nicholas Bacquie, Odera Adimorah, Samuel Nwaokpani, Sele Akioyamen—your euphoric endorsements had me blushing in front of my computer screen at four in the morning.

Sometimes, the words stopped. The cursor blinked and blinked. Burnout crept in alongside skeptical twilight voices. I am thankful to all my companions who rejuvenated me with food, time, much-needed distractions, and endless encouragement: Akailah and Traven Smith, Clarity Nwaokpani, IK Okoro (all those existential, engine-revving midnight chats on the balcony), Paul Soladoye, Priscilla Larbi, Tolu Akinola, and many, many more. Daalụ niile.

I am also grateful to the CBC, the Commonwealth Foundation, and the Writers' Trust of Canada for the opportunities they've offered me these last few years. Your calls and emails marked some of my most exciting days, and your work to support writers is so deeply impactful.

When I was seven, I handwrote my very first story—a ridiculous if earnest piece about a boy disowned for spending bread money on ice cream—and afterward spent most of my prepubescent years continuing with other ridiculous stories on a slow, cranky desktop computer my parents got me. Mom, Dad, you filled my early years with books, allowed me my earliest creative space. Because of you, my siblings, and everyone who is family, I write, love, and feel loved. Endlessly. Even on the decidedly non-angelic days. Life's icy periods would be utterly unmanageable without your warmth. Thank you.

Photo credit: Samuel Nwaokpani

VINCENT ANIOKE is a Nigerian Canadian software engineer and author. His short stories have appeared in *The Ex-Puritan, The Rumpus, The Masters Review, Carve Magazine,* and *Passages North,* among other literary journals. He won the 2021 Austin Clarke Prize in Literary Excellence and has been shortlisted for multiple contests, including the 2023 RBC Bronwen Wallace Award for Emerging Writers and the 2021 Commonwealth Short Story Prize. He reads literary submissions for *SmokeLong Quarterly* and *Split Lip Magazine*. Find him on X (formerly Twitter) at **@AniokeVincent**. | **vincentanioke.com**